T0208551

HEME INC.

MARK ROBERTS

BALBOA.
PRESS
A DIVISION OF HAY HOUSE

This is a work of fiction. All of the characters, names, incidents, organizations, and dialogue in this novel are either the products of the author's imagination or are used fictitiously.

Scripture taken from the King James Version of the Bible.

Balboa Press books may be ordered through booksellers or by contacting:

Balboa Press
A Division of Hay House
1663 Liberty Drive
Bloomington, IN 47403
www.balboapress.com
1 (877) 407-4847

The author of this book does not dispense medical advice or prescribe the use of any technique as a form of treatment for physical, emotional, or medical problems without the advice of a physician, either directly or indirectly. The intent of the author is only to offer information of a general nature to help you in your quest for emotional and spiritual well-being. In the event you use any of the information in this book for yourself, which is your constitutional right, the author and the publisher assume no responsibility for your actions.

Print information available on the last page.

ISBN: 978-1-9822-0634-5 (sc)
ISBN: 978-1-9822-0636-9 (hc)
ISBN: 978-1-9822-0635-2 (e)

Library of Congress Control Number: 2018906945

Balboa Press rev. date: 11/19/2018

This book dedicated to my wife Sharon and my family who had faith in me all the way through the process.

PREFACE

IN THE BEGINNING GOD created the heaven and the earth. In heaven he created the celestial angels and christened them his warriors

1:5 And God called the light Day, and the darkness he called Night. And the evening and the morning were the first day.

1:6 And God said, let there be a firmament in the midst of the waters, and let it divide the waters from the waters.

1:7 And God made the firmament and divided the waters which were under the firmament from the waters, which were above the firmament: and it was so.

1:8 And God called the firmament Heaven. And the evening and the morning were the second day.

1:9 And God said, Let the waters under the heaven be gathered together unto one place, and let the dry land appear: and it was so.

1:10 And God called the dry land Earth; and the gathering together of the waters called he Seas: and God saw that it was good.

1:11 And God said, Let the earth bring forth grass, the herb yielding seed, and the fruit tree yielding fruit after his kind, whose seed is in itself, upon the earth: and it was so.

1:12 And the earth brought forth grass, and herb yielding seed after his kind, and the tree yielding fruit, whose seed was in itself, after his kind: and God saw that it was good.

1:13 And the evening and the morning were the third day.

1:14 And God said, Let there be lights in the firmament of the heaven to divide the day from the night; and let them be for signs, and for seasons, and for days, and years:

1:15 And let them be for lights in the firmament of the heaven to give light upon the earth: and it was so.

1:16 And God made two great lights; the greater light to rule the day, and the lesser light to rule the night: he made the stars also.

1:17 And God set them in the firmament of the heaven to give light upon the earth,

1:18 And to rule over the day and over the night, and to divide the light from the darkness: and God saw that it was good.

1:19 And the evening and the morning were the fourth day.

1:20 And God said, I will create the first four magical tribes. And God created the elf, vampire, dwarf and werewolf. And to each he gave a task. The elves task was to create life. And the elves said Let the waters bring forth abundantly the moving creature that hath life, and fowl that may fly above the earth in the open firmament of heaven.

1:21 And elves created great whales, and every living creature that moveth, which the waters brought forth abundantly, after their kind, and every winged fowl after his kind: and God saw that it was good.

1:22 And God blessed them, saying, Be fruitful, and multiply, and fill the waters in the seas, and let fowl multiply in the earth.

1:23 And the evening and the morning were the fifth day.

1:24 And elves said, Let the earth bring forth the living creature after his kind, cattle, and creeping thing, and beast of the earth after his kind: and it was so.

1:25 And the elves made the beast of the earth after his kind, and cattle after their kind, and everything that creepeth upon the earth after his kind: and God saw that it was good.

1:26 And God gave the dwarves and the werewolves charge of his earth and he made the vampires his earthly warriors and healers. And God saw everything that had been made, and, behold, it was very good. And the evening and the morning were the sixth day.

2:1 Thus the heavens and the earth were finished, and all the host of them.

2:2 And on the seventh day God ended his work which he had made; and he rested on the seventh day from all his work, which he had made.

2:3 And God blessed the seventh day, and sanctified it: because that in it he had rested from all his work which God created and made.

2:4 These are the generations of the heavens and of the earth when they were created, in the day that the LORD God made the earth and the heavens, and all that inhabit both.

CHAPTER 1

*"In the beginning we are all clay. We all await
a master's touch to be born into greatness"*

"YOU ARE THE LAST hope of all the beings on this planet and you must be strong. You must find your own path. We can teach you, but we cannot lead you. Your path is your own to choose. Many others will try to sway you. Some of them you must learn to trust, and others will be your most deadly enemies. Give in to your destiny now or it will destroy you. You my son and all creation this is the will of God Almighty."

The telephone rings and the piercing high-pitched sound startle Remy Robon from his sleep. A sleep once again troubled by a repeating dream or maybe it was more like a nightmare. Remy always finds himself in a meadow full of snow and a strange man is speaking of the choices that Remy must make in his life. A man he had never seen with a voice he has never heard. Nonetheless, this dream feels more real than anything else in Remy's life. Lately, the dream has come more frequently and has increased in intensity. Remy always feels as if he can smell the meadow and touch the snow. He shivers at the thought of the cold. Yet it reminds him so much of his home in Canada. The crispness of the air gives him a great feeling of oneness with Mother Nature.

Remy immediately pulls his two 9 mm Glocks from under his

pillow and scans the room tracking for any movement. He then reaches out and picks up the phone fully awake and mutters "Good Morning." as he looks at the bedside clock checking the time.

"Good Morning, Boss. Its 5:00 AM, I called just like you ask. Good job, huh?" says Dingham.

"Thanks for listening so closely, Dingham. Is everything ready at the base camp?" Remy asks as he walks over to the window surveying the countryside.

"Jesus Christ. Here I am in another war-torn country filled with disease and pestilence. How many was it now, five or six at least and always another hot sweltering country with poor irrigation, huge bugs and deplorable sanitary conditions. Just another shit-hole assignment that was given to him by the Heme Corporation and as always because someone else could not get the job done." Remy thinks to himself looking out the window at the street people waking up. Every single one of them trying to get ready in their own personal way to survive yet another day, one way or another. Remy sees the homeless appearing from beneath the cardboard boxes they have used for shelter. He watches as they relieve themselves and walk to side walk troughs to wash their faces and hands.

"Same shit different country." Remy exclaims aloud.

"What you say, Boss?"

Remy realizes Dingham is still on the line and replies "Nothing, Dingham. Is everything at the base camp ready?"

"Yes, for the second time, Boss. Are you, all right? This not like you. You did have a lot to drink last night." says Dingham

"I'm all right, thank you for asking. These are strange times. Just have a lot on my mind these days. Call ahead and let the camp know we are coming and tell them to be on their toes. I do not trust the warlord."

"Okay, Boss."

"I'll be down in thirty minutes, see you in a bit." Remy says hanging up the phone. "Dam, come to think of it, I do have headache. I cannot even remember what we were drinking. Guake must have drunk about two or three bottles of that shit and he wasn't even drunk." Remy notices a stench in the room and realizes after a few moments, that the stench is coming from him. "I need a shower."

Remy Robon went to the Air Force academy where he trained to be a military nurse. Many people have asked him why he had not become a physician. His answer has always been, for all intense purposes, a military nurse was a field physician. They do about everything a physician does without the glory or the title. What he has never said to anyone was that he never thought he could make the grade as a physician. Now he knows better. Remy knows he is one of the best at what he does. He is a bizarre mixture of healer and killer. When Remy graduated, he was recruited by the Heme Corporation to set up hospitals in countries ravaged by war and poverty. Places where both his skill sets would come in handy. The Heme Corporation is a worldwide health maintenance organization that bids for foreign and local contracts. The Heme Corporation has been in existence for the last three hundred years. They provide health care to all the third world countries as well as in the United States and Europe at a fraction of the cost of other organizations. Still the corporation has prospered in the global market and has become the largest health maintenance organization in the world. They have built and supplied hospitals in every corner of the globe. They also provide the security to oversee these facilities. In most of these countries, the different warring factions ransacked most of the first hospitals leaving nothing for those who really needed the medical care and medicines. The Heme Corporation then created a private military force to protect their assets and soon found that was not enough. The security force could protect the property, but they had no understanding of the medical needs of the population or the medical staffing needed to operate one. When the Heme Corporation identified this as a roadblock to giving needed healthcare to the masses, they began hiring nurses out of the military academies in the early nineties. Nurses it seems have a better overall perspective of the issues. The corporation had tried physicians at first and they found out quickly, the physicians were easily bribed with money and seduced by the opportunity to gain power in those countries. They also had no ability besides providing direct care to the public. Nurses seemed more committed to making sure the people got what they needed. Nurses could think outside the box, they expect the unexpected and were more effective than any physician in most situations. They are incredible at improvisation. Remy has been with the corporation for three years. His job is to create a safe environment for the hospital staff and then oversee the construction of the facilities in some of the most violent places in the world. When the facility is completed, Remy sets up a security detail, makes sure the hospital has the appropriate staffing and moves on to his next assignment. Remy is now in a country that has been at war since the early 1990's. This country has endured twenty years of trying to kill one another over tiny parcels of land. As with most of these countries, the central government has no real power and the local warlords run the provinces. Moreover, just like in any war-torn country the women and children are the greatest casualties. Because of the lack of medicine and medical care, they die of the most curable diseases and minor injuries. Not to speak of the raping and brutality that is heaped upon them daily. All this suffering, so a few men can say, "I've conquered. What a fragging waste of life".

Remy turns from the window and puts out his clothes for the day. "God, its hot today, must be a hundred degrees already." Remy says as he goes into the shower hoping to cool off a bit. His taunt flat muscles initially rebel against the cold by tightening up as the frigid water cascades of his skin. Soon he feels somewhat cooled down, nonetheless, he is perspiring as soon as he turns the water off. However, he does feel to some extent refreshed. Remy quickly dons his uniform, a black matte jumpsuit with built in body-armor and a pair of rubber soled jump boots. Remy checks his weapons which consist of two shoulder holstered Uzis, two Glocks and various sharp-edged weapons secreted in his uniform. His Uzis are double clipped with silencers attached. A special edition he had helped create. Each weapon has double clip with 100 armor-piercing shells however, the weapon is only twelve inches long including the silencer and weighs about a pound. The weapon is made of blue stainless steel and is extremely durable. This weapon is so silent, that it has been outlawed in almost every country in the world. Most Special Forces team members across the globe are now equipped with one or two of these weapons. The patent alone has filled his bank account with a fortune. Remy puts on a vest that covers the Uzis' from view. You would think looking at him in all black that he would be unbearably hot however, the uniform has a built-in cooling system. The cooling system is powered by motion. As you move the micro tubing throughout the suit forces cooled fluid up and down the artificial arteries and veins that outline it. Like a built-in temperature controlled vascular system. The Corporation is very adept at this kind of technology. It is one of the reasons they are so powerful. There is not a country on this earth, which does not purchase something from them.

Most people think it is a joke when Remy tells them what he does for a living. Hearing that his chosen profession is nursing gives rise to most people automatically thinking he is either gay or lying. No matter what changes and what you do to enlighten people old prejudices diehard. Prejudices, that Remy has no problem at all correcting either verbally or physically. Remy graduated as the valedictorian of his class at the Air Force academy. He is an accomplished pilot, an expert at Aikido and a small weapons and explosive specialist. Remy also is the owner of a very short temper. The last person, who had the misfortune of calling him gay in jest, was hospitalized for months. Many others were not so lucky. Remy has no tolerance for such things. Bigotry, prejudice and taking advantage of people has always filled him with rage. A rage he channels into violent behavior against the transgressors. Remy enjoys the violence, he enjoys using his unique ability to injure, maim and kill people. It was as if he were born to do it. Born to right the injustices' human beings heaped upon one another every day. The last weapon Remy straps on is a short sword, a gift given to him while he trained in Aikido in Japan. Once his weapons are in place and he checks them, he starts down the stairs. If you did not know he was armed, you could never tell. Ninja-like the weapons seem to just melt into his body.

Outside, Dingham sits in the land cruiser waiting for him. His Boss has always perplexed Dingham. Dingham has never met a man who could be so ruthless, tearing men apart at a moment's notice, yet so kind in every other way. With women and children Remy seemed like the father we all wish we had. Nevertheless, in true battle he is as vicious as he can be kind. Remy would cut you down without a thought for the most trivial of reasons, especially if he felt dishonored in any way. Honor was everything to Remy. Remy was a true enigma. Dingham owed this man his life. When Remy found him, he was in the gutter a drunken fool with no future, but an early death. The street gang, whose turf he had trespassed on caught him and was beating him to death. Everyone in town knew that you did not go near the MI2 after dark, however, Dingham was quite drunk, and drink makes you careless. From out of the shadows came Remy. Like some avenging angel, he intervened. Dingham had never seen a person move that fast; it was as if he were dancing. So, fluid, so deadly, within what seemed like seconds four men were dead. Remy had ripped out the throat of two, ripped out one's heart and eviscerated the last. Dingham had thought Remy used a blade, he later found out he had used his bare hands.

Remy reaches the land rover and jumps in. He slaps Dingham on the back and says, "Time to party Big Guy."

"Anything you say, Boss" He answers as they drive away. "You sleep good, Boss?"

"As well as could be expected."

"I know what you mean. You drink a lot last night."

"Yes, that is true. I have this splitting headache to prove it. It was kind of dumb to challenge Guake to a drinking contest." Remy says opening the coffee Dingham brought for him. As is always his habit, he smells it first. Satisfied it's not poisoned he sips it and savors the taste. He has always loved the pungent taste of coffee. It has always relaxed him.

"Boss, why do you always smell everything you eat or drink? You don't trust Dingham?"

"It's just a habit. My nose has never steered me wrong. If it does not smell right do not eat or drink it. The one time I did not use this skill it almost cost me my life."

"What happened?"

"I was at a dinner with some dignitaries of a country I was sent to set up a hospital in. They had tried to bribe me, and I politely refused. After one sip of the wine I knew it was full of poison."

"What you do?"

"I have an antitoxin unit implanted in my body just for this reason. I hit the button the computer quickly identified the poison and the antitoxin was immediately deployed into my system. I then feigned blacking out and was carried outside. They thought to bury me in the courtyard. I killed the men who carried me out and then I killed everyone but the nonmilitary women and children in the house. No one has ever tried to bribe me or poison me again."

"You think there be trouble today, Boss." Says Dingham changing the subject quickly.

"Most definitely. The biggest warlord in this province is going to try to stop the construction of the hospital and I cannot allow that. I will not allow the women and children of this country to suffer any longer because of greed. Greed is what motivates the warlord and the politicians of any country. Greed and power that is, what a fool this warlord is. He allows the people in his province to die for no reason. He uses them as cattle and slaves." Remy says staring off into the foliage taking another sip of his coffee. "He could easily have the people eating out of his hand if he just helped feed them and kept them safe."

"We lose a lot of money, huh Boss."

"This has nothing to do with money, Dingham. The people of

this province need a hospital with a clinic just to keep them alive. When we came here two months ago there was an epidemic of cholera, measles, venereal diseases and small pox. With the medicines we have provided, we have been able to wipe out these epidemics. No more children lost to poor prenatal care because almost everywhere in this province the women are now registered with the corporation. I don't give a damn about the money, Dingham you of all people should know that." He says looking directly at Dingham.

Something in Remy's voice makes Dingham hit the brakes and he pulls over to the side of the road too afraid to go on. He has seen Remy kill men for less than this.

"Why did you stop the car?" asks Remy sensing Dingham's fear. For some reason the scent of fear has always filled Remy with energy and the feeling of power. The scent sends a warm feeling through Remy's body. A feeling that makes him pulsate with power. He wonders if a predator feels this way during a hunt.

"I just do not want to displease you, Boss." Dingham answers head down. "I have seen what you do to people who displease you."

"Lighten up, Dingham. I trust you enough to let you in; I was just making a point. Come on we have a job to do"

Dingham exhales noisily and restarts the land rover, as if he had been forgiven the worst of sins he continues.

"You did call ahead and tell the camp I'm on my way?"

"Yes, Boss."

"Whom did you speak to?"

"I spoke to Guake."

"Good, let's get this over with once and for all." Says Remy

The road is extremely bumpy and filled with huge potholes, which make the ride to the hospital site very uncomfortable. "Shoot." Remy thinks to himself. "I don't remember being comfortable, ever."

They soon reach the work site and find the workers scrambling about. It seems the Warlord has again sent some men to harass the workers. This has become a weekly ritual. For some reason the Warlord does not want this hospital built. He has done everything in his power, short of a military action to prevent its completion. However, every time he attempted something Remy has been ready and put plans into place to stop him before any real damage could have be done to the people that work here or the work site itself. Nevertheless, each attack has made Remy's anger escalate.

"This Warlord is really started pissing me off." He thinks to himself. The Warlord had even tried to bribe him over the past year. He had offered him money, women and power. It seems the Warlord already had most of the politicians on the payroll. The Warlord even offered part of his drug operation with a full cut of the profits. "What an idiot".

On arrival to the compound Remy notices two new guards at the gate. Remy has made it his business to know everyone who worked on a site. He also went out of his way to have thorough back ground checks done on his employees and he never hired a local for security details.

"Excuse me how long have you been working at this site?"

"Who the hell wants to know?" replies one of them. Dingham almost swallows his tongue.

"Excuse me, what did you just say?" says Remy getting out of the vehicle and walking in front of them.

"What you can't hear. I said..." Remy slits his throat and has already grabbed the second.

"Since he can no longer hear me, I guess you and I can have a chat. Now who hired you to work on this compound?"

Gurgling from the pressure on his throat he wheezes "Guake did"

'Really, when was that?" Remy asks taking a little pressure off, so he can speak.

"He hired us last night in town."

"Where?" Remy says exerting some pressure and then releasing it slightly.

"In the cantina."

"I see." says Remy snapping his neck. "Ok Dingham something is a foot. Drive slowly into the compound."

After surveying the work-site, it dawns on him that his security detail is nowhere to be found. He only sees the people Guake has hired. This is extremely strange, especially since he had Dingham called ahead.

"Stop the car" he whispers and Dingham complies. "Something is not right here, Dingham. Take the car back to the city and I'll call you later."

"Boss, you crazy?" Dingham doesn't even finish the statement and Remy is gone."

"Whoa, shit this is serious. I outta here." and he turns the vehicle around and speeds off.

Meanwhile, Remy has slipped into the foliage. Soon he has arrived at the window of the compound where his soldiers reside. He looks through the window and sees almost all of his security force slaughtered in their beds. "This is an inside job. Someone is a traitor." Remy thinks to himself and immediately becomes alert and checks his surroundings closer. He clears his mind and begins calculating all his options and possibilities. Anger will not help him avenge his men.

"Where is Guake?" he says to himself as he heads towards the command center. He then hears Guake's voice barking out orders in the native tongue. Orders it seems that are clearly being given to the warlord's men. It takes Remy no time to realize Guake has betrayed the corporation. Guake must have been a plant by the Warlord. Remy shrugs; it means nothing to him, because he does not trust anyone anyway. Since he was a boy, he has only had himself. Only three people in his life have ever kept their word. That is exactly why he always has a plan B.

Remy pulls out his radio and says, "This is wolfhound, I repeat, this is wolfhound." The radio crackles to life and a voice responds.

"We read you loud and clear, wolfhound. Over."

"All the puppies are asleep, and the wolf is loose in the yard, do you read me."

"Affirmative, wolfhound. How big is the pack Over?"

"Maybe 50 to 75 cubs."

"What do you suggest, wolfhound. Over."

"Four packed birdies and two hawks. Over."

"Sounds good, where do you want the hawks? Over."

"Have hawks raid the wolf lair and open the door for later. Over."

"Copy that, birdies play in your yard? Over."

"Affirmative. ETA? Over.

"Fifteen ticks. Already airborne, Over."

"Good job, Den mother. It will be lit up when they arrive, Over."

"Good luck, wolfhound. Transmission ended."

Remy smiles to himself because he has anticipated something like this happening for several weeks and had the corporation put a destroyer about thirty miles out from shore. Close enough to help but far enough to seem harmless. This Warlord was in for a rude awakening, the corporation is never denied once they have a project to complete. Something just like this had happened in Bangkok two years ago. The warlord there had bribed the Corporation representative just like here. The Warlord thought he had it all figured out, just like this one. Then Remy was brought in to find out why the hospital was not being completed and all the medications kept getting stolen. The fool lied to Remy and then tried to get him to join in the deal. Remy killed him on the spot and then hunted down the Warlord and executed him in public. Greed kills every time. No difference this time Remy thinks to himself. Except, this time it was personal. They had killed his men. Remy pulls out his Uzis and heads off into the compound. He chuckles to himself, because he loves this he loves the smell of impending death.

"Hey, Guake." Remy says opening fire on a group of the Warlord's men. "Show your traitorous face, it's time to die." Remy runs around the compound jumping from the shadows cutting men down getting Guake's men confused and making then chase him. After killing several of the Warlord's men, Remy runs into the command house and barricades himself in. All of the Warlord's men led by Guake pour into the courtyard. Guake steps forward and says "This can be easy or hard, Remy. The command house is surrounded, and you have nowhere to go. We both know the command house is bulletproof, but I also have four men with bazookas here. Now join us or die. There is so much money to be made in this country, the people have no choice. Any woman you desire, power and land. You can be a king here."

You know Guake, I told you when I first got here the lives of these people meant more to me than money, I guess you didn't listen closely enough. Plus, I thought we were friends."

"I have one friend, Amigo and that is money. We did have some good times though and that is why i am giving you a choice."

"So be it. You should choose better friends."

There is an explosion of phosphorus that rocks the compound. Men begin running to and fro screaming as they burst into flames. Like many of his assignments he had personally laid phosphorus charges in a hundred feet circle around every command house he had built while no one was around. The command house was always away from the construction of the hospital and away from the barracks. When he left he removed the charges, well when he did not have to use them. Soon many of the warlord's men fall to the ground their lives ended horribly. The explosion took all of them by complete surprise. Those who are not injured are totally disoriented and begin to just run away. Remy begins to laugh. These are not warriors, they are just bullies. At the first sign of real battle, they are running like children. Remy is suddenly disgusted as he watches them run. "You can beat children and rape women, but you cannot stand in combat." He says as his radio crackles to life.

"We're here, Wolfhound how do you like your food?"

"Well done, thank you." Says Remy

The war birds strafe the rest of the survivors and then land. Sixty men hit the ground full speed and mop up whatever is left of the rabble.

Remy comes out of the house and greets the commander.

"Commander Sauer, how are you, Sir?" he says with a salute and then a handshake.

"I'm fine, Remy. What the hell happened here?" Commander Sauer says looking around at the devastation.

"Well, Sir about two weeks back, I intercepted a courier from my compound going back to the Warlord. In his possession was a full set of plans of the compound and a schedule of the times the medications would arrive. Only six people knew this information. Unfortunately, even though I tried, I was unable to persuade the courier to talk before he expired. Therefore, I developed a plan to set up the traitor. Guake, was one of the men who had been entrusted with this information and now I see he joined the Warlord for money." Remy spits as if he had something sour in his mouth as he places emphasis on the word money.

"You know, Remy not everyone is strong enough to be priceless. Most of us have a price; it just needs to be established. We know you have a bank account full of money from your military inventions. You have no love ones to use against you, damn, to think of it I do not think you even have any friends that you care enough about to be used against you. You do not trust anybody and what I saw upon landing proves you did not even trust us. Phosphorus mines for Christ sake. You killed at least seventy-five to a hundred men instantly. I know you; there was no need for us you could have mopped up by yourself. My God, Remy, what has happened to you?" The Commander says placing his hand on Remy's shoulder.

"Nothing has happened to me. On the other hand, a significant number of things have happened here and to the people who inhabit this country. I need you and your men to be witnesses to the atrocities that have happened here. Beginning with the fact my men were butchered in their sleep by Guake and the Warlord's men."

"What do you mean beginning with?"

"Oh, commander since I came here six months ago I have seen many other hideous things. Things that make you lose faith in human beings." Replies Remy.

"War can be hideous."

"These things have nothing to do with war. Please follow me."

"You kept proof." Says Commander Sauer

"Yes, I kept proof of all the atrocities that I have seen. Follow me, Sir. See what I've seen then you can judge me."

First Remy leads him to the barracks where forty men lay dead shot while they slept. None here died a soldiers' death, they all were dead before they had a chance to defend themselves. That could only happen if they were all drugged. Now he realized why they all had drank so much the night before. He probably was supposed to be sleeping while all this transpired, but his implanted device had counter acted the drug. Another thing Guake has to answer for. A warrior should not die like that. Death in battle was clean. This was murder. The warrior's code had been broken. The Commander looks in amazement at the carnage.

"A soldier should not die like this." he says, "Not without a fighting chance."

"My sentiments exactly, Sir, none of the men here were given a chance at a clean death." answers Remy "Come with me there is more, much more."

Remy leads the Commander down into a makeshift morgue. Inside the morgue lay the bodies of women and children in different stages of decapitation and amputation. Children of all ages lie headless.

"Why did you show me this, Remy? This is horrible!" exclaims the Commander.

The commander's second in charge looks at him and is given a hand signal for silence by the commander. A signal Remy does not even understand but notices.

"I showed you the handiwork of the Warlord and his men so that you would realize I was quite merciful to his men." Remy says staring at him, ignoring the gesture, but realizing this is not the first time the commander has seen something like this. As always, he files that information away in his mind for use on another day.

"I get your point." replies the Commander. "Now what?"

"Now we end this once and for all. I think by now the Warlord should be softened up enough, don't you?" Remy says with a devilish smile playing on his lips.

"You're quite right, Remy. Let's finish this."

"The warlord thought if he moved his compound I would not find him. But we all have our spies and my spy told me his new location yesterday."

"And we sent our planes in too soften him up. That is as per your request, of course. You are a better tactician then I gave you credit for, Remy, much better." Replies Commander Sauer smiling and to himself. "A much better tactician than any of us gave you credit for. You remind me of someone Remy. I just cannot put my finger on whom."

"Well let's see if it worked, Sir." Says Remy.

CHAPTER 2

"Man is capable of more evil than he can dream of"

"WHAT ARE YOU DOING here?" the Warlord says agitatedly to Guake. The Warlord's name is Alexandro Diego. He is a ruddy complexioned hulking man with jet black hair that always looks wet. He weighs closed to three hundred pounds and constantly sweats profusely. Alexandro's father had always said he would never amount to anything. He was a waste since birth his father had said. But, look at him now. It took him ten years, still Alexandro had created a small empire using drugs and smuggling. Alexandro Diego is the most hated man in the country and he is also the most dangerous. In the beginning, his pipeline into America had always been fragile. Running smoothly one day and not running at all the next. This frustrated him greatly. Nothing seemed to work. Bribing politicians, threatening law enforcement agents, even making deals personally did nothing. His luck changed after he met some strange priests about five years ago. It all began when a mysterious temple appeared in the middle of the jungle with a bunch of albino priests. The same priests who had approached him with quite a generous proposition. They had opened a pipeline that runs like a rolling river. Alexandro Diego now makes close to six million dollars a month and with that kind of money, he soon saw his power start to really grow. In return, he helped; these priests start a druid-like religion in this country, a religion that included ritualistic human sacrifice and mutilation in its ceremonies. Since then Alexandro's power had grown to the point where the president of the country does whatever he asks and looks away from his affairs. Not too shabby for a Harvard graduate, who majored in economics. Whose father thought he was worthless. The same father Alexandro had murdered himself. From the moment they arrived, the priests of the temple were always by his side constantly giving him instructions and setting up more ways for him to make money. Alexandro had made a pact with them, power and riches for human bodies. It seemed like a good deal at the time and everything had been working well. That is until the Heme Corporation sent Remy Robon in to set-up a hospital. The last two people the Corporation sent were easy to bribe and now worked for him in the pipeline to the States. He thought Remy would cave in just like the others. On the contrary, he did not instead; Remy had started to meddle in community affairs. The people started to look up to him and they no longer feared Alexandro and his men. The people have started to refuse to give their children and women to the temple. Alexandro cannot afford to lose all he has gained because of one man. Alexandro had tried to bribe Remy with everything from woman to diamonds. Each time he attempted a bribe Remy told him where to stick it. He had tolerated this behavior, because he was just trying to do business. Enough of the bullshit, no one tells Alexandro where to stick it. Therefore, Alexandro bribed Guake and ordered him to kill Remy. Seeing Guake in front of him without Remy's head was a bad sign.

"We lost all the men at the compound." Guake says.

"No, you lost all the men at the compound. We could see the fires from here." Alexandro says reaching for a glass of wine and sipping it. "You told me that you had everything under control. That if, we left it in your hands, not only would we make money, but I would also have Robon's head on a platter. Well, I am losing money and men and I do not have Robon's head on a platter. In fact, we do not even know where he is. Am I right?"

"No, we don't." Guake answers nervously looking away and starting to perspire heavily.

"How the hell did you get out before he killed you?"

"I had some tunnels dug underneath the camp. When I heard the first explosions I jumped into one and headed back here. That's when I looked back and saw the Corporations troops arrive."

"Now let's see, Robon is alive with about two hundred trained soldiers with him. He also knows it was I who engineered the attempts on his life and the death of his men in the compound. Knowing Robon, I would say he is a little piss off and he is coming for me. That I should thank you for because I intend to kill him myself."

"My Lord, Remy is unlike any warrior I have ever met. It would be better if you have him killed from a distance." Says Guake nervously.

"So, you fear him."

"No, My Lord I respect his abilities. Abilities I have seen firsthand."

"Are you trying to tell me what to think? Well let's see if his abilities are as good as you say when he gets here…."

"He will never find you here, My Lord." Says Guake

"That is probably true. Thanks to these priests' advice to move the compound yesterday. These caves are the perfect defensive position."

Standing to his left are three men about six and a half feet in height. Two of them have gaunt features with pointed ears and cold pink eyes. They are arrayed in dark robes, each a different variation of maroon. They are extremely beautiful and graceful. Just looking in their eyes could easily enthrall a person. They have a magical quality about them. The one standing in the middle however, has a more rugged look to him. Tanned and muscular, more akin to a warrior then a priest and his eyes are coal black. He steps forward and says "Diego, this is not the time to allow your temper to override reason. We have lost this battle. Nevertheless, we have not lost the war. Let it be, you will not beat Robon by being impulsive."

"I'll do whatever I please, Priest Fica. I have a thousand men and Remy has a mere two hundred. The mathematics is simple. If they attack us, we will crush them. Besides, I have a fortified position. I hold all the cards here." Alexandro says rising from his seat looking up at the priest. "You are here to advise me not to control me. No one controls me, no one."

"This is not an idea of control. It is an idea of restraint. You have amassed power, money and land with our assistance. We must show restraint to protect it. The Corporation we can wait out. They only want to build this hospital and move on. They do not care about your drug trade."

"We, we what? I care. To keep power over my men I need to show strength always. I cannot hide every time I am attacked or run when challenged. I will lose their respect and their fear of me." Replies Alexandro looking Fica directly in his eyes. "Maybe it is you that fears this Robon. Is there something you are not telling me?"

Fica looks at him unfazed and says, "We fear no one that walks this earth. You are making a grave error in judgment here and what you bring on yourself is your own affair. Nevertheless, even though we think you are foolish we have backed you in all your enterprises and will continue to do so."

"Of course, you backed me in all my enterprises. But you did not answer my question? Do you fear Robon? Yes or no?"

"As I said we fear no one on this earth, Diego. We have given you what you needed to become what you are. Do not take prudence for weakness."

"And I gave you what you needed for your experiments and your church. I smell fear upon you. Your words are brave, but your actions are weak. I need you no longer, priest. I can solve this problem myself. Go back to your temple and shake in your boots. I expected more backbone from you."

Fica's body becomes tense with anger, but before he can say

anything one of the other priest touches his arm. After eye contact with the other priest, Fica visibly relaxes.

"As you will." Fica says and turns away. He signals to his fellow priest and they walk out together. As soon as they reach the safety of the corridor leading to the temple, the other priests remove the albino masks and pink contacts.

One of the other priests stops in front of Fica, who is visibly upset and says, "I thought you told me this operation was under total control. Evidently, it is not. That fool will fall to the corporation's forces with little effort on their part. His men are not warriors they are rogues and bullies, who will run at the first sign of real battle. Once again, Robon will triumph. These fools are no match for him or the trained warriors that come with him. We have chased Robon for years and this was our best chance to kill him without the other tribes even knowing of his existence. You know as well as I do that until he claims his birthright, we cannot personally intercede, it is the law. Though we care little about the law, we must keep up pretenses to achieve our goal. I want him dead before that, you hear me dead! You will pay the price for your incompetence, Fica. Now we must go, the half-breed comes. His tracking abilities are without equal and we do not need him hunting us. Not now, before we are ready. The council will not be pleased with you Fica. You were never my choice for this operation and your performance has proven I was right. We will lose much today, this had become a place we could rely on. I will contact our warriors and they will take care of what you could not. That news will also not please the council. Come we must hurry to the temple. It is time to leave that human dog to his fate."

Meanwhile, Alexando has lost his mind to drink and anger. The need to kill Remy has become an obsession. "I want every man ready for battle. This time there will be no mistakes, everyone dies."

Alexandro's captains nod and run out to prepare their men.

"My Lord, I agree with the priest. They will look for us at the old command post and find out we are not there. This is a perfect place. It is away from the main road and no one knows of its location. We stay low for a week and then Robon is alone again. We have someone close to him. We only need to wait." Says Guake

"What do you mean we have someone close to him, you work for me." Alexandro says walking up to him and pointing a finger in his chest.

"Yes, My Lord I work for you. But they are here and everywhere. You need not have spoken to them like that. It's not a safe thing to do. There is more to them then you know."

Alexandro paces away from him, laughs heartily, picks up a bottle of scotch, and drains it in one swig.

"Is that so? So, you have become enthralled by those self castrated priests as well. Guake, something is going on here you don't understand because you're less than a man. Robon is a man; he lives or dies with his actions. You are a pussy! You hide in the shadows and kill men. You give orders for death however you do not administer it. I have had enough of your ball-less behavior." Alexandro shouts as he throws his knife into Guake's throat. Guake falls grabbing at his throat feeling his life flowing through his fingertips all for money.

There is a loud rumble as missiles raining from the sky begin striking the camp. Alexandro goes to the window to see two jets strafing the camp. "Shit I shouldn't have killed you so soon, Guake. I probably could have used you as a shield. It does not matter Robon and his soldiers are going to die. Next to die when I finish with Robon is those fucking priests" he says as he opens his weapons closet and hurriedly stocks up on ammunition and weapons. As he heads up the tunnel towards the temple, he hears another roar. Alexandro turns and races down the tunnel that leads to the temple at a speed that belies his bulk. As he reaches the surface, he sees the whole temple fly away. Alexandro chuckles to himself and says, "No wonder they built it so quickly." Surveying the yard, he sees many of his men already dead from the surprise bombing. "Those priests were a lot of things and thorough was one of them. How the hell did Robon find us? I guess he has a spy network himself. No matter,

Remy Robon dies today." Alexandro thinks to himself running into the fray as the helicopters with the corporation's troopers land.

Remy is in the forefront unloading his weapons on his attackers shouting, "Show no mercy to these dogs!"

The troopers quickly over run the whole compound and control the base in minutes. The reality of this situation is Diego's men are farmers and bullies against warriors. They fall and keep falling until they turn and run. Then they are all cut down like pigs in the slaughterhouse. Alexandro seeing no chance of victory rushes back into the tunnels. Looking for a place to hide until the battle is over and he can try to escape. Alexandro has some money hidden in the mountains and accounts in Switzerland. He will just cut his losses and start somewhere else. Alexandro has no more words of bravado because reality has finally sunk in. They never had a chance against the Heme Corporation's forces. All his dreams of power are coming to a pitiful end. Again, he wishes he had not been so impetuous and killed Guake. If there was one thing he did well, it was to escape. The priests were right, and he was a power-hungry fool. Behind Alexandro he begins to hear shouts and he knows if he does not find a place to hide soon, he is dead. He makes a turn into the cave they used to throw the body parts of all the sacrifices not used by the priests. The stench is unbearable. Alexandro begins to vomit and continues until he is retching. He had never been in this cave; he never knew it was this horrible. Men, women, and children's body parts are thrown about in huge piles. "My God, what have I done? What did I allow those butchers to do?" Alexandro thinks to himself as he falls back against the wall. He is startled by movement to his left and gets up quickly.

It is Remy Robon. Remy punches him in the face sending Diego's weapon sprawling out of his reach. Remy kicks Diego's weapon away and throws his own gun down.

"What's wrong, you allowed this? You led your own people to slaughter. Why did you allow this to happen? Was it for power, for money? Look at all these pieces of humanity strewn about like garbage. Their souls cry out for vengeance. Do you hear it Diego?"

Alexandro backs away from Remy his eyes' wide in terror because he suddenly does hear voices begging for revenge. "This cannot be real, I must be going mad from the grotesque sights in this cave, or is it you. Are you some type of demon?"

"Yes, Diego, I am the demon sent to bring you down. I gave you many chances to change your ways. But, you would not listen to me. You could have been the hero of the people instead of the scum that you are. Come Diego, fight me man to man, not through puppets. I have heard you fancy yourself a warrior. Time to prove it here amongst the dead you created from your greed."

Alexandro pulls out his bayonet and charges Remy who deflects his blade with the tip of his short katana.

"Good, you at least have spirit. Maybe you will even die well."

"You are a madman Remy. I did not know what I was allowing. They said they needed subjects for medical studies. I didn't know."

Alexandro says feinting and dancing back and forth trying to gain an advantage against Remy. Remy's eyes are like burning coals searing into Diego's soul. Remy's gaze never wavers he does not even blink. This unnerves Alexandro as he tries to find an opening in Remy's defense.

"But you did know Diego. You let them have your women and children. You gave away whole families, as if they were nothing more than chattel. These were your own people. You were born here. You need to pay for that and you will," replies Remy.

"No, I swear. I did not know. This is the first time I have even seen this cave."

"I find that hard to believe, Diego. Puppet you may be to those priests, but, you have to take some of the responsibility for what has happened here."

"I only procured for them. I was never personally involved."

"There was a little boy, Diego. A boy named Manuel. He used to run errands for me. That was until he disappeared one day. I asked his mother where he had gone. She told me that the priest at the Temple had recruited Manuel to work in the fields. She explained your soldiers offered him twice the money I paid him. His family was poor that type of money could feed and clothe them for months, so he agreed and left with your soldiers. Two days later, she was told he was killed in an accident and was given his pay for a week. A week later, his decapitated body was found somewhere in the jungle. I knew it was Manuel because he was still wearing the bracelet I had given to him. Explain that Diego. He was twelve years old. Killing him made it personal to me."

"You see it was Manuel's own choice to go. I always gave them a choice. I did not make him take the job." Says Alexandro panting.

"Enough games Diego, you will never admit your guilt. It is time to die. And you're going to die just like these poor people, piece by piece." Remy says severing Alexandro's knife hand from his arm. Diego roars in pain as his hand hits the ground, but before he can move, his left leg is severed at the knee and he crashes headfirst into a pile of body parts. He screams again "No. No, you are the devil incarnate. Robon, you need killing!"

"I need killing. It was not me, who became a traitor to my people or used their deaths to make a profit. You did."

Alexandro smiles through his pain and says, "They know about you Robon."

"Who knows about me?" says Remy suddenly confused by Diego's words. "Who knows about me?"

"They know about you and your life will soon end. Because they are everywhere." answers Alexandro "Everywhere. You will die. I now realize Guake was right." And Alexandro begins to laugh like a madman at the realization that he had no control over anything. He had been a pawn all along.

"I do not understand what you are babbling about."

"You will soon. They are about to take over this world and they have hundreds of enclaves like this. They want you dead and they will succeed. You are going to hell."

"You first dog." With that, Remy cuts his head off as the rest of the corporation's forces enter the cave and most of them start vomiting immediately at the sight and smell of the rotting body parts.

"Get out all of you, except you Julio. Please film this cave and then leave. Julio gets up and shakily does as he ask as the Commander steps into the cave and exclaims "Mother of God, what type of sick bastards would do this?"

"I don't know Commander, but I'm sure as hell going to find out. Enough pictures burn the room and give these people peace." Remy says striding out of the cave with the Commander behind him.

"You still think I'm cruel and inhuman after what you've seen this day?" says Remy.

"No Remy, I don't. In fact, you have done an incredible job under extreme circumstances."

"I guess I'll get a medal or something." Answers Remy sarcastically.

"No Remy, no medals. But I do have new orders for you."

"Yea, what hellhole are you guys sending me to this time?"

"Why do you always think in a pessimistic manner? Remy, you are to go to the corporate offices in New York." He reaches out to Remy's shoulder and continues, "They're going to promote you to a stateside position where you'll earn allot of money and your ability to plan can be put to better use. You deserve it boy. You have busted your ass for the corporation for the last three years. We owe you."

Remy stands in shock. He never thought this would happen. He always envisioned himself dead in some jungle. You know another patriotic fool off saving the world.

"Remy, did you hear what I said to you?" The Commander says awakening Remy from his musings.

"Yes, I heard you. There must be something to this. What else do they want, maybe a quart or two of blood?"

"Why would you say that? No tricks boy, a straight promotion. You can enjoy life a bit now. Why are you so skeptical?"

"I said that because nothing good ever happens to me without a price. That price is usually paid in blood."

"Well maybe your luck has changed." Says the Commander smiling.

"Okay, let me just oversee the clean up." Remy says striding away.

The Commander looks after him and says, "Always the suspicious one, Remy. But your instincts are right, you just don't know how right. Still it's strange that you would talk of a blood debt. More and more I think we are missing something with you." He looks back into the cave and says, "I must let the Queen know of this. They are loose again."

Remy helps with the clean up and then heads back to the hospital. As he arrives, he sees the bodies of his men all loaded on the carrier for transport home for burial.

"I have not lived up to my duties." Remy says. "However, I will avenge you when I find those priests."

Dingham comes running across the field and says, "Bad business, huh boss?"

Remy looks at him and something does not seem right. His intuition is trying to tell him something, but he cannot quite place the feeling. "Yea, really bad business, what are you doing here? Didn't I tell you to wait in town?"

"I know, Boss, but I just wanted to make sure you okay."

"How did you find me here, Dingham?"

"I followed the fires, Boss. It's not hard."

"I see." Says Remy feeling a little disoriented for some reason.

"What do we do now, Boss?"

"Well, at least you'll have a job when I'm gone. I spoke to the Commander and he is going to give you a job with the corporation." Remy says lying.

"Why, boss? Ya going somewhere?"

"Yes Dingham, I have been recalled to the states for another assignment."

"Boss, you can't leave, the people depend on you to protect them." Remy notices that Dingham's scent has changed. Almost like dead flesh rotting away.

"Dingham are you ill?" He asks baffled by the change in scent.

"No Boss, why you ask?" answers Dingham stepping noticeably down wind.

Remy takes note of this and says, "No reason, you just look a little pale."

"Well, Boss, it's all this business. Ya know with Guake being a traitor and all. I mean who can you really trust these days."

This statement sends a shiver down his spine. He had given strict instructions that no one was to tell of Guake's betrayal. Everything crystallizes in one moment. The men in the alley when he saved Dingham were there as a trap for him. He had just killed them all. Dingham had radioed the base before they had departed this morning and said everything was okay by that time everyone was dead. Dingham has been a spy all along. Watching him and plotting against him at every turn. Remy does not outwardly react and says, "I guess you came back to help with the fighting instead of going back to town when I told you."

Dingham smiles and backs up making hand signals to three farmers whom are working by the roadside. "Enough with the bullshit, Guake did what I told him to, he belonged to us you see. This time there will be no mistakes. You will die." With that, Dingham starts to change into some type of demon. He now has sharp fangs with clawed hands and feet and his voice has become more of growl. Remy looks over and sees the other three undergoing the same transformation. He pulls his Uzis and opens fire hitting them all point-blank in the head and chest; they all fall but rise again. Dingham says, "New weapons can't kill us half-breed. Only the old weapons can kill us. It is time for you to die."

Instinctively Remy draws his short sword cleaving the first in twain. He spins and beheads the second astounded at his own prowess with the blade and his somehow augmented strength and speed. Remy hears the Commander barking orders as the beast that was Dingham charges forward and rips open his back with razor sharp claws. The third beast comes charging forward and is skewered through the throat by Remy's bayonet.

"You have no idea of your birthright, boy". Growls Dingham turning for another pass. Remy flips his sword as if he had done it a thousand times and twirls in front of himself forcing the beast back. Dingham then leaps at him; however, Remy turns ever so slightly and eviscerates the beast in one stroke. Bleeding profusely, he staggers over to the beast. "What are you?"

"I am the creation of the elder ones." he coughs blood spewing from his mouth. "Their time has come again. They will not be stopped this time. You will die with at least that knowledge."

Remy has other questions, but his answers die with Dingham. He feels faint as he turns to walk away because of the massive loss of blood. It's very strange though, he doesn't feel much pain. Remy's last conscious thoughts are of many men running to him led by the Commander as he plummets into darkness.

CHAPTER 3

"Through blood and fire we are reborn. Our
bodies tempered, our hearts filled with hope anew,
our purpose clear and our spirit reincarnated."

REMY TOSSES AND TURNS in the cryogenic chamber. Hideous dreams
of an all-out slaughter are flowing through his mind. A battle is going
on around him. Skies full of smoke and fires burn all about. Fairies,
werewolves, ogres, elves, vampires and dwarves are battling to the
death, no guns, no bombs, just plain cold steel. Blood of a thousand
colors is spilt all around him as he gives orders in the fray. A woman,
skin of ivory, eyes black as coal dressed in all black armor with a red
dragon crest upon the chest is in the center of the battle swinging
two short swords like a maestro swings a baton. All the while, a huge
grin resides on her face. Remy is attracted to her like no other woman
he has ever known. He fights his way over to her slicing through the
throng with his own double blades. When he reaches her, she has cut
down the last of her antagonists and she turns to face him covered with
blood. They sheath their blades in unison and stare into each other's
eyes. Soon they are locked in an embrace kissing passionately and
ripping each other's armor off. They make love amid the dead bodies
as the battle rages on. Never has Remy felt so satisfied or so safe. She
kisses him after their mutual climax gently and smiles revealing fangs
saying, "Welcome home, My Lord."

Outside the cryogenic chamber the flight physician frantically administers a sedative to calm Remy down. "He's going crazy in there. He has already received enough sedative to knock out a bull elephant. This is no ordinary human, Commander. By God's name he's going to rip the chamber apart."

"Who said he was human?" replies the Commander. "We recruited him from the human world."

"Have you ever seen a human who could tolerate the blood of life? That must intrigue you."

"No, I have not known a human to live after receiving the blood of life and yes, his existence intrigues me. When you brought Remy to us, his spine was completely severed, and both his lungs were punctured. How he even lived that long I will never know. However, we gave him the blood of life while he was being prepared for surgery and he began to heal at an accelerated rate, even faster than us. His lungs started repairing before my own eyes and his spine reconnected it seems on its own. Therefore, I placed him in a cryogenic tank to accelerate it more and he has almost totally healed in just eight hours. Almost like the Elves, but that is impossible, you know as well as I that we have never been allowed to mate with the elves because of the curse. All the children born from these unions become mad and die of synaptic seizures."

"You're a genealogist, look at him; he has the traits of all the four base tribes. I have always held Remy in high regard. He is very intelligent, loyal and innovative. After I watched him battle the shape-changers, I knew he was more than I had ever hoped. I must admit I stopped to admire his prowess instead of helping him. For some reason, I knew he would be the victor. It was incredible Vaft."

"How so?" replies Vaft?

"His speed was that of a werewolf and his strength as much as the most powerful vampire.

It was as if the Emperor were alive again. He used the old style of the spinning blade. Thinking of it brings great joy to my life again. I so miss my sword-brother Vincenzo".

"There must be another explanation, Commander?"

"Yes and no, but the only true explanation is Dewa."

"That's a possibility, but we all thought him dead at least thirty years. He was quite mad you know. We should never mate with an elf, it's too dangerous."

"You are correct, he was mad, nevertheless, he escaped and was never found in the Canadian wilderness. There is a tribe of werewolves there who coexist with some of the last dwarves. Dewa could have gone there, found his peace and mated. You know the dwarves are the masters of the mind. Maybe they placed a block in his mind to prevent the madness or maybe they just healed him."

"Or maybe the legend of a serum to prevent a vampire from becoming feral actually exists. As you well know, the shape-changers emit a pheromone that inhibits a werewolf from changing. Maybe Dewa's father was able to create a serum to prevent Dewa from needing to become feral using the same process." Says Vaft.

"That is true, Vaft, but any serum created can be duplicated. The elves would have the serum by now and would have tried to create an army of hybrid vampire/elves. That is unless he died with that secret. Nonetheless, maybe a vampire and an elf had a child and that child impregnated a mixed dwarf and werewolf child before the madness took hold."

"Again, that is possible. That child would have the aspects of all the tribes, but some of those traits should have manifested by now. However, this is all far from conjecture. I do have the results of the blood tests back." Says Vaft

"Yes, I know and that's why I have taken such a keen interest in Remy's past. I looked at Remy's records and he does not exist until high school in the state of Washington. Which I might add is just forty miles from the Canadian border. Only one hundred miles from the dwarf and werewolf camp we just mentioned. If he does have the bloods of the four first tribes, then he is the link between the past and the future. He is the only hope of mankind and the peaceful tribes of the Old Era."

"Then he is the one spoken of in the prophecy."

"Possibly, however, there is no doubt he is of royal blood and that he is part of the magical races."

"If this is true the Queen must know." Says Vaft

"The queen will know soon enough."

"Do you think the queen will accept him?"

"The queen does not have a choice; she is one of the last thousand fertile females left. You know the last chemical war waged by the Elves left most of our males sterile and the first generation of males completely sterile. There has not been a life mate ceremony in a century. We are but forty thousand strong not counting the clans in Europe and Asia and the Elves know it. They are willing to wait until we all die off before they take over this planet. We are the only protectors of God, the old ways and humans. The Queen must accept the truth, the Emperor has been dead almost a millennium. In all that time she has not found anyone appropriate to even have a child with. She makes the laws, she must abide by them."

"You speak words that could be construed as treason by some. There are still a lot of zealots amongst us especially in Europe and Asia, your words could cost you your life." says Vaft looking at him.

"I'll take my chances if it means the peaceful races will survive. Did you send the blood sample to the Queen by special courier as I requested?"

"Yes, I did My Lord. It should have reached there by now. Once they analyze the sample, they will come to the same determination we have. This man carries the blood of all the first four tribes including the Elves and can possibly mate with anyone without the madness because the blood is mixed. All the blood types found seem to be of royal origin. I personally have traced the DNA to all of the first tribes' royalty. He essentially is a prince to all the tribes."

"I expected to hear that from you once you had finished your examination of his genes because I already felt that in my heart."

"By the great ones it has just dawned on me. He is as important to the Elves as he is to us." Vaft exclaims.

"That is where you are wrong. He is a danger to the Elves

because any one he mates with would create mixed blood, which the Elven Elders would never permit. Well that is only a problem for them if vampire blood is included. They have many half-breeds in their tribe that are accepted. Based on this attack they know or have guessed about Remy's lineage. They hoped to kill him before he knew of his birthrights or his powers. That clearly indicates their plan is not a peaceful unification. What they desire is total dominion over this planet with God and all of the first tribes' dead at their feet." Replies Commander Sauer.

"That is true. But, they had so many chances to kill him. Either he is the best warrior alive or they are losing their touch. Still many high-ranking Elves have mated outside the tribe with dwarves, werewolves, and others."

"But never a vampire and always by force, none of the other tribes would mate with an elf under any circumstances. Hell, the elves still raid the other tribes' encampments. We are all like garbage to them, no more suitable to mate with than a wild beast. Not fit for anything but death. We stand in their way and they will not stop until they find a way to destroy every single one of us."

Sariel erupts out of her sleep drenched in perspiration. She has just had a dream that felt so real her heart is still pounding. A man like no other man had fought by her side and then made love to her on the battlefield. The dream was so tangible she had climaxed for the first time since Vincenzo had died almost a millennium ago. Could it be true, could she have another life-mate? She thinks to herself. "No, it was only a dream," Sariel says aloud composing herself. She rises from her bed and goes into the shower hoping she can wash his touch from her body. Nevertheless, she can still feel his caresses, kiss and his passion. The water seems to accentuate those feelings. She just cannot stop thinking about him. It is almost maddening, the need she has for this person that does not exist, or does he? She thinks as she steps out of the shower and dries herself slowly.

"It's not so bad to feel this good." Sariel thinks to herself. Looking into the mirror at her almond shaped green eyes, her Asian features and long red straight hair. She sits still staring into the mirror brushing her hair. "I have been without physical pleasure for so long; I almost forgot how good it felt. Forgive me, Vincenzo, but I think my time of mourning has ended at last at least in my dreams." Sariel gets up quickly and heads to her closet. She squeezes into a sweat suit as she prepares to go for a run around the park. Being a warrior, she is in splendid physical condition. Long flat muscles and wrist strength created by millennia of sword play. Maybe a little physical activity would keep her mind occupied. Some group of kids always tried to mug her in the park. Sariel could be just a warrior for a change. These forays were her only escape from her position of authority. She sneaks by her bodyguards and runs through Central Park in the middle of the night. It drives her security team crazy. The Haxe Building where she lives overlooks Central Park. Still her security staff understands why she is gone and stay within fifty feet of her at all times. They allow her the illusion of freedom from her position of authority, an illusion is better than nothing. They allow her to hunt. She never kills any of the people that attack her. Not killing them takes more prowess than killing them. However, they would never allow harm to come to her.

In the last millennium, there have been three attempts on her life by the elves. The first was right after Vincenzo died. To Sariel it was as if it happened yesterday. Vincenzo had been a very public man, a driving force in government and business. His funeral was a state event. Hundreds of politician and royalty from all over the word attended. This of course included all of the tribes. The law of God forbids aggression during gatherings, including funerals. Nevertheless, when did the elves ever abide by God's law? As her carriage pulled out of the cemetery and holy ground an ogre hit squad attacked. Commander Sauer, who oversaw her security detail, expected this foul play and had secreted warriors in the brush near the cemetery. The hit squad never had a chance as soon as they attacked they were hacked to pieces. Pieces that were sent back to Naline, the elven leader, with a note. "This could be you."

The second attack was during a trip to Europe for a vampire clan council. Naline had a battalion of shape changers take over the private airport her plane was landing in. Little did he know but the vampire clans in Europe did not take kindly to this overt military action? They called ahead, and the shape changers were crushed between the landing forces and the European clan.

The last attack about a decade ago came during the summer solstice. A group of trolls were sent underground to dig up into the Haxe building with the help of some vampire traitors. There objective was to kill Sariel, Dr. Vaft and Commander Sauer all in one move. It might have been a successful operation if the three of them were soft politicians. The three of them drew blades like in the days of old and killed the vampire traitors as well as all of the trolls except one who they let live to speak of the folly of a direct attack on the vampire royalty.

Her phone rings as she finishes getting dressed. When she picks it up she suddenly feels a chill in her bones.

"Hello."

"My Lady I know it is early, but we received a blood sample from one of Vaft's patients about two hours ago. After analysis, it is confirmed this patient has all the genes of the first four tribes, including the Elves."

"That is impossible a vampire and elven mating would result in a mad then dead child."

"Well my Lady, it evidently happened. I am checking now to see if the blood of each is of royal descent. I will know soon." says Dresa

"You know what will happen if he has royal blood from all of the tribes?"

"Yes, Milady the prophecy would be fulfilled and there will be war, a war to end all wars."

"Much worse than that is the immediate threat of every tribe having the right to claim him as royalty offering him a throne and a mate, every tribe that is, including the Elves. This being becomes the pawn for domination of this planet."

"We cannot let this happen, Milady. The Elves cannot know of his existence, he is probably our salvation as well as the salvation of all the peaceful tribes." Replies Dresa.

"We don't know what will happen. He must choose his own path. That is the way of God. This man has no idea of our world. Just finding out who he is will be hard enough. He will initially struggle with just our laws and ways."

"True, Milady, but he has responsibilities to live up to. It is his destiny."

"Destiny or not, I will not force his hand."

"He must come to you sooner or later. He is the prince."

"That is true, but it will be his choice to do so. If we are to rule together, he must come freely."

"I will assign a special guard for him. One that will test him in many ways, Milady." says Dresa

"No. I will have Commander Sauer choose his guard. It is his duty to do so." Replies Sariel.

"Yes, Milady, as you wish."

Sariel begins to quiver inside at the thought of meeting a man she already feels intimate with. She asks Dresa reluctantly. "Who is he and what do we know about him?"

"His name Milady, is Remy Robon and he's on his way here now. He sustained life-threatening wounds during battle, Lord Vaft gave him the blood of life at Commander Sauer's request, and Remy started to heal at an accelerated rate. Remy was hired by the corporation out of the Air Force academy to be a point person for our hospital corps. It seems Remy while protecting one of the sites was attacked by four shape-changers, but was victorious somehow."

"Four shape-changers you say?" Sariel exclaims.

"Yes, milady, no one has done that since the Emperor." Dresa pauses at the other end of the phone realizing she may have just incited her mistress's wrath. "Forgive me milady, I did not mean..."

The Queen cuts her off and replies, "We all heal in time Dresa. You have been my personal confidant for two centuries. That will never change. This man may be the answer to all our prayers. However, it is quite clear that the Elves know of his lineage. Do you have a picture of him?"

"Yes, Milady, look at your computer screen."

Sariel almost faints at the sight of Remy's picture. It is the man from her dream. It cannot be. She stops her thoughts and says to herself "You are a queen pull yourself together."

"Milady, are you, all right?"

"I am fine. You said he was attacked by several shape-changers and survived. How many attacked him again?"

"Four, milady."

"You did say, four?" replies Sariel with an audible gasp.

"Yes, milady four shape changers. He killed all of them with a blade."

"With a blade is the only way they can be killed, Dresa. But no vampire has been able to kill four shape changers alone. Not even Vincenzo."

"That is true, Milady. However, Remy does have the blood of all the first tribes running through his veins. Which makes him like no other vampire we know?"

"Yes, his prowess would be that of the werewolves. The only interesting point is that he did all of this without the blood of life. He did this without the aid of the four first tribes' magical powers. He did this as a human."

"That is true, milady."

"Now as he starts to claim those powers he will become an even more formidable warrior." Says Sariel.

"Almost like a Celestial, I would think milady."

"Please bring me all the data we have on Remy Robon, he sounds like an interesting man. Oh, and Dresa, bring a pot of coffee and some Danish, I'm starved." and to herself "An interesting man, indeed."

CHAPTER 4

"Rebirth is always a painful process."

AS THE PLANE LANDS at Kennedy airport, Remy wakes up with a start. He jumps up from his seat and is gently pushed back down by Commander Sauer who says, "Take it easy son, you've been through a lot."

"Where are we, Commander?" Remy asked looking around the plane, which is taxiing into a hangar.

"We are in New York, Remy. You slept most of the way. I cannot blame you after those creatures attacked you. Dr. Vaft here patched you up pretty good and gave you a sedative. This is why you might feel a little groggy and disoriented for awhile." Commander Sauer says pointing to Vaft who is sitting across from them.

Vaft waves back at Remy with a faint smile on his lips. Remy looks at Lord Vaft and knows he has seen him before. He quickly orients himself to his surroundings and says aloud.

"Where were my injuries? If I remember correctly my back had been ripped out by that beast. I mean I thought they were mortal wounds. I really didn't expect to wake up this time."

Commander Sauer and Vaft just glance at each other and Vaft says "You had some lacerations on your back which I was able to use a new plastic technique on. If you notice, they are almost completely healed by now. I also placed you in a cryogenic tank to accelerate the healing process."

"'Oh, man that means I've been out for a week again." Remy says.

"More like eighteen hours." Says the Commander Sauer. "It seems you heal very quickly."

"That I find hard to believe, Commander. If you read my dossier, you know I required cryogenic healing four times and each time it was for at least a week. Moreover, when my heart was punctured, it was three weeks. How I even survived that time I will never know. I must have been God's hand on me. The only difference this time is I do not feel the disorientation I felt after cryogenic healing. In fact, I feel brand new as if I've been reborn."

"You may be right on the money with that statement, son." Commander Sauer says as the plane comes to a halt.

"It time to embark on your new life, Remy. One you were born to live."

"What do you mean by that Commander Sauer?" asks Remy.

"Oh, let's say your life is now going to be very different."

The plane hatch opens, and four armed men step into the cabin. Remy instinctively rolls and pulls his weapons and shouts "Get down Commander!"

The Commander is amazed at Remy's speed. Vampires are fast, but werewolves have much faster reflexes. Remy's speed rivals some of the best werewolf warriors he knows. He just files that information in his mind and salutes the armed men by pounding his fist against his chest. The men return the salute by pounding their chest with their weapons.

"Remy, it's ok. These are members of our elite security team. The reason why you have never seen them before is quite simple. You have never been stateside long enough to spend any significant time at Heme building. They are here to escort you to the Heme building to see your pal, Martin. Get used to this; you are part of the upper echelon now. This is one of the perks. In addition, there has already been one attempt on your life that we know of. I will not allow another on my watch. These are my handpicked warriors." Commander Sauer says gesturing to the security staff to check the perimeter.

"Sorry Commander." Remy says holstering his guns and getting up. Remy notices the security team wears not only traditional weapons but also a pair of double swords and that is quite peculiar in the middle of New York City. "I guess it's just my nerves, Commander."

"Nerves can save your life. There nothing wrong with a little fear of the known and the unknown." Replies Commander Sauer

"My advice is to keep that attitude and remember to use your senses. Don't trust anyone till you smell them." says Vaft.

"Smell them?" answers Remy quizzically.

"That's right do not trust anyone until you smell them. If something smells rotten. It is rotten. Remember your battle with the shape changers". Says the Commander. "Remembering can keep you alive."

"There are many races on this planet who would like to see you dead, especially after what you did." Says Vaft

"I did my job. That is all, just my dam job." Replies Remy in a metered tone.

"Which it seems was more than enough to piss off a lot of folk." Says Commander Sauer "Time to go."

Outside the plane is a limousine with a full escort of police cars. It makes Remy truly feel like royalty. To top it off, at least two or three of the escorts have addressed him as "My Prince". They all get into the limousine and head towards midtown where the Heme Corporation's main building is located.

"Commander, can you explain why did those men address me as "My Prince?" Asks Remy pouring himself a glass of red wine and reclining back in his seat.

"Well, it's true in a way. You are a prince to these men, but you do not know why. It has to do with your blood. We tested it to give you a transfusion and found out some interesting things. Martin will explain everything to you in detail when you reach the Heme building. Please be patient." He answers looking directly at Remy.

"Okay." says Remy and he turns to Vaft. "You know, doctor, I just realized who you are. You are the utmost authority on genealogy in the world. Doctor Antonio Vaft. I have read a lot of your work. You have some very fascinating theories about evolution and man's place in the chain."

"That is true, my prince. However, I am one of the authorities not the most prominent. I would not have thought that the study of genealogy would interest you."

"Everything about genealogy interests me, Dr. Vaft. However, I disagree. I have compared your work against other genealogists and yours has always been succinct and easily understood. While others seem to speak in generalities, your work seems to unravel those generalities into specific genetic calculations in nonprofessionals' terms. Only someone who truly was an expert on a subject could relay information that complicated in such a clear way. Based on this information I would like to ask you a question."

"Anything, my prince." replies Vaft who is truly intrigued by this young man. It always refreshing and flattering to a scientist when someone shows genuine interest in his or her lifetime work.

"What is your professional opinion concerning my genetic heritage? Surely, you were the one who took my blood sample and analyzed it. Based on my rapid recovery you must have been absolutely captivated regarding the origins of my genes based on the way I healed so quickly. Virtually like finding a new species. Almost like your life work walking in front of you."

"You know young man, what I find more interesting is the way you carry yourself. Based on your file you were brought up from meager beginnings; nonetheless, your whole manner is that of an aristocrat. You ask questions expecting answers because you asked the question. I have watched you and you poured yourself a cup a wine and sat back in your seat and started asking questions. Such confidence and power of presence for a person who grew up without a family and no formal etiquette training, I find that quite alluring. It just adds some truth to a couple of my own theories. One of which is when you are born you already have the complete knowledge of everything. It just that your environment dictates what you need to know to survive and your own personal gifts are enhanced. Now back to your question. Of course, your miraculous recovery peaks my scientific interest. Investigations of your blood sample brought to light that you are something of a prize to several groups in this world because of your rare mixture of genes. So rare you seem to be an original. Those genes my prince, make you the savior of several races and possibly the end of another. Your blood is so rich with history and it will begin to shout out for knowledge of days gone by. These are becoming exciting times, indeed. Your whole existence is a riddle for some and a blessing for others. No matter how anyone looks at it, you are more gift than a prize." Says Vaft sipping his wine.

"My heritage sounds more like an enigma than a reality." Says Remy with a chuckle.

"More of an enigma than you may ever know, Remy." the Commander adds sipping his wine.

Remy pauses and looks down into his cup and says, "You know, Sir, this is really becoming a little strange. You know me I am just a grunt doing his job for the corporation, nothing more and nothing less. I have always tried to do my best. Maybe I was brought up a little more moralistic than other people, but that is just the way I was raised. I have given all I have to help others. I have been true to the company and always worked towards advancement. But to be raised to this level so quickly is somewhat surreal. Seriously, Sir, you have never lied to me. What the hell is really going on?" Remy says finishing his wine and pouring another.

"That my son will become quite apparent in a few moments we have arrived."

The limousine heads into an underground parking lot. As soon as they enter, the gate is closed. Remy has been here once, and he remembers how impressed he was by the tight security. Looking around he notices more extreme measures in place with a lot more men and women patrolling the perimeter. Everyone is wearing double blades, no guns. It is as if they expect a full-scale attack by an army. However, if they only have swords on what type of army are they expecting? As Remy disembarks from the limousine, every person bows as he passes him or her. Remy is escorted quickly to the elevator bank by several guards along with Commander Sauer and Lord Vaft. They all enter the elevator in silence. Remy could swear there are two or three guards on top of the elevator.

"Commander Sauer, the elevator feels as if you have two or three guards on the roof." He says jokingly.

In a deadpan voice Commander Sauer replies, "There are and two below." Vaft gets off on the twentieth floor. Remy makes a mental note of this.

"Dr. Vaft is your lab on this level?" Ask Remy.

"Yes, my laboratory and an infirmary. We always take care of our own, my prince."

"I will speak to you later, Dr. Vaft. I have a couple of other questions for you." Replies Remy.

"I am at your service, Milord." Says Vaft bowing as the elevator door closes.

Commander Sauer gets off on the fortieth floor and says, "Embrace your destiny. Your time has come."

Soon Remy reaches the floor beneath the penthouse. His friend Martin's office is on this floor. This is where he was recruited to work by the corporation five years ago. Remy remembers that day vividly. Martin had come to meet him after his graduation from the Air Force Academy. He told Remy that he could serve his country better by working for the Heme Corporation. Martin explained the Corporation had a deal with the government and recruited directly from the academies and the Corporation only wanted the best of the best. After Martin explained what his job would entail Remy jumped at the chance. To him it was a way to pay back all the people who had helped him through the years and to channel his propensity for violence in a constructive way.

The guards escort him to the office they turn and leave after they bow. Martin sits in a high-backed chair looking out the window with his back to Remy the same way he sat when he hired Remy five years ago. The silence seems to last an immeasurable amount of time.

"Martin, what's going on here? This is a little weird even for me." Remy says sitting down across from the desk breaking the silence.

"Well Remy, there is a war going on for the domination of this planet and you are now a key player." Replies Martin spinning his chair around to face Remy it has been close to five years since he first met Martin and it seems as if he hasn't aged a day.

"What war? There are no countries at war now."

"A war to end all wars has been ongoing for several millennia. A war no living being on earth and in heaven can afford to lose." Replies Martin.

"No shit, Sherlock."

"No shit, Remy. You still have a very dry wit" Martin says getting up. "Do you have any idea why you are a key player?"

"Not really. This is all like a really bad dream. Finding out would probably be the best ending to a fun filled day"

"You do have a point; it is a dream that can become a nightmare for many quite quickly. But I ask you now, why do you think you are a key player in this war to end all wars."

"Well, after a talk with Dr. Vaft, I think it has to do with my gene mixture. A mixture I have no idea about because I have no idea about my heritage."

"That is precisely why you are here. I happen to know everything about your heritage and your genes."

"Did you know these things when you hired me?"

"Actually, I had my suspicions. However, I never dreamed they would be true about you. Hiring you was either dumb luck or spiritual intervention. You should know you were not my first choice. I was looking for a person to be a liaison between the Corporation and the countries we serve around the world. A person to build relationships and from what I knew of you, it was apparent destruction was your forte not building. Again, to my amazement you proved me wrong and became one of our best operatives."

"So, I guess you're a little taken aback by my accomplishments."

"Some of those accomplishments yes, but not all of them. I hired you because you interviewed well and spoke plainly. You seemed to have a good spirit and exhibited an excellent work ethic. Those are some of the things I rate higher than others. Plus, I allow my personal feelings to sometimes rule my decisions. You just felt right."

"So, you hired me on a whim. You took a chance. I thank you for that."

"I should thank you. You have an excellent record of service and have on more than one occasion, gone beyond the call of duty. You have endured many injuries for the Corporation, some of them life threatening. We could ask no more than this from anyone."

"I just did my job. So, what has happened so drastic it changes my status in life from grunt to prince."

"We now through some research and guess work can piece together what must have happened. Basically, what your gene pool is and where it originated."

"I see. Dr. Vaft seems to think my genes are unique."

"That is true. You do have a very unique set of genes. So unique, that when I explain them you might say I'm full of shit or just plain crazy."

"After what I have gone through in the last day or two nothing could sound crazy. Shit, I watched men turn into monsters right in front of my eyes." Replies Remy looking down into his hands.

"What I'm going to tell you is going to sound ridiculous, but, you're going to have to believe what I say and fast. We do not have much time and the attempt on your life means they know who you are."

"This gets better every minute. I have now heard that statement from three different people. Who exactly are they?"

"Oh, you ain't heard anything yet; to coin a phrase here we go the down and dirty version. Before humans were created, God created four great races. These races were Vampire, Werewolf, Dwarf and Elf. Each of these races has magical powers, so to say. Each one of these races was fashioned to be the servants of God. We were to be his guardians and creators of life on earth. The Vampires were his soldiers and healers; they can become feral when needed in battle. Controlled ferocity is what makes them the perfect warrior God's celestial soldiers on earth. Many think this is shape shifting, but it is only an augmentation of strength and sometimes size. The legends are true Vampires do require small amounts of blood to survive. However, every single other myth is true of our cousins the Elves. You see the Elves were God's chosen his favorites. Their function was to create life on earth. They are very fair skinned people and cannot stand being in direct sunlight for extended amounts of time. This is where the word "fairy" was born. They need flesh and blood to survive, not just blood alone. The flesh and blood they crave the most is human. Most of the stories you have read about human beings found with their throats torn out are about them, not the Vampires. Like the Vampire, these beings have pointed ears and fangs. They hide their appearance behind plastic surgery and disguises. They may well be the greatest scientists and surgeons in the world.

The Werewolves on the other hand were created by God to protect the woodlands and be great hunters. It was their function to make sure the wild life prospered creating food for all. They can shape shift into whatever animal is their totem, not just wolves. This allows them to run amongst the animal tribes and cure disease or lead them to food. Some of the first amongst them can change into any animal at any time. They are quite a peaceful people. Despite that, of all the first tribes they have the greatest prowess in battle. The blood lust after however, sometimes last for days. Therefore, they cannot be God's warriors. Sometimes they would lose control and become filled with a blood lust that could never be satisfied no matter how much they killed. It was then they needed to be hunted down and destroyed another task given to us by God to keep the balance. The Dwarves tasks were to till the soil and to create tools and weapons. They are the masters of the fields and earth. Mother earth bends to their nurturing touch. The dwarves are additionally the masters of the mind and manipulation of it. They too are a very peaceful people at heart. Both the werewolves and the dwarves have always lived in harmony because they are both so close to mother earth. These are the most primal of the first four tribes. Moreover, whether you believe me or not there is a true mother earth. These two tribes worship her and protect her at all cost. Neither, dwarves or werewolves got along well with the Elves or the Vampires. That is because Vampires and Elves are quite aggressive and warlike. The Elves knew this and constantly tried to turn the dwarves and werewolves against us to no avail. After some time and God's help the four tribes learned to live in harmony, sharing all their special gifts with one another freely for centuries. The elves however have always preached domination over the rest of us. They thought we all were inferior to them. The Elves have always thought they should lead us all. To that end the Elves soon created four new forms of life. They created the shape-changer, the troll, the ogre and their crowning achievement human beings. God was overjoyed with their work and infused these beings with intelligence. The elves were not happy with this because their overall plan was to overthrow God and reign as the rulers of this planet. In addition, several celestial angels did not approve of God's decisions concerning human beings. The celestial angels already felt they had been replaced as God's favorites by the Elves. The celestial angels were God's first creation. The celestial angels were the first true tribe, whom were given dominion over heaven. The first of them to fall from grace was Lucifer. They all felt Jesus was one of them and in his reincarnation; he did become one of them. Some of the celestial angels never forgave God for allowing him to perish at the hands of earthly creatures without a fight. You see the celestial angels are God's personal warriors. The Elves tried to persuade the other three races to join them against

God and could not. Therefore, they turned to their creations and were successful recruiting the shape-changers, the ogres, the trolls, and a couple of disgruntled celestial angels to their cause. The humans, however, chose the side of God. What the Elves did not know was God had foreseen their treachery and had given human beings free will to choose. God of course knew they would choose him over them. This was another reason for the Elves to hate God even more than ever. There were many battles fought on earth and in heaven with victory not certain for either side. Finally, a force led by Emperor Vincenzo of the vampire clan crushed the rebellion. He led God's forces against the Elves and their allies and won. At the same time the archangel Michael led heavens forces against Lucifer. Most of the celestial battles are chronicled well in the bible. A battle that raged for years, bloodier than any other battle this planet has known. A battle that saw hundreds of thousands of beings killed or maimed from all the tribes. Very little is documented about those battles that took place here on earth. That is the way God wanted it. Once the battle was over the Trolls and Ogres were banished to live under the ground and the Elves were banished into the mountains in Switzerland. The Celestial angels who chose to overthrow God were banished to other realms by God himself after most of their powers were stripped from them. Most wondered why all of them were not put to the sword at the end of the war, but King Vincenzo was in union with God and that was not God's wish. God felt they would atone for their sins over time. However, that was not to be. The elves continued to plot against God and vowed vengeance against the rest of us. A century later, they created a virus, which made most of the first three races sterile. There are now maybe forty thousand of us left, while the Elves, Trolls Shape changers and Ogres have proliferated freely."

"Now hold on one minute, are you telling me all the stories I read as a child portraying elves as heroes were blatant lies?" says Remy walking over to the bar pouring two bourbons.

"Yes, what I'm saying is they are deceivers and have infiltrated mankind and fed them propaganda to make them malleable when the time came for the second war. Think about it would human beings follow vampires, werewolves and dwarves into battle. I think not. You see the Elves never forgave God for creating vampires. Vampires are the only entity standing between them and total domination over this planet. As long as enough Vampires live, they can never take over this realm and they know it. The elves are not true warriors. They are priests and scientists. That is why they created Trolls, Shape-changers and Ogres to fight the other three races. Shape-changers were created with specific chore, to kill werewolves. Because they emit a pheromone which prevents a werewolf from becoming feral, making them less effective in battle. It also works on some vampires. The Trolls are strong enough to fight the Vampires and the Ogres were created to destroy the dwarves through guile."

"Martin is that why those creatures have such a sickening smell."

"Who are you referring to?" Asks Martin

"I would guess the shape-changers that attacked me of course." Replies Remy

"So that is how their pheromone smells. No one except the King Vincenzo has ever survived an attack. That is good to know. I will alert all of the militia."

Handing him the bourbon, Remy asked "Why create man? I mean man seems to serve no military purpose. All of the first and second races could defeat the humans with ease."

"You're right. Man was not created to be a warrior he was created to be the perfect slave for the Elves. A being that is intelligent and delicious to boot, imagine that, a slave who sees to your every whim and then becomes dinner. Quite ingenious don't you think?"

"So that's what was happening in Thailand. The warlord was in league with the Elves and they were living off the population and creating shape-changers."

"I must admit, you are pretty quick on the pick up."

"Right, somehow, at this point I do not really think I have much of a choice. Now, how am I involved in all of this?"

"Well, you are involved because you are the son of royalty."

"Is that why all these people keep bowing and calling me prince?"

"Exactly, your father was the offspring of a Royal Elven and Vampiric union. A union that God has always been forbidden. What you have to understand is God had to leave some safeguards in place when dealing with these two powerful races. Elves are not able to become feral and Vampires are not able to become feral until they are adolescents. What happens when a vampire and elf mate, is as the children of this union reach puberty, they start to go mad because their feral side is suppressed by the elves' inability to become feral. Until one day they have to become feral as part of the birth gift of the vampire clan and then it happens. They have what is called a synaptic seizure, the brain over-loads and they die horribly. It is the reason these unions were outlawed by the clans."

"Does something like that also happen when the other races mate?" asked Remy downing the rest of his bourbon and pouring another. "Would you like another, Martin?"

"Yes, thank you, but to answer your question in a word no. The other races can have mixed offspring without them going mad or dying, however, the offspring usually lose one of the birth gifts given by God. It seems no being can have more than one of these special abilities at one time. But, then we don't know about you, of course."

"What does that mean?" replies Remy handing him another drink.

"Well with you it's kind of different. You are one of a kind. No one can predict if you have all or some of these gifts."

"Understood, nevertheless, if my Father was an offspring of this union, how did he survive long enough to sire me? He would have had a synaptic seizure long before he could sire me."

"There are many theories concerning your father. The one I believe is his father, who was a brilliant scientist, created a serum which would prevent your father from needing to become feral."

"If that's true, then the Elves would have killed for that secret, Martin."

"They did, they killed your grandfather like a dog in the town square with his wife full of child watching. They were so in love and would not be a pawn for the Elven council. He would not tell them the secret and since these unions are forbidden by the Elven council, he was put to death publicly. My theory is he injected your grandmother with the serum once he knew she was pregnant. He may have been the elves greatest scientist and he still remained loyal to God."

"Who killed my grandfather?"

"Naline, Clan Master of the Elves."

"Was this before or after the war?"

"This was years before the war. Before anyone knew of their treachery."

"You sound like you were there Martin." Says Remy chuckling while sipping his drink.

"I was there, Remy. I am thirty centuries old."

Remy almost chokes on the bourbon. "No kidding." he wheezes. "You look pretty good for someone who is three thousand years old."

"Most of the people you have seen today are at least eight hundred years old. Lord Sauer is thirty-five centuries old himself."

"That is extraordinary." There is a silence between them and Remy asks, "Martin what is wrong?"

"I still cannot believe I was so blind when I was young. I hated your grandsire just because he was an elf. Prejudice we vampires are taught from birth. Hate all Elves. I held that hate for no good reason, because he had never wronged the vampire nation or me. I loved your grandmother, but she loved him." Martin says getting up and looking out the window. "She risked all for him. It was not until that day that he was executed that I realized how much he loved her. He died with such grace and strength. He challenged Naline to battle even though he was not a warrior. He never had a chance. But, he fought bravely for close to ten minutes. That may not seem like a long time for a normal person. Yet as a warrior you understand he fought from his heart because he did not have the skill to win. Your grandmother was the King's sister and the Elves dared not touch her it was vampire business not elf business. If they had tried, the King would have destroyed them there and then. King Vincenzo had learned to accept his sister's love for Dewa, the first and he and Dewa had become friends. King Vincenzo, I found out later, begged Dewa to allow him to be his champion for the challenge. Dewa a man of true peace said "I will not allow you to start a war that could end existence because I fell in love with your sister or because we share a friendship. This is my burden to bear, mine alone. God will choose the fate of my wife, my child and me." Now that all was in the open your grandmother went before the council and they stripped her of her rank. They had no choice the law is the law. It was during the trial we all found out they had been married and she was with child. Some wanted her killed on the spot, but none wanted to test the tolerance of the King. He had allowed the council to adhere to the law and that was all he would allow. After the trial and a long talk with her, I took her as my own knowing her love did not belong to me. Three months later, Prince Dewa the second was born. I came to love him as my son and she came to love me as I loved her. His mother died in the same battle that King Vincenzo died in and I raised Dewa as my own. One day after a gathering of the First Tribes he just vanished. Last, I heard some twenty- five years ago he had gone to Canada to live with an Indian tribe. Now I know the tribe was filled with werewolves and dwarves."

"Hold on a second. The child was born in three months."

"Pregnancy is a lot shorter for the first tribes. God wanted us to proliferate as quickly as possible."

"I see. What you are saying is that my father mated with someone who has dwarven and were blood creating me. And apparently that blood is that of royalty as well. Martin, think about what you're saying. Let's look at all the facts before us, shall we. I am way past puberty and to my knowledge I have never become feral. I have shown a natural aptitude for medicine as demonstrated by my nursing degree and as you well know I have a great propensity for violence. Still this is all pretty hard to believe, that I could possibly have the blood of all the first tribes pumping through my veins or for that matter that there is even all the other tribes." Remy says getting agitated.

"Well first our puberty comes at about a century. You have already had encounters with at least three of those tribes. Vampire, human and shape-changer plus there is much more to it than that."

"What else could there be? Will I grow a tail soon?"

"No, I do not think so." Replies Martin with a chuckle. "Now that the blood of life has been introduced into your system, you are going to start experiencing some changes in both your appetites and biological make up. Some Halflings never have those changes."

"Really, is there a book I can read to find out what those changes may be?"

"With you no book could predict what physical changes you may have."

"There is a prophecy that explains all of this."

"Good, what is it?"

"I do not know exactly, you're going to have to find the dwarven elders and ask them. God entrusted them with this secret."

"All right, let me get this straight, I am the so-called savior of several races on this planet and I may be the only one of my kind."

"Right." says Martin slugging down his drink.

"And now you're telling me that I am going to undergo some physical changes in a short time that you are not sure about and I need to find the dwarven elders to learn about this prophecy. Which apparently was written about me many centuries ago?"

"I think that about sums it up nicely."

"I think something is definitely wrong here, Martin. My parents dumped me in an orphanage when I was a baby. I am not somebody who is special in anyway. I think you guys have the wrong man or you are just wishing I am that man."

"Oh, I think a review of the blood tests performed on you will change your mind about the fact you're the wrong man. Genetically at least, I do know you are somewhat of a genealogy buff. So, you will understand the basic chemistry profiles as well as the DNA testing results. Open your mind, Remy. The fact of the matter is your father placed you in safe hands knowing the Elves would try to kill you once they knew of your existence. He knew you were safe in that orphanage. He basically knew you were safe until you tasted or were given the life-blood."

"Everyone keeps talking about the blood of life or the life-blood. What is the life-blood?"

"The blood of life comes from one of the first four tribes and must be given freely to another."

"What of the need for blood to survive? I will not kill humans to live."

"As I explained to you, vampires require ingestion of a small amount human blood to survive. Therefore we chose to take over the medical affairs for the planet. It is how the Heme Corporation began. The planet's populace donates blood to us for distribution though out the planet. This gives us more than enough to synthesis into these." Martin pulls out a maroon pouch and pours out what looks like blood red jellybeans. "Each one of these is equal to a pint of human blood. It of course is not pure blood. It is a synthesized form of human blood we had to create about ten or twelve centuries ago, so we could survive. One of these per week is enough to sustain us. We have no need to slaughter humans to live."

"What happens if vampires don't ingest some human blood?"

"We become uncontrollably feral. No intelligent thought at all. A complete animal, which's only thought, is to fulfill its blood need by any means necessary."

"I guess that is where the human stories of vampirism come from."

"Exactly, some us went rogue especially in Europe and Asia. But that doesn't happen anymore."

"But if you have a means to create synthetic blood, why continue to control health care throughout the world."

"Think about it. The elves control races through pestilence and disease. It is our way of keeping a balance. Why do you think you were recruited in the first place? Elven nests are found mostly in under developed countries...." Martin says.

"Where the elves can live off the population and have raw material to create more warriors to battle us. I'm thick sometimes, but I do get it after a while." says Remy pointing at his head.

"Now the life-blood is not the same as these capsules. The life-blood comes directly from one of the first tribes and must be given freely to another. In your case, Commander Sauer chose to give you his own. It seems when you were attacked by the shape-changers, you were gravely wounded and required a blood transfusion. As you know, Commander Sauer is very fond of you and he ordered Dr. Vaft to give you a pint of his blood. He did this because of the fighting style you used against the shape-changers. It reminded him of the King. He hoped beyond hope you were half vampire because he thinks highly of you. There are many vampires who have bred with humans creating a danipiru. Commander Sauer never expected you to be who you are. You survived, so you could not be human. Commander Sauer then had Vaft do the gene testing and here we are."

"So, it was my Vampire genes that made me heal so quickly?"

"No, it was your elven genes that did that. We heal fast, but not that fast. The only way to kill an elf is to decapitate him. They even grow back limbs. Can you see why God did not want these two races to mix? It would create a mighty powerful warrior with the ability for mortal wounds to heal completely. Most of those wounds with the help of cryogenics could be healed within hours. If that being could procreate and became disloyal to God, they would storm heaven."

"Okay, fine. I get the point. But before I embark on my destiny, I would like to try to locate my mother and father."

"I am sure no one will have a problem with that. You deserve that much. Plus, you are a prince only the Queen could naysay you anything you chose. The Elves need at least a decade to prepare for the final assault. Believe me, we have time."

"What final assault?"

"Well, the elves have patiently been waiting centuries for most of the first tribes to die off. We are not immortal. Our life span is about forty to fifty centuries. In ten years whether we like it or not their tribe and their allies will outnumber us close to ten to one. Doesn't matter how great a warrior you are, sheer numbers will win the day."

"So how could I possibly be a threat to them?" says Remy?

"Just your presence is a threat to them. The races will rally behind you. They almost had the other races turned. They will never turn them now because the prophecy seems to be coming to fruition, a prophecy that both binds us all and brings an end to the Elves existence here on earth. Now that the Elves know you exist they are going to try to kill you anyway they can."

"Why? Am I not a prince to them as well?"

"Listen to me very carefully. As I explained earlier mating between elves and vampires is considered taboo. An elf would not mate with a vampire due to plain old bigotry. They think we are an inferior species. We are like animals compared to them. There council has placed a death sentence on anyone who does mate with a vampire. It is why your grandfather died. You are the culmination of their greatest fears. They do not want you to rule them. It would be a sacrilege. They just want you dead. Welcome to the most wanted list."

"What the hell does that mean, Martin?"

"Well we vampires have been hunted for centuries. The elves have gotten the humans to fear us and love them. It was a struggle just to survive in the beginning. Then Emperor Vincenzo got us involved in human politics and placed many of us in important positions. To coexist with humans, we signed treaties and kept to ourselves. Because of our prowess in the use of medicine, we have proven to be necessary to humans. Yet looking pass that Emperor

Vincenzo felt if we learn to live with the humans' side by side they would not fear us as much."

"Fear, is a dangerous emotion. It leads to irrational thought and rash actions. The Emperor was a wise man indeed." Replies Remy.

There is a knock at the door and Martin puts his finger to his lips. He reaches behind the desk and throws Remy a sheathed sword. Remy pulls out the blade and on inspection it looks like a roman sword, sharp on both sided and about two and a half feet long. The blade's balance is magnificent. Remy finds great comfort in the feel of this sword.

"Martin, aren't we in a highly secure area?"

"Remy, when shape-changers exist you must always be careful. They are masters of disguise and deception."

"But they stink. Whoever is outside that door smells to sweet to be a shape-changer." Says Remy.

"You can smell who is outside the door?"

"Can't you?"

"No, I cannot. That would be more of a werewolf trait." Says Martin

"I guess I do have a little werewolf blood."

Martin waves his hand for him to be quiet. "Who is it?" asks Martin

A woman's voice answers "It is Kirstyne and Kiree." Martin rushes to the door and opens it bowing. Two stunning women walk in, both about five feet nine inches tall and dressed in black medieval battle armor. Kiree has auburn hair and Kirstyne's midnight blue-black, both pulled back in tight long braids. Both wear a circle of gold and rubies on their brow. They too wear double blades. These women seem to exude an air of royalty as they seem to flow into the room perfect posture, graceful stride and lots of presence.

"My Prince" they say in unison bowing deeply, the entourage with them also bows saying "My Prince."

"My Prince, the Queen has sent us to prepare and escort you to the ball tonight." Kiree says

"I was getting to that, My Prince."

"Martin, give me a break, not you too."

Martin whispers "You don't understand vampiric law. If I do not address you properly, I will be beheaded. There is no bending the law here. Everyone is held to the laws of the clan. Even you got it. There's a lot for you to learn in a very short time."

"I see. So, the law includes the royal family."

"There are some exceptions. Being of royal birth does allow you a little leeway, my prince."

"Listen, I haven't been in my apartment for about eight months. Plus, I don't even have any clothes fit for a ball." Remy says shrugging his shoulders.

"That has all been taken care of Milord" answers Kirstyne.

"How do you know my size? Or even what I would like to wear?"

"Again, Milord that has been taken care of you no longer have to worry about the mundane things in life. What you require will be made available upon request. Your clothes, your food and any other physical need will be seen to. Besides you will no longer be residing at your old residence. You will be having new living arrangements more fitting to your station." replies Kiree

"All right, fine. I get it choice for me no longer exist. I really am enjoying this situation more and more each second. Wait till I speak to the commander. But first, Martin please have someone stop by my apartment in town and bring a black cedar chest to my new home. Also, there is a safe in my closet and the combination is 6-45-6. Have them bring the contents to my new residence."

"It is done, my prince." Martin says with a big smile.

"See you later, Martin." Remy replies icily "Oh Martin what type of blade is this? It looks like a Roman foot soldiers blade, but it's much longer."

"Milord, that is a vampiric blade made by the dwarves just for us. Keep it for now soon you will make your own blades."

"I see, this is one of your blades." Says Remy looking at the blade.

"Yes, it is. As you can see, milord, all vampire warriors carry two blades. It is my second set of weapons, not my battle blades."

Remy looks at all the warriors and sees that Martin is totally correct. They all carry two blades, but no guns. Strange he thinks to himself. Aloud he says "Interesting."

"You must go now; you have much to do before the ball. I will see you then, My Prince." Martin says bowing.

They leave the office and get aboard the elevator. Remy soon feels a premonition of danger and checks his weapons. The elevator reaches the garage floor and Remy's senses go wild. Something is not right. He turns to Kiree and Kirstyne and says quietly "Something is amiss, be ready. The scent in the air is different than anything he has ever smelt." All of Commander Sauer's and Vaft's warnings come to mind as he smells this new odor.

"What scent, Milord. I smell nothing?" asks Kiree

"Just be on your guard."

They walk out of the elevator after the doors open and there are no security officers to be seen. Remy remembers quite clearly how many guards were present when he came and he's sure they were not called away.

"Kiree, did the rest of your security team go in the other elevator?"

"Yes, they did, Milord. They should reach the ground floor in a few moments. Why?" She asks.

"Remind me to give you some lessons in effective security protocol later. But for now, draw your weapons and stand ready."

"But, my prince, this may be one of the safest buildings in the world. Our security protocols are second to none." Says Kirstyne.

"Well if you think your protocols are the best, you have another thing coming. From what I have seen I personally could have gotten into this building, killed whomever I wanted and walked out like it never happened. Enough talk draws your weapons."

"Yes, my Prince." They say in unison drawing they're weapons.

Suddenly from the shadows come ten beings with axes and

spears surrounding them. Most of them are about six feet in height and emit an acrid stench. They are covered with down-like brown hair and wear dark green battle armor.

"So Kirstyne, what are these things?" says Remy opening fire with his two Glocks knocking down six of the creatures who immediately get back up.

"They are Trolls, my Prince, dirty filthy Trolls that will only die by the blade." She answers

"Halfling, you will die today!" shouts the lead Troll as they charge forward.

Remy draws the sword Martin gave him and beheads the first and hamstrings the second. To his right Kiree throws a dagger into a Troll's throat and parries the next one's spear. Kirstyne lets out a war cry and disembowels another leaving five standing where there were ten. Remy presses the attack slicing an arm off another troll and spinning on the balls of his feet he lays open the troll's throat. It's mind-boggling the rush he feels as he engages in battle. As if this were what he was born to do to wreak total exhilarating havoc upon his assailants? The sword in his hand feels as snug as an old friend. He only wishes he had two blades. One feels as if it's missing the other as if they were brothers. He uses an open palm technique on his next attacker splintering his nose, grabs his head and snaps his neck as if it were a twig. He is astounded by his newfound strength and speed. It is as if he were augmented in some way.

Kirstyne is pressed against the wall fending off two attackers. Remy notes that Kiree is engaged with the last of the troll's and is in control of the battle. He leaps letting out a war cry he never used before and cleaves one of the beast from head to waist.

The second troll turns to him with a look of fright and screams "You must be the legend. You are the one." He drops his weapon and bows at his feet." My Prince I will serve you to my death I swear." says the Troll.

"Why?" replies Remy looking closer at the Troll. On closer

inspection it seems they are quite humanoid under all that hair and the stench comes from their clothes.

"Because I have seen werewolves, elves and vampires in battle and you have their prowess. Besides the war cry you just used was a werewolf's war cry, my prince. A vampire would never use it in battle."

Suddenly, the ham-stringed Troll throws its spear through the bowing Troll's back.

"Traitor, he is the enemy, fool." Exclaims the Troll as it throws the spear.

"No, he is our salvation." The dying Troll says being held by Remy. "Remember, we are not all like this, Sire. Please forgive him; he has been poisoned by years of elven propaganda and by hate. But, I remember the teachings of the prophecy and my spirit rejoices. Some of us will welcome you as our prince with open arms." He coughs blood as he continues "Some of us need you very badly, my... my." He goes limp in Remy's arms as the elevator opens and the guards rush out. Remy walks over to the crippled Troll.

"Why did you kill your own kind?"

"He is a fool to think our people would be accepted by the Vampiric nation. All Vampires look down on us as if we were vermin. We are slaves to them, who are only good for work and to kill. Kill me and end this farce. I am a warrior and I'm not afraid to die." says the Troll exposing its neck for the deathblow. Everyone is silent just observing the situation. Nonetheless, the vampire bowmen have they're arrows notched.

"You have never met a vampire like me. What is your name?" Remy asks to the surprise of all even the Troll.

"Is this a trick of some sort? Do you mock me for some reason?" answers the Troll quizzically.

"No." Remy says reaching out his hand looking directly into the Troll's eyes. "My name is Remy Robon and I would ask you again what is yours. I swear no harm will come to you."

The Troll looks back into his eyes and is startled by the sincerity of these words. It reaches out for his hand and she is taken to another place. Just Remy's touch fills her with an incredible calmness and love for this man. She replies "My name is Ejam, Milord. I am a female warrior of the Clan Smit and I will serve you until my death. For my sword-brother was right. You are the one and I am the fool."

The vampire guard is lost for words. No vampire had touched a Troll in friendship since they were created by the elves to kill the werewolves. They instinctively bow in unison.

"Get up all of you. Realize the death of these Trolls was pointless and engineered by the Elves. Get her some medical attention, now. Take her to the medical suite to be cared for by Dr. Vaft." Shouts Remy. They all scurry to pick up the Troll and carry her to the elevator as Martin with another group of guards arrives.

"Thank God your alive, Prince Remy." he says and then seeing the Troll shouts. "Put that filthy thing down and hack it to bits."

"Do no such thing. Take Ejam up stairs and have the medical team tend to her wounds as I ordered you to do. In fact, contact Dr. Vaft and tell him to care for her personally." says Remy looking at Martin and then Ejam who bows her head to him. The guards hurry into the elevator.

"Do you know what you're doing, my Prince? Trolls are dirty filthy things. It would have gutted you the first chance it got."

"I don't think so. Every being deserves a chance, Martin."

"That's not a being. That is a thing created in a test tube by the elves to kill werewolves and anything else they order slain, my prince."

"I see so even though they are sentient beings we should treat them as animals because the elves created them. They are still God's children."

"I didn't mean it that way, Milord. I just meant you should be careful. They are still our enemies."

"Let me ask you something, Martin? If any of the races swear on their Clan is it binding till their death?"

"By the law of God and the Covenant yes, it is, my Prince." Martin says bowing.

"Then as all here can attest to the fact, Ejam swore allegiance to me until her death. So, I don't think there is much to worry about." answers Remy with a smirk.

"I don't believe this you become more of a dam legend every day, my prince. But I don't think this will sit well with the council or the Queen for that matter."

"I did not ask for their permission."

"Gee, you sound more like a vampire prince every minute, Milord. But there is a second part to what you have done."

Before Remy can answer Kirstyne begins to waver and fall. Remy sees this and catches her as she loses consciousness. He checks her and discovers she has sustained a stab wound to her shoulder, which is bleeding profusely. From his own training as a nurse, he knows an artery must have been severed by the blow. How she stood for as long as she did he'll never know. He quickly rips off his shirt and packs the wound with a pressure dressing stopping the bleeding. Yet the sight and smell of the blood fills him with a hunger he has never known.

"She is wounded. We must take her to the med-lab at Haxe building" says Martin.

"Why not here?" asks Remy

"There are better facilities at the Haxe building, Milord."

"Give me a couple of those blood beans to give her." Says Remy. Placing them in her mouth, he notices she gains a little color and her heart rate has decreased. The bleeding has also lessened.

"Let's go." says Remy picking Kirstyne up as if she were a rag doll and running towards the limousine that drives up. "How far is it to the Haxe building?"

"Five Minutes maybe less. In fact, that's where your new home is." answers Martin as they speed away.

CHAPTER 5

"The strongest loves are born through hatred"

EJAM IS CARRIED INTO the infirmary where Vaft is waiting. Vaft thought it quite strange that Remy had singled him out to care for this Troll. "The prince must trust me immensely to give me this task." Vaft thinks to himself. Vaft is filled with a great sense of pride and duty. "Whatever the prince asks was his command without question." Vaft instructs the guards to place Ejam on the treatment table and tells them to leave.

"Do you not fear me old man? Like all the rest of your kind." says Ejam venomously "I am just a beast you know."

"Well I have learnt to treat any being fresh from each initial encounter. You are a young female to me who needs medical assistance nothing more and nothing less."

"You are unique amongst your people. Most vampires find us revolting. Down stairs an order was given to drop me and chop me to pieces." She replies.

Vaft smiles and says "Remember young lady, your people have killed many of the tribes on the orders of the Elves. If you changed positions, you would feel and act the same. My prince has requested I care for you as if you were family. That is quite an honor for one who has killed her own kind and tried to kill him. Don't you think?"

"I owe him my life. He could have slit my throat when I offered it to him; instead he held out his hand and touched me. I have never felt such power and strength before. I have pledged myself to him and I will honor that pledge to my death." She says quietly. Her anger blunted by his words.

Vaft looks at her and knows in his heart she means what she has just said. Yet something else is amiss, but he can't quite pinpoint it. There is something about her speech and her mannerisms.

"What is your name and what clan do you belong to?" he asks inspecting her leg seeing it has almost healed. Trolls heal as fast as the Elves. "What a lovely weapon they have created." he thinks to himself.

"I am Ejam daughter of Eji Clans master of the Troll tribes. My Clan is the Smit."

Vaft almost faints. He understands Eji is considered the Troll king. "My Lady, please excuse our crude handling of you. I had no idea." He claps his hands and four female guards enter the room. "Please take the Princess and bathe and groom her."

"But she is a Troll, Milord?" exclaims one of the guards.

"No, she is the Princess of the Trolls and under the protection of Remy the Vampire Prince. Do you have any other questions?" Vaft says coolly looking directly into her eyes.

All four bow and say "It will be an honor to care for you milady. Please excuse our comments. We meant no offense, Milady."

"Sir, you honor me excessively. Trolls have never been treated with such respect not even by our creators." says Ejam.

"Then milady." he says taking her hand and kissing it. "Then it is about time. I have found my Prince to be of very special stock. His decisions could save a world. He is quite a breath of fresh air don't you think?"

"More then we may ever know, Milord." she replies as two guards help her to the next suite where the groomers are waiting to bathe and clothe her.

Vaft turns to the guard who made the comment and says "One moment Isla. I would like you to find the queen and ask her to come here. The Queen and Commander Sauer need to know what has happened. This is a very rare occasion indeed. I'm sure the Prince had no idea what he was doing when he spared her life."

Isla looks at him with a quizzical look and says, "I don't understand Milord?"

"That is because most of us have forgotten the old codes of honor. By the old codes when you save or spare someone's life of the opposite sex who is of royal birth they have the right to choose you as their mate. The old customs are still in practice by all the tribes closer to mother earth then we are. I am sure Ejam knows her rights and may well claim our prince as her mate."

"She can do no such thing Milord. He is a vampire. We don't mate with Trolls."

"Your prejudice is showing. Beside my dear, she is no ordinary troll. She happens to be the troll princess and I'm sure you know the rest. It will be up to the Prince to decide. Also, the Prince may have many wives. It is his right, unless he finds a life-mate. At which time he will cleave unto her for life forsaking all others. Now go and bring the Queen here and tell her it is urgent."

As Isla leaves the room Ejam is helped back to the table. Her feral beauty astounds Vaft. She stands six feet tall with an athletic body, long and sinewy. Her long tawny hair pulled back in a braid now accentuates her soft but strong facial features. Her eyes are the liquid gold of a lioness and her smooth caramel skin is likened to silk. They have dressed her in a black silk robe, which flows about her like smoke. She is breathtaking.

Ejam notices Vaft's awe and says "We were bred to be sex toys for the Elves you know. We are their personal play- things. That is why they force us to let our hair grow to cover our features and bodies. To make us look fiercer to their enemies, the vampires, werewolves and dwarves. The elves always took most of the female children at birth and made them their body slaves leaving only enough females for us to be breeders. They also created half breeds to use as jailors for my people by offering them Elven rank. My father had only one female child and refused to let the Elves have their way with me. So, he proclaimed me a boy and made me his head warrior, so it would not be questioned. He trained me to be his best warrior and told me to guard against letting anyone know I was a woman. This is the first time in my life I have dressed like a woman and felt like a woman. It feels strange, but good."

"I am glad for you. It must have been difficult to hide your gender from the elves."

"They never questioned my father's loyalty. In addition, maybe the prince will notice me as a woman." She says looking into the wall mirror admiring herself as a woman for the first time in a long time.

"Speaking of that, Milady I hate to be so forward, but I must ask you a question."

"Yes, Milord."

"Well I was wondering if you were going to invoke the right of mating with our Prince Remy? I mean he did spare your life and I am sure you know the customs of the clans very well." Asks Vaft.

"Yes, he did, and I am aware of the custom. We have always tried to keep with God's laws and have awaited his arrival to liberate us. Even at the risk of punishment from the Elves. We pray to him in secret. We pray that he sends us a savior and I know the prince is that savior."

"That must have been quite difficult, princess. The elves would have killed you all if they knew." Says Vaft, quite taken aback by her words. Who would think a creation of the elves would believe in God, his laws and the prophecy. "I can see how you would think of the prince as a savior, but I ask again will you invoke the right of mating with the prince?"

"I really had not given it much thought. But now that you mention it I guess I must give it some thought."

"I could not help watching you admire yourself in the mirror nor was your statement "I hope the prince notices me" lost on me"

"I can honestly tell you I have never been with a male of any race.

But if I were to mate he would be the one, Milord." Ejam hesitates and then answers as the Queen walks into the room.

The Queen is dressed in a long maroon gown with a low neckline. Her long red hair held by a gold and ruby tiara. Ejam immediately assesses the queen and notes she has an athletic build and moves like a predator. But what the Queen has in abundance is presence. She exudes regality from her pores as if she were borne to be served.

Even Ejam bows as the Queen enters the room reflexively. Her mere presence seems to demand the utmost of respect. Vaft begins to speak and the Queen silences him with a look and says to Ejam.

"Welcome to our world. I have heard how you and your people are treated by the Elves and I admire your peoples' courage in enduring those hardships. I am Sariel, Queen of the Vampire nation. It is a true pleasure to meet you." Sariel says reaching out her hand.

Ejam takes it and holds it gently. The feeling she feels is disorienting. It is the same feeling she felt when Remy touched her except much more intense. The Queen is using her own spirit to look at Ejam's spirit. They look into each other's eyes and seem to bond on the feral plane. Like sisters of the earth. The way God meant it to be. She sees them in a lush meadow holding hands and dancing in a circle. They exchange thoughts and return to present.

"I see your spirit is clean and true. It is all a sister of the earth can ask from one another."

"That is the first time I have been in touch with a kindred spirit. I feel truly honored that you chose to bond with me on that level, Milady."

"You do realize that I had to do that. Before you had reached this room, I was notified that the prince had spared your life. We are having a ball tonight and all the tribes will be present."

"Milady." Ejam says stepping back. "The Trolls will serve the Vampire nation against the Elves you have my word on that."

"Thank you and your name?"

"Ejam. Milady."

"I thought you were born Ejamine." Says Sariel looking directly at her.

"That is true, Milady. But no one knew my true name except my father and a precious few. The elves would have known I was a female and taken me from my father."

"Ejamine, we of the vampire clan have spies everywhere. There is not much the elves know that we don't know. We knew you were female. So, I am sure the Elves know as well."

"How could the elves know? Who of my clan would betray my father?" says Ejam her anger rising.

"There are ways to find things out without anyone betraying anyone, young lady. Some have the power to reach into a mind and pluck answers out. Of course, there is always a price for the use of this gift."

"If the Elves knew all along, why let the charade continue so long?"

"Because it served their purpose to them you were just another bartering chip to hold over your father if they had to. It is the way the elves do things. By allowing you to feel comfortable, you will never see them pulling the rug from underneath you. It is why they agreed to you leading the strike team on the prince. Be truthful the prince had already defeated four shape-changers by himself. They rate shape-changers as their greatest warriors. They did not expect you to return."

"Those son-of-bitches knew the prince was an accomplished warrior and told us we were the first attack team to confront him. They threw away my warriors."

"No for them it was another test of the prince's prowess. If you defeated him then he was never the threat they thought, he was, and he was lucky against the shape-changers. If you all died you could be used as martyrs."

"What an incredible waste of the warriors of my clan. The elves really do think of us as refuse."

"What did you think of the prince's prowess in battle?"

"Quite frankly, milady, he could have taken us alone. The battle itself took minutes and he defeated six of us by himself. He apparently has had some Asian training. Aikido mixed with the Yangjia Michuan Jian traditional sword style. It was amazing to behold."

"So, you are saying he could have defeated all the warriors in your attack party without much effort."

"To be honest, Milady, he could have taken twice as many warriors if he had carried double blades. He was like a fluid shadow. Here then there."

"He defeated six of you with one blade?"

"Yes Milady, one blade. And that blade I am sure is not even his. With his own blades he would be magnificent to watch."

"What else do you think of him?" asked the Queen astonished at the statements made by this warrior. A warrior bred and trained to be the best of her clan.

"He has a good soul. He should have killed me for what I did, but he chose to spare me. If fact he ordered Lord Vaft to treat me as family."

"He is quite special I hear." Sariel says turning and pacing slowing towards the Vaft's desk.

"Who is, Milady, the prince?" asks Ejam.

"Why of course the prince. You see I have not met him yet. We have just identified him as the prince by a blood sample. He actually was working for us in a different position and we didn't even know he existed. He started out with no affiliations, but he seems to be building quite a contingent." Sariel pauses and continues "Are you a part of that contingent?"

"Milady we have bonded on a feral level you know my thoughts already on this matter." says Ejam uneasily.

"Yes, that is true, but I would like to hear it from you personally as a woman and as a warrior." Sariel turns slowly and looks at her.

"If he chooses me I would be honored to be his mate, Milady. And if he does not I will die by his side as a warrior. I would not hold him to the right of mating unless he chose to." Ejam says looking directly into her eyes.

"You of course understand how the Vampire nation would view this."

"Yes, and he is worth it. I know he is worth it. I don't know him well, but he now resides in my heart and soul, Milady."

"You also know you are not his life-mate. So whatever time you share with him is borrowed."

"I know, Milady."

"Well I guess that makes everything clear. Would you join us at his banquet tonight as my guest?"

"I would be honored, Milady." Ejam says curtsying

Sariel turns to Vaft and says "Please see to it that she is provided with garments that befit her station and have an extra setting placed at my table. Also, tell her of the plan. Good day, Princess." and she turns to walk away but stops and says not looking over her shoulder to Ejam "You know I will fight for him, Princess?"

Ejam answers "He's worth fighting for Milady. I understand." Sariel does not say another word she just walks out of the room.

Ejam turns to Vaft and says, "I must ask you a boon."

"Yes, Milady."

"If you could help me get word to my people to let them know that the child of the prophecy exists."

"That can be done, Milady. We have people in the compound."

"You mean you knew we were in slavery all this time?"

"We were never sure. The Elves love to play mind tricks and could have portrayed your people as slaves while they were not. It would have been a great ploy to have us think that and take you in to find we had let a wolf in the door. Only what you have told us is real." Says Vaft

"How could you believe me so easily? I am the enemy. Plus, what you just said could be true."

"I doubt that. The Queen is a pureblood vampire of the highest order much like a priestess. If she connected on the spiritual plane with you and says you are clean. Then you are without question clean."

"I still could be a threat to the Queen."

"If we thought that, would the Queen have seen you without any guards? I think not."

"I think two of the best warriors on this planet stood before me. We do our homework and know of both the Queen's and your prowess in battle."

"That is a very interesting thought. However, that never crossed my mind."

"We know that you and the Queen were by Emperor Vincenzo's side at every battle."

"As it should always be, and we will be by Prince Remy's side when the time comes, Milady."

"As will I, Milord."

"Well my lady you must begin to prepare for tonight."

"Milord, do you think the Vampire nation would accept me as the prince's mate?"

"By the laws of God, you have all the right to be his mate, Milady. Plus, I must add that the alliance of our tribes could signal the destruction of the Elven clans plans to dominate the world."

"Oh, after I get word to my people. I am quite sure they will agree, Milord. And if they do I will need a large favor."

"As you wish Milady our resources are your resources short of an act of war."

"I still cannot understand how you could trust me so easily, Milord." Replies Ejam.

Vaft hesitates and then answers. "My prince trusts you after making physical contact with you and I have found he has a refreshing way of reaffirming faith in people. He has reaffirmed my faith. Given me hope where I had none. He truly sees the good or bad in people and acts upon it. He adheres to the laws of God without knowing. He does it from the heart and soul not from the mind. For the prince there is nothing to think about, there is no other clear choice. It either is what it is or it is not. No gray areas and no need to vacillate or play games of politics. He takes command and defends the weak without being instructed to so. The prince is willing to die for what is right. So, I trust you to do as he would because he has touched your heart and soul."

"Thank you, Milord. I will never betray that trust. My people will never betray that trust."

Vaft looks at her and smiles. "Then my lady we have much to do before the ball."

CHAPTER 6

"The world sees what it wants, but you must be true to who you are"

THE LIMOUSINE REACHES THE Haxe building within ten minutes. Remy was shocked that they had a full police escort all the way. Screeching to a halt in the garage the limousine's doors burst open. Kirstyne still lies unconscious on Remy's lap as the medical team rushes out to meet them. Remy lifts her as if she was an infant and places her on the awaiting stretcher. The team quickly inserts intravenous lines and takes her vital signs. Within seconds, they are wheeling her away. Remy is drenched with blood from both Kirstyne and from the Trolls. What a sight he is to behold. Shirtless with a sword strapped to his back and both his glocks on his waist. The people in the lobby do not even seem to notice what he looks like and bow to him. Commander Sauer walks forward followed by six guards and says, "Are you injured, my prince?" surveying him for wounds.

"No, I am well, Commander."

"That is good, my prince."

"What is this place?" he answers looking around at the splendid marble workmanship.

"This is the Haxe Building. It has been here for close to two centuries. It will now be your home, Milord."

"I see. If this is home, then I should be safe right."

"Yes, Milord this is the best guarded building in the world."

"Then what are they for?" he asks gesturing to the six men who have surrounded him in a defensive position.

"These men are a precaution my prince. I have personally decided to take charge of your security measures. It seems you have been lacking the proper protection." Commander Sauer says looking directly at Kiree, who bows her head.

"What the hell is that supposed to mean, Commander?"

"It's meaning is very simple. Your personal guard exhibited poor judgment regarding your personal protection and that could have caused your demise. You have had security details before, Milord. You know the drill. Never let your client enter an unsecured area. Never. The follow-up group should have been the initial group to arrive from the elevator shaft and after they checked the area you should have been brought down. I thank God that you are able to defend yourself however; this could have turned out quite badly. There is always a price to pay for failure."

"What are you talking about? These women fought well and protected me with their lives. I do not wish to have them punished."

"Milord, is that an order? "Says Commander Sauer

"If that's what it takes. Then yes, damn it, it's an order. I've never seen people more hell-bent on killing their own kind in my life."

"My prince you do not yet fully understand the ways of the first four tribes yet. We are bound only by God's law and by that law you now own Kiree and Kirstyne body and soul forever."

"What the hell are you talking about? They are not pieces of property?" shouts Remy.

"That is the law my prince if you spare someone's life they are indebted to you for life." says Commander Sauer

"Great. So, what of Ejam the Troll I spared?"

"Oh, that is different my prince because she is royalty. She can claim you as her mate." answers Commander Sauer with a chuckle.

"You are joking, right?"

"No Milord and you have no idea the ramifications of your actions. This coupled with the fact you are emitting pheromones that say you are ready and willing to go to all the females of the first tribes. That makes you quite a paradox to most females from those tribes. They do not know whether they should kill you or mate with you."

"How do you know she is royalty?"

"Lord Vaft found out while questioning her and one of the guards told me."

"That's pretty dam quick. It's only been about ten minutes."

"Information travels fast, Prince Remy. Especially information that is important."

"Why don't we go to where ever I'm going to live to discuss this further? I need a bath." says Remy.

"As you wish, Milord, and by the way the box you requested is in your chambers." says Commander Sauer who signals the guard to check the apartment before the prince arrives. He turns to Kiree and says, "This is how it's done, remember that."

She bows her head and replies "Yes, milord."

They quickly get into the elevator and go to the floor beneath the penthouse. Remy audibly gasps as the elevator opens. Before him, is a full floor suite exquisitely decorated in French provincial décor? The ceilings are easily ten feet tall and the carpet has the look of well-groomed grass. Remy is amazed at the opulence of this dwelling.

"This will now be your home, Milord "says Commander Sauer. "On the table are a book of tribal etiquette and a book with the laws of God that we all live and die by. Up to this point, you have been exempted due to your ignorance of our ways. After this evening, you will no longer be exempt. You will be held to the codes of honor in this book and the laws of God. You are the Prince of a great and powerful people, a people who would die for you in an instant. Soon you will meet many tribes who will swear allegiance to you. I know Martin explained a great deal to you, Nonetheless, you are possibly the most important being on this planet. You must place the needs of all the people of this planet above your own desires and wishes at all times. You will have many tests of your strength, mind and your spirit coming in the next couple of months. How you deal with them may heal or destroy a world."

"I never asked for this yoke to be placed upon me, Commander. As you well know, I have always tried to be an honorable man. Nevertheless, this is a bit much for any being to understand in less than two days. Don't you think" Remy says taking off his weapons, which Kiree takes from him and he sits on a bar stool. Kiree goes into the next room and returns with a basin of water and starts to clean the blood off Remy's back and chest.

"Time is a luxury we no longer have, Milord. The elves have already tipped their hand by having you attacked by those shape-changers and trolls. The next attack will be with ogres we just don't know when. They are testing you for a weakness. Their plans were almost complete, and you are greatly upsetting those plans. Just your presence has now created an alliance with the trolls. Something none of us could have accomplished due to bigotry. Most of our people think trolls are dirty filthy murderers and as you know prejudice does not just disappear overnight. It will take great strength and courage to keep this alliance viable. It might have been just dumb luck, or it could have been divine intervention. A marriage to Princess Ejamine would solidify the alliance completely." Commander Sauer says sitting across from him.

"You must be kidding me I don't even know that woman. And I thought her name was Ejam?" says Remy pouring a glass of red wine and sipping it. He finds it very interesting how he has always hated wine being a beer man, yet all of a sudden it is all he craves.

"Her full name is Ejamine. She is the daughter of the Troll Clans master Eji of Smit Clan. However, knowing someone has nothing to do with royal etiquette Milord. The Trolls are great warriors and would be splendid allies against the Elves. This is not personal it is what you might call a business deal in a way more like a merger of sorts." says Commander Sauer pouring himself a glass of wine.

"Oh, I see. Now marriage has become business as usual. Like two corporations involved in a takeover."

"It has been that way for centuries, my prince. You are a learned man, I am sure you known that more human alliances were made through marriages than treaties."

"That is true. It was also true that those marriages were binding until death. What happens when I find true love?"

"You of course can marry or mate with as many females as you like until you find a life mate. When you find your life-mate you are no longer bonded to your wife or wives. You will also have no desire for anyone else. It is the law of God, which all the tribes understand. If Ejam is your life mate, then that is the will of God and must be accepted by all without question."

"What about how I feel? Does that count at all here? Basically, I have been alone all my life. Making all my decisions alone and all those decisions were made for my well-being. Now you tell me I must marry a woman I do not even know to solidify an alliance. I find this all quite interesting indeed."

"You may find it interesting, milord. However, we find it necessary. We need as many alliances as we can get. Your presence indicates the final conflict approaches."

"I've been hearing a lot about the final conflict today. Can you explain to me what the hell it is?"

"All these things will be explained in time. As you said yourself we have expected too much of you to soon and I agree. Anyway, back to Ejamine."

"You speak of her as if she were property. Does she have a choice in this matter?"

"Yes, she does have a choice and she chooses you, milord."

"You asked her already? You guys are pretty dam pushy. It must have been only about thirty minutes since the battle. Your people have already interrogated her and obtained this information?"

"It is a matter of etiquette, my prince. You should know the importance of immediate debrief. Tonight, at the ball she may claim you and we needed to be prepared."

"Prepared for what?" exclaims Remy.

"An official announcement of betrothal, my prince." Commander Sauer answers laughing aloud and everyone in the room soon joins him in his mirth.

"I am glad that everyone finds this amusing. So, I don't even have to ask?" Remy says

"No, it's all been arranged."

"That's another line I have heard all day."

"My prince, as young people are so good at saying just go with the flow."

"Commander, I have a question."

"What is that, milord?"

"Why do I love red wine all of a sudden?"

"Because it is not red wine it is synthetic blood. Now that your vampire and elven genes have been awakened, you need it to survive."

"So, this is all part and parcel of who I am."

"Yes, Milord. Any other questions?"

Remy just shrugs his shoulders. "How will I feel when I meet my life-mate?" he says draining his glass and pouring another. Without Remy even noticing, Kiree has waited on him hand and foot since they arrived in the apartment. Now Kiree brings out a tray of almost raw roast beef that is sizzling and places it before him. He reaches out with his hand and ravenously begins devouring the meat. Then he stops himself looking at Commander Sauer who is smiling.

"I see your feral side is showing Milord. Let me explain that before I explain how meeting your life-mate will make you feel. All the first four tribes have a feral side. The elves have had their feral side suppressed by God and the dwarves feral side has been channeled into constructive behavior. However, vampire and werewolf tribes let it free without restraint. It's what makes us God's true warriors. The werewolf has chosen the natural path and will only fight when provoked because they can easily lose themselves to their feral side.

The vampire on the other hand has chosen the path as the protector of all the races and has learned to have great control over our feral side. You have the blood all the tribes running through your veins, which make you a great warrior. The werewolves are much stronger and faster than all the tribes. In the past one of the gifts was lost when any of the tribes mated. The werewolf can shape-change at will and become feral immediately. Whereas, a vampire becomes feral only under duress or after the very special battle training that all the clans must undergo. It seems you have the werewolf gift of immediate shape-change and ferocity."

"I have not shape-changed. What makes you think I can?" asks Remy.

"Well the first thing is that you are able to tolerate the blood of life. The second is films from the surveillance camera, which revealed you shape-changing against the trolls. You shifted from normal to feral at will and totally ended it within seconds. No vampire or werewolf can do that. It is proof you still have both gifts. While others have lost one gift or both." answers Commander Sauer.

"So, what your saying is that I shape-changed without a thought." replies Remy aloud. "So that's why I felt much faster and stronger" he says to himself. "But what beast did I shape shift into?"

"Actually, you did not change into a specific animal. Your skin color just got darker and your fangs were showing. We noted that you had talons and had grown in height and girth. Nothing as pronounced as when a werewolf changes or as inconspicuous as a vampire. Somewhere in between I would say."

"Something new again then."

"Yes, my prince something new. That is exactly what I am saying, and neither vampire nor werewolf can do that even under duress. It is one of the things that seem so unique about you. You also have shown the gift of healing from the elves. Only time will tell if you have the dwarven gifts."

"What gifts do they possess?"

"They possess many gifts some physical, some mental and some mystical. When you meet with the dwarven elders, they will explain their gifts much better than I ever could."

"Another mystery to unfold I guess."

"Now I will tell you about finding your life-mate. It is very simple; the first physical contact of any kind with your life mate and you will want no other for life. It is like finding the missing part that completes you. There have not been many life-mates over the past century amongst our clan; I guess that is due to the decrease of our numbers."

"Or due to just plain bigotry. It seems the only tribes that have any sense are the werewolf and dwarf tribes. They do not seem to have any problem mating or living with other beings. They just coexist without trying. This is something the vampire nation will need to learn about if we are to survive."

Commander Sauer looks at Remy flabbergasted by his observation. Here was a being no older than a quarter of a century and he was already wiser than beings that had lived for two millennia. So, innocent and noble Remy is. Commander Sauer's only hope is that he does not become tainted by the amount of hate and bigotry he will go up against in the clan.

"My prince, you make a good point. But as I said before true prejudice dies hard."

"For this planet to survive, we must all understand that we are a part of the whole? Not a completely separate part. We must learn and teach tolerance."

"I agree, milord. Maybe our life mates are from other species. We just never made ourselves available to the other tribes."

"Or to any of the beings created by the elves."

"Again, you have a valid point, Milord."

"So, let me ask you a question in regards to this life- mating?" says Remy.

"Sure, my prince."

"Would you dream of this person even before meeting them?"

"That is possible, my prince. Have you had a dream of someone?"

"Yes, I have. I was engaged in a battle and I made love to a beautiful woman with dark red hair and eyes like smoldering green coals. Her skin was the color of cream and she used two swords in battle. We fought side by side. I know she is my life mate I can feel it. The truth is she looked allot like Kiree. She said, "Welcome home, My Lord.""

"If Kiree was your life-mate, milord we would not be talking now. If you know what I mean." Says Commander Sauer chuckling.

"I understand." Remy says glancing at Kiree, who blushes.

"Well you must be tired, my prince. Kiree will see to your needs from this point on. Guards will be posted outside your door and on the window ledges. I will see you later this evening at the ball. Kiree I will need a quick word with you."

Kiree walks over to him as Remy heads into the bed chambers. "Yes, Milord."

"This will sound strange to you. But the clan needs to know if the Prince is fertile. I know you are fertile at this moment."

"So, you are asking me to have sex with the Prince to see if he is fertile? What if I am not impregnated?"

"I ask this of you not order you."

"You are aware that I have never been with a male before? This is quite awkward."

"He is very attractive, and I can smell your pheromones when you are near him. It is obvious that you would like to mate with him."

"Commander I am afraid I may have feelings for him that are stronger than physical mating and what if I am his life-mate?"

I really do not think that is possible. I'm pretty sure it's someone else. Once again, I am asking not ordering. Let nature take its course and see what happens."

"Yes, Milord. I will see." Kiree replies and heads back into the bed chamber.

Commander Sauer bows and leaves quickly sweating profusely He says to himself as he leaves "I must speak to the Queen immediately. If what I think is true, the meeting between the Queen and Remy could lead to disaster if it happens to soon."

Inside his room Remy strips and steps into a huge bathtub. The whole idea of "his room" is foreign to him. He has always shared a room with someone. Be it at the orphanage or at some barracks in the military. Even his apartment was just something to have because he never really stayed there much. In the past five years he basically has lived hotel to hotel. Looking at the bathtub, he would swear it was a small swimming pool. Remy looks in the mirror next to the pool and the wounds on his back are gone. Not healed, just totally gone. "That is some plastic technique Dr. Vaft has." He says to himself. The water is hot and soon he begins to relax reflecting on the last couple of days. He looks up and sees Kiree smiling at him from across the pool. To his amazement she drops her robe revealing her body to him. He finds himself completely mesmerized by her beauty and just stares at her as she wades over to him.

"Kiree, I do not expect you ….........."

She cuts him off with a passionate kiss and says "No milord I want this. I have never been with a male before. All I have done for centuries is train to fight in the upcoming war."

"Is that all your allowed to do? Train to fight a war. What about love, relationships and happiness."

"We are the chosen of God. It is our path to defend the weak against harm. I do not begrudge my life. I feel honored that I can make a difference."

"Kiree, you are a beautiful woman. I am sure some vampire is going to be upset that you are with me."

"I doubt that. The vampire world is different than the human world. Our rules are different. We do not abide by the moralistic mumbo jumbo that man does. Every being has a choice in our world. Nonetheless, I know there are females who would take my place without hesitation."

"What do you mean take your place? I do not understand."

"I am a virgin because I am one of the few who can bear children. It is the law that as the prince you are sworn to propagate our race. The fact you claimed me as your life time servant basically set up this moment. I belong to you body and soul until I can repay a life for a life."

"Belong to me. What the hell does that mean?"

"Vampires have blood debts. These debts are created by risking your life for another. We are all proud warriors and would rather die than accept help from another. So, when it is offered it creates a blood debt. These debts can only be paid by doing the same for another. That is what I owe you."

"But that is a debt paid for on the battlefield not in the bedroom, Kiree."

"Oh, but milord you have responsibilities as well, especially, in the bedroom." She answers with a sheepish grin playing on her lips.

"Are you saying I have a responsibility to impregnate the females of the clan?"

"Yes, Milord. We must increase our numbers if we are to survive. The needs of the many outweigh the needs of the few. We are slowly dying off; we need fresh blood to continue to exist. Your blood line will be able to reinvigorate our people."

"So, I am basically just a stud to you. A man whore." Says Remy visibly angry."

"No, my prince. To me you are more than that as well as any female from the clan knows you are more than that. Since meeting you I have wanted you and when you had my life spared it made me want you even more." She says, and she reaches down and begins stroking his already rising member.

Remy's mind and body explode with a primal need for this woman. Never have his sexual urges felt so strong so primordial. "Kiree, I have not been with a woman for awhile I may not live up to your expectations." says Remy massaging her breast gently.

"I have no expectations Milord?" she says as he lifts her and carries her still wet to the bedroom.

"Good, maybe we can create some." he answers closing the door behind them.

CHAPTER 7

"Patience is a learned behavior"

FICA IS OUT OF breath as he rushes to the council hall. Once he had received the summons to appear before the council he has run about five miles at top speed. Fica still cannot believe Remy is still alive. Four attempts have been unsuccessful to take his life over the last month. He had been told not to personally be involved so he got others to do his bidding. The first being those trained killers in the alley in which he had planted Dingham. The next was an explosive in his car, which Remy found by scent. Then the two direct attempts by the shape-changers and the trolls. Both attack teams were the best of their species. All were battle proven. It all just seemed like a waste of time and resources to him.

"They should have allowed me to confront him. I would have killed him in an instant, am I not the only half-breed with werewolf blood. No elven warrior can best me in battle. I am the best warrior we have. Don't these foolish old men understand, I and only I can end this quickly and decisively? I am the most skilled warrior this clan has ever known. Have I not proven myself over the centuries? They still don't trust me because I am not a pure bred, but I am more loyal than most of them." Fica thinks to himself as he hurries along. He soon arrives at the doors of the great hall.

The Elven complex is deep within the Swiss Alps. It was literally cut into a mountain after they were exiled by God and the vampires. It took months to create this cavern. Impregnable to attack once sealed off. That is impregnable to all but an all-out assault, which could bury their kind forever. Yet, they know that will never happen because the other tribes would find that plan of attack distasteful and against the Laws of God. If the situation were reversed the Elves would have buried the vampire's centuries ago. The hall itself is a fantastic structure. It is has been crafted entirely from marble.

Its majestic cathedral like appearance would fill most with awe. The elves are masterful craftsmen. In addition, they have the ability to create their own work force from scratch. They are incredible biogenetic engineers a gift from the most high that could not be taken from them. Fica walks in as Naline is addressing the council. Naline is the great Elven elder. Naline sat at the table of the great clan council before they were exiled. His hatred of all species besides elves is unmatched. Naline stands six foot five inches tall and his appearance is that of an athletic fifty year old, although he is close to twenty centuries old. Naline's long gray hair is braided and hangs down his back held with a golden clasp adorned with emeralds. He is dressed in an emerald green tunic to match his sparkling green eyes. His voice booms throughout the hall.

"My brethren we are so close to the completion of our plan to destroy the vampires and take over this realm. However, there is something or rather someone who now jeopardizes our plan. As the prophecy has foretold a being has been born with the bloods of all the first tribes. He has been tested in battle by some of our warriors and has proven to be a worthy adversary. He is not to be taken lightly."

Torm the second elder stands to be recognized and then says "He is but one being. Surely he can be killed."

"Four attempts have been made on his life this month. Two of those attacks were by our own warriors the shape-changers and the trolls. In both cases the warriors were killed almost single handedly by Remy Robon."

Torm laughs aloud and says "What one or two warriors. That is no threat to us."

"More like four shape changers and six trolls by himself including Eji's son, arguably, his best warrior. As I said Remy Robon is not a being to be trifled with. No one has had that prowess since the emperor."

A hush rolls over the council-room and Torm looks around and then sits down feeling like an utter fool.

Naline looks around the room and says "Now if there are no more interruptions I will continue. Our spy has informed me all of the bloodlines are noble in origin, which means there is two ways to deal with him. One is to kill him and we have not been very successful at that and now that he has been accepted by the vampire clan it will be near impossible. The second is to have him betrothed to a female of royal elven blood and make him conceive a child of the same bloodlines. This will make him honor the offer of an Elven throne."

"An Elven throne are you out of your mind?" says Torm as the room erupts. "No vampire will sit upon the Elven throne in my lifetime." There are shouts of agreement throughout the hall.

Naline motions for quiet and then says "Remember he has Elven blood too and he has only just become aware of his vampire heritage. It is new to him. He would not know who is right or who to follow. Think if we had known, we could have him here at our council now a loyal elven citizen. The vampires just beat us to the punch or they were very lucky. What I propose is to turn his loyalty to us and make him an enemy of the vampires. I am sure we could persuade him into thinking our side is the correct side." Naline pauses for effect. He watches the crowd and sees many murmuring agreement.

"What elven bloodline runs through his veins?" asks Casset, the third elder of the council.

"Your bloodline, Lord Casset, your son is his grandfather." Replies Naline. Again the crowd starts to shout and protest against Naline's plan.

"Listen to me." Shouts Naline quieting the hall. "Would you punish someone for someone else's crime? Lord Casset is one of our most prominent and loyal elves. What his son did has nothing to do with his bloodline a son who paid for that treachery with his life. Let's not fool ourselves we all want Robon dead anyway. But we need to stall for time until we are completely ready. Haste was the reason for our downfall last time. Let us not go down the same road. Had we been better prepared and not go against our own teachings, the other clans would be our slaves by now."

The hall is silent. Everyone is quite aware their defeat was because of poor planning and no patience. Something Naline preached and was ignored by the council.

"Naline, you have a point. We do not know he has become absolutely loyal to the vampire clan and he would be a great addition to our warriors. I think your plan may have merit." Says Sonnel the fourth elder of the elven council.

Naline smiles to himself, because his greatest rival had agreed to the plan. He would think Sonnel would never agree to his plan. Sonnel may well hate the vampires more than anyone. His whole house was killed during the war. His wife and all his children were lost in battle.

"Good. Then I propose we offer Princess Ave as his betrothed at the ball in his honor tomorrow."

"That is preposterous?" shouts Torm, Ave's father. "Not my daughter. The thought of such a mating goes against our own laws. Thou shall not mate outside of the clan."

"Let's make that let's not mate with a vampire shall we. As you all know we have several well accepted members of our clan who have mated with dwarves, werewolves, trolls, humans and ogres." says Naline

"This is true." Says Werg the fifth elder. "But as you well know, Naline the only reason we do not mate with the vampires is because the offspring die horribly as soon as they reach puberty. What assurance do we have the offspring of the union between this mixed breed and Princess Ave will not die the same way?"

"My spy has told me a test mating has been done between a fertile vampire female and Robon. The spy is now trying to find out who it is. We wait three months and we will know one way or another. Now let us be truthful hatred and loathing goes both ways. As much as we loathe the vampires, they loathe us. If they are willing to take this chance, we can do no less. My brethren this being will either join us or destroy us. We must be proactive in our plans related to him."

Fica is silently smoldering. Princess Ave was to be his betrothed. Enough he says to himself. "I demand to be recognized by the council?" he shouts.

All eyes turn to him and Naline says "You are recognized, Fica."

"My Lords, there is another way to keep this being at bay. We can send Ogres to capture the vampire queen. When they find out and start to negotiate, I can challenge him to combat for her life."

A hush rolls over the council and Princess Ave who has secretly loved Fica for years feels a twinge of pride that he would speak up for her in front of the whole council. It shows great bravery and stupidity at the same time. In fact, it is exciting her to no end. Fica looks at her and she smiles bowing her head.

"What you propose could lead to all out war. A war we are not prepared for yet. The Vampires still are formidable foes. Stealing their queen may force them to forget the laws of God and openly attack us. They may even be able to reenlist the European and Asian tribes. Is this what you want? Does Fica speak for every one?" Says Naline as he looks around the room and notices everyone's head bowed.

"I see." he says "You all do agree, but do not want to go against my wishes. Remember while I may be council leader this is not a dictatorship. We vote on everything. That is our way. But I must say one last thing. Our plans have worked perfectly to this point and we have had absolutely no elven casualties and have become a strong vibrant race on the brink of victory. We have always thought of the whole instead of the one. We shall now have a closed ballot vote upon Fica's plan." The box is passed to each of the council members and is soon filled with ballots. There are sixteen council members and the council leader who only votes when there is a tie. The ballots are collected and are counted quickly. Nine to seven in favor of Fica's plan. Fica leads his partisans in cheers. Naline steps up to the podium with a heavy heart. He remembers his dwarven classes so long ago, when he learned of the prophecy. "It shall begin with disagreement and foolhardy pride."

"A decision has been made and we of the council will abide by this decision. So it has been decided so it shall be done." Naline says hitting his gavel against the podium three times.

Eji stands and request to be recognized. Naline nods in recognition.

"My Lords I understand Fica's need to fight Robon. Especially, since he had three chances to kill him and did not."

Fica feels a jolt in his abdomen from these words and says to himself." You will pay for your insolence old man. Pay dearly."

"Robon has taken my son's life. I should have first right of combat to avenge his death. I will challenge him at the dinner while the ogres take the queen. If I win nothing has been lost, if I die we have the queen to barter with and Fica gets his wish. It is my right by the Laws of the Clan."

Naline looks about the council and notices most agree with Eji as they nod in agreement. He thinks to himself that maybe, just maybe his people original plan of patience and stealth can be returned to. Eji is a mighty warrior, much better than even Fica.

Naline says "Let us put it to a vote as before." They all agree and the box is passed around once again. The ballots are once again collected and counted. It is unanimous for Eji to challenge Robon. Naline smiles at Fica whose face is filled with rage.

"A decision has been made and we of the council will abide by this decision. So it has been decided so it shall be done." Naline says hitting his gavel against the podium three times. "I also have the other surprise set up to be a diversion."

"That is good, Lord Naline." Says Sonnel. "I hope they burn in hell."

"Enough we must prepare for the surprise and of course the banquet. I adjourn this meeting. All go in strength and health." All bow to the speaker and head off into groups to discuss what has transpired.

Princess Ave runs to Fica and kisses him deeply. They part and she says "Thank you Milord, for saving me from that fate."

"But for how long will that be, Milady? If Eji or I fail in battle Naline will revert to his first plan and the council will have to agree, it is only logical." Fica says his body tensing from her touch. He has never been intimate with Princess Ave and actually is startled by her public display of affections. Nonetheless, he has loved her for years and was just waiting for the mating time to make her his wife.

"Oh there is another way, Milord." she says reaching down caressing his thigh and smiling at him.

Visibly uncomfortable Fica begins to perspire as he feels himself becoming aroused and he replies "What is that, Milady?"

"If I am already pregnant, I cannot be betrothed to anyone but the father. That is the Law of the Clan."

"I see, Milady. Then you are proposing........"

"No Milord I am saying I want you to impregnate me and be my mate as is my right as princess. I am ovulating right now. I know I am ready."

"Milady, you take great risks in public?" he says looking about. It is then he realizes everyone has left the council chamber and they are alone.

"What public? There is no one here. I knew that already because I have dwarven second sight." Says Ave.

"Then you are a half-breed like I am."

"Yes and our child will have all bloods except for vampire and will be the next Emperor of the Elves. Come we have much to do, Milord." she says taking his hand and leading him to her chambers.

CHAPTER 8

*"Personal needs are but wishes, however
the needs of the many are reality"*

COMMANDER SAUER RUSHES TO the Queen's chambers. Outside her door are four of the best warriors the earth has ever known, all female, mute from birth and loyal to only the Queen.

"I need to speak to the Queen. It is a matter of great importance."

One of the guard's nods at him and heads through the doorway while the other three block his path being his sister gives him no privilege nor would he ask any. The queen must be protected at all times. She returns soon and he is ushered into the Queen's chambers.

Sariel sits with her back to him working at her computer without turning says "What is so important brother, that you would disturb me so close to the prince's announcement dinner."

"I only have one question, Sariel."

"And what is that, Sauer?"

"Have you dreamt of him?"

She stops typing and turns to him and says "Yes."

"Yes, is that all you have to say?"

"What else do you want me to say? Yes I dreamt of him."

"Then you know you are life-mates and that you cannot make physical contact if our plans are to come to fruition."

"I thought I could at least look at him for awhile. Just to see if he were real and not a dream." She says wincing at the words.

"Look at him for awhile! Are you kidding me? He would long to touch you in any way possible and once he touched you all our plans would be over. The truth is I do not think any warrior or group of warriors could stop him from getting to you. He is quite a warrior."

"So I have heard."

"What were you thinking?"

"Sauer, since Vincenzo died I have not had anyone. I love this being without seeing him and I am jealous Kiree is with him now. It should be me in his arms not her. If I had no restraint, I would be slitting her throat now. The feeling of jealousy is maddening. I do not want anyone to even touch him. I have been cursed again by the pains of finding a life-mate. My feelings for Vincenzo have been replaced completely with feelings for Remy. Only this time you see its worst, much worst." Tears begin to well up in her eyes. "It is not fair Sauer; I have given my all for the clans. There must be something for me?"

Commander Sauer reaches out and hugs her trying to shush away her tears.

"I know it is difficult, but it won't last forever. We must know if he is fertile so he can be your true mate. You know that. Plus strategically we must get him to mate with Ejam to solidify her peoples' loyalty."

She jumps back and says "That will not be difficult. She loves him already. We bonded on the feral plane. She would die for him now if need be. She has already pledged herself to him heart and soul." Sariel hesitates for a moment then says "She is also quite beautiful."

Commander Sauer pours two cups of wine and hands her one smiling.

She takes it smiles and replies "So you're right. You're always right. It gets disgusting after awhile."

"I know. But, that doesn't change anything. You cannot be in the same room as Remy, even for mere moments. He has already exhibited unmatched senses. He'd pick up your scent in a second. He has already started to be inquisitive about the woman in his dream."

"So what do you suppose we do?" Replies Sariel

"Well Kiree looks just like you. If we place a veil over her face no one would know the difference. She makes an appearance greets everyone and then leaves. That shouldn't take longer than an hour at the most."

"The Prince will know the difference."

"I will explain to him that this is a security protocol. He is a soldier first. He will agree these are not the times to place you in jeopardy."

"Kiree is also the daughter of the elves spy you know."

"That is true which is why it's probably safe to use her in this situation. Plus I doubt the elves have enough balls to use the dinner as a cover for military action." says Commander Sauer.

"Never underestimate those elves. They are desperate. They have attacked Remy at least twice that we know of and probably more times that we do not know. From the pictures of the cave and the encampment we've been able to deduce that they had set up one of their fake temples. They tricked a human into supplying them with raw material to feed them and to create shape-changers. The elves must have been there for at least two or three years based on the amount of body parts found. They must have known that Remy was a threat to at least the set-up. They then took normal steps to kill him and it did not work. That is when they decided to use the shape-changers. They must have gotten desperate, that not usually their style, unless they figured out who he was." Her eyes widen and she says "Which I think is exactly what happened by the last attempt. It is only because of his prowess in battle and God's protection that he is alive today. I have watched him on tape of his battle with the trolls over and over. You are right he is magnificent and without double blades."

"Quite true I watched the tapes myself and was impressed by

MARK ROBERTS

his prowess. None the less, he will need special training to be the best warrior possible."

"As you know, their spy must know everything and has passed it on to them. We knew of the troll attack, just not when. Again Remy passed the test and we got an added pawn with Ejamine and possibly her people."

"He loves you. You know that?" says Commander Sauer looking at her. "He would die for you right here and now. No woman will take him from you once this is over."

"True, but it doesn't stop the thoughts brother. Moreover, when will this be over? The elves still have many trumps to play and we still have no control over the European and Asian Clans. Our only advantage is that the summer solstice is six months away, so they cannot try to bring a wraith across to aid their cause."

"Everything will become clear soon. The words of the prophecy are starting to ring true."

"That is true. Anyway, unless he is also a champion in the art of lovemaking, I think it is time to summon Kiree. I will tell her of the plan and let her dress here. Three of my personal guard will be with her at all times."

"Oh Dresa will love this, her only child a pawn in a game where she has chosen to play both sides of the board."

"The best part is she actually thinks she is my confidant. She has been our best pawn in this scenario. She has fed the elves the exact information we wanted." Says Sariel

"Well, she never was very bright. However, until this is over I have taken over the prince's security myself. There will be no more slip ups."

The infliction in his voice makes her smile and say. "You care for him. Can it be the ice king has finally thawed?"

"He is extremely important to our plans and of course to you." He says meekly looking at her. "All right I do care about him. He is special almost like a son to me. I will not let him die for nothing. I have already lost one son."

"All these years the both of us have been filled with bitterness and hatred. We have tried to save a world that does not care if it is saved at all because it is our sworn duty. Yet, look at us. I mean really look at us. Not just you and I, but all the people he meets. All of us are fundamentally changed forever after being around him. Look at Lord Vaft I have not seen him smile in a century. Yet, he is once again filled with purpose and energy. He sees a light at the end of the tunnel and that light is Remy. He is like a breath of fresh air. Remy has no entrenched prejudices, no petty hatred. He has not learned how and so he will not tolerate it. Hatred has always been a mature disease it only grows with time. If the elves learn he is this way, they will use his heart to destroy him. It will be their only weapon. We both know Remy must be taken to the werewolf and dwarves camp to meet his destiny as soon as possible. He needs to learn a lot in a short time because I am sure the elves have stepped up their schedule." she says picking up the phone and dialing. It rings ten or twelve times before it is answered which makes her even more jealous.

Remy answers a little out of breath. "Hello, may I help you."

Sariel quivers at the sound of his voice and hesitates. Remy repeats, "Hello, is anyone there."

The authority in his voice startles her.

"Yes, may I speak to Kiree, please?" she says.

"Just a moment, please hold while I get her for you." Sariel hears giggling in the background and then a kiss and is more infuriated.

"Hello, this is Kiree."

"Kiree, I need you in my chambers now."

"Yes my Queen." answers Kiree her heart in her mouth. She hangs up the phone and immediately begins to get dressed to leave.

"Where are you going Kiree? There is at least two hours before the ball." Remy says grabbing her hand and smiling.

"I have been summoned by the Queen. Even though I do not want to leave you, I must. She is the one person not even you can protect me from." She kisses him deeply and says "I could never have had a better first lover than you. However, we will never be like this again. Just remember you are the Prince of Princes and must save this world for the children of tomorrow. I hope you will forgive me when all is done." she then turns and leaves before he can say a word.

Remy sits on the bed and says to himself "Forgive her for what?"

The tears flow from Kiree's eyes as she heads towards the Queen's quarters. She thinks to herself "I can't believe I made love to him. I barely know him. But my heart, my body and my soul are filled with him. I feel obsessed with him. I never thought I would care for him the way I do. I did not expect him to be loving and kind. I was not prepared for him to make love to me body and soul. I was just to be the test vessel for his seed, nothing more. It will be torture to see him with others. I will never want another unless he is my life-mate. By God what have I done to myself?" She says as she hurries along to the Queen's quarters.

"So is all ready with Ejamine's people?" asks Sariel

"All the arrangements have been made. It will be very tricky, but it seems to be working. Lord Vaft has been in constant contact with her people." Replies Commander Sauer.

"She of course will follow her heart and we will have an ally for eternity. Remy has no idea I suppose."

"A little, I left a book of etiquette for him to read. Once he reads the book he'll understand. He already understands the gravity of the situation and what he may need to do. Why do you keep calling Ejam, Ejamine?"

"Because that is her real name her birth name as a woman."

"I sense you admire her."

"Well, from all our reports she is an accomplished warrior and strategist. She also hid herself as a male during all these years. That must not have been easy."

"I agree. Plus it doesn't hurt that Ejamine is as attractive as she is." Commander Sauer says winking.

Sariel looks at him and hits him with a pillow. "You will never change you bastard. She is so stunningly beautiful an elf lord would have quickly claimed her as his concubine."

"There is one more thing, Sariel." Commander Sauer says becoming serious again.

"What is that?"

"Only Ejamine's father knew she was female. A father's love for his daughter has and will be stronger than for a son. He will seek revenge by the word of God."

"That is ridiculous. They are the allies of the elves. They don't believe in God."

"Based on the tape you are wrong. The last troll that died swore allegiance to Remy based on the prophecy. That means the first teachings continue in that tribe. This of course makes me wonder are they allies by their own choice."

"Then it is a good thing we have tried to do what we have chosen to do for their clan. Let's hope we are successful in our endeavor. But I somehow think the elves no more about Ejamine than you think."

CHAPTER 9

"Appearances can be quite deceiving"

DRESA HEADS DOWN THE corridor dressed for the evening in a pale yellow gown with gold accessories. She is a tall stately woman who walks with great grace. Her purple eyes and long raven hair help her stand out from other women and she knows it. She is a woman who feels the power and energy of the events unfolding and relishes a time of change. Dresa has always thought the elves were the most beautiful race God had created; she even fell in love with one. She does not see him often enough, however that will not last forever. The last time she saw him, was in the Bahamas six months ago. They had spent a week together making love and making plans. Soon the Elves will be the masters of this planet. Soon the vampire clans will be extinct. The clan has never given her what she deserved. Had she not figured out all the genetic change serums the elves had created? Wasn't it she who created a serum to combat most of them and still she had no seat on the council. Still she was treated like a mere lackey. The will all perish for that affront; all that is except her and her daughter. She will rule by his side and the earth shall bow at their feet, as it should be. God should have never cast his favorite children down. Soon even God would feel the vengeance of the elven clans and it will be a vampire that aided them in their cause. She turns into the room beneath the communication area and opens a door, which no one knew existed. In this room is the equipment to communicate with the Elves by bouncing off thirty to forty satellites making it impossible to track or pinpoint. Plus, with the signal originating from beneath the COM center there was no way to discern a difference. She steps inside and touches the wall illuminating the room. She punches in the codes and a connection is accomplished. The COM light starts flashing and she clicks on the speaker.

"Is all ready, my love."

"Yes, milord." She answers filled with a sudden gush of lust for this being. "The upper gates have been opened and the attack team has access to the Queen's chambers."

"Good, my love. May I have a dance tonight at the ball?"

"Milord, you may have anything you wish."

"I will see you soon, Milady."

"I will be waiting as always."

Kiree reaches the Queens chambers and the guards allow her through. The Queen is not dressed as Kiree expected. The Queen is arrayed in battle leathers and her swords.

"My Queen." bowing deeply. "Why are you not dressed for the ball, milady?"

"Because I am not going to the ball tonight there is something afoot. Kiree, you are going to masquerade as me tonight. There is a plot to kidnap me and you are to be my decoy. The elves have not seen me in public for years and you are almost my twin. I am not in complete agreement with this plan. But, the survival of our people depends on what happens here tonight."

"It will be an honor to serve you in this way my Queen."

"This may be hard for you to understand. Nevertheless, I feel compelled to tell you this. Your mother may be part of this plot to kidnap me."

"That cannot be milady. My mother is loyal to you and the vampire clans."

"Be that as it may, we have intercepted transmissions from here to the Alps and your mother's voice signature was identified." Sariel presses a button and Kiree hears her mother giving vital information to someone."

"Why do you tell me this, milady?" Says visibly in pain from what she has just witnessed.

"Because if the elves succeed in kidnapping you I want you to have a secret edge, a very sharp edge, indeed you do not recognize that voice, but I do. That is the elf leader himself, Naline."

"Thank you, my Queen and my mother?"

"Will be dealt with later after all has transpired I promise you she will not be killed."

"If the council chooses death for her, I would like to be the one who carries out the sentence."

"As you wish, Kiree." Replies Sariel feeling her pain.

"Thank you, My Queen."

"I see the glow about you."

"Yes, my Queen, I have conceived as I was instructed."

"You have conceived? How do you know so quickly?"

"I feel it, milady. He was kind and gentle. Every woman should have as her first lover a man like Remy. He was patient and caring throughout" Kiree smiles.

The Queen is spilling over with a jealous rage at this statement and is stopped in mid-word by her brother.

"Good job Kiree. I take back what I said to you earlier. You have done the clans a great service." Says Commander Sauer looking at his sister.

"Yes, Kiree." The queen says her temper dying down. "A great service to all the clans."

"My Queen, I must tell you that I am honored to carry his child even though we will never be together again. I understand politics very well Milady. And I am also honored to be of service to you and the clans this night. But, what of my mother right this minute? As a traitor to our people she can do our people great harm? She knows so much."

"We have known about your mother for awhile. She only knows what we want the elves to know." Says Commander Sauer

"My, Queen I apologize for her. She has been blinded by their beauty and tricked by their cunning."

"Your mother acts on her own, child. She is in love with a man of great power and strength. I almost understand why. She feels slighted for not be placed on the council or sub-council. Unfortunately, we could not take the chance of her having that type of access to information. It is no reflection on you. You are a loyal subject of the clans. I know that." Says Sariel

The Queen looks at her and a tear falls from her eye. She reaches out and hugs Kiree. Kiree is flabbergasted. The Queen touches no one ever. Sariel steps back and says, "I have more heart than my people could ever know, Kiree. I know how you feel about him so I will bestow the truth upon you. Your mother is the consort of Naline, the great elven elder. She does what she does for love. Your mother has always thought the elves were a beautiful and intelligent people and has always admired them. We have formulated a plan where Remy will mate with Ejamine tonight and then leave for the werewolf and dwarf encampment. We need the trolls as our allies and have taken special precautions to protect them against retaliation from the elves."

"Milady, I must say I'm not too happy at the thought of Remy mating with a troll to be honest. How about you?"

"Me? Me? I do not think I can be objective about Remy. You see everything points to him being my life-mate. It is why you must masquerade as me tonight. It is too early for us to meet. He must mate with Ejamine tonight and nothing must stop that no matter how it tears my heart apart I have to let it happen for the good of the clans. Do you understand?"

"More then you know My Queen."

"Good, I have chosen my burgundy dress with cowl for you to wear. It will cover your head and face. It is my right to cover my face as a royal single person. You will stay at the ball for exactly two hours and then return here. Half of my security contingent will be with you at all times."

"I hope you are removing yourself from the building my Queen." says Kiree.

Commander Sauer smiles to himself and says aloud "I guess one mistake is too many, huh little one?" Commander Sauer trained both Kiree and Kirstyne to be warriors and has been like a father to them both. Both of them lost their parents in the war. Kiree is overflowing with joy, because this statement means he forgives her.

"Thank you Milord, never make the same one twice if you live through it. I will make no more mistakes."

"I will be going to the stronghold to bless three new births." Says Sariel

"That is wonderful, My Queen three births in one day."

"You will be next, Kiree three months from now. You carry the seed of a new era within you." Says Commander Sauer.

"An era of peace I hope milord."

"Come, my queen. We must go. Kiree you be careful I have not been a godfather yet." Commander Sauer says winking at her.

"Yes Milord." she says her eyes burning bright with pride. Sariel and Commander Sauer leave via an old elevator shaft only known to the royal family. Commander Sauer's nose starts to twitch and the hair rises on his neck as they reach the communications floor. He stops the elevator between floors and says, "We have visitors my Queen."

"Who?" She asks.

"Smells like some ogres and elves."

"You just may be a little jumpy. Both races are invited to the ball as you well know and are already in the building."

"That is true, my queen but no one invited them into the communications center with the smell of steel and leather."

He opens the top of the elevator and the four guards he placed up there snap to attention. Two stay on top and two automatically jump inside with the queen.

"If anyone comes near this elevator they are to die. I do not care who it is. Do you understand me?"

They nod in unison. Commander Sauer takes out his com-link and places it in his ear. "Power team set for big game on com floor. Move quick Move strong." He says climbing through the doors above the elevator that has begun to descend. He thought it would be a good idea to set-up three teams. Each team has different abilities and tasks. A power team, stealth team and a quick team. "Stealth team head for the Queen's chambers and Quick team hit the roof." This is Commander Sauer's worst nightmare. If the elves are only five floors beneath the queen, then Dresa let them in. "But where?" he thinks to himself. "Where?" It is then it dawns on him that the laser system in the ventilation shafts has a bypass on this floor and only the royal family knew of it. That is except for Dresa. "Now that bitch needs to die." he spits as he pulls out his blades.

He activates his comlink again. "Power team, ETA."

"We're on the other side of the floor, Milord. There is nothing suspicious except the smell. The COM center is untouched."

"Where the hell are they?" he says looking around. He sees an opening he has never seen before in the ceiling. The hole is teeming with the scents of elves and ogres. No more than a ten-minute head start he figures by the smell. "Get over here ASAP; we got rats loose in the house and their going for the queen."

Kiree has just finished getting dressed and all she can think of is Remy in her arms. He was so gentle and loving. She twirls about the room in an imaginary dance with him. She could not have chosen a better person to mate with the first time. "This child will be strong." Kiree thinks to herself rubbing her abdomen.

Kiree walks across the room and looks into the mirror at herself, quite happy with what she sees. The burgundy gown looks glorious on her. Would he notice? Would he know? She starts to look around the Queen's suite. She has only been in the Queen's chambers twice before and she has always been surprised by its sparseness. There is very little furniture, simple and comfortable. She now realizes how different then the rumors about the Queen really are. In God's name how lonely must her life be. Add to that the pain of knowing your life-mate exist, yet, you can do nothing about it. Kiree's revelry is shattered by the sound of her com-link crackling to life on the bed. She rushes over and puts it on. "Yes."

"This is Commander Sauer. You have to get out of there, now. There are ogres and elves moving in on your position. We are coming up through the elevator shaft."

"I am moving now, Milord." She says as the door comes crashing in. She sees all four of the Queen's personal guard dead on the floor. Through the doorstep enters Fica flanked by eight ogres with battle-axes.

"Good evening Milady. We have come to fetch you. We have much to discuss. Please come along quietly. If not then by force it of course is your choice." he says bowing with a smile.

Mustering all her resolve Kiree covers her face and head with the cowl and says, "You have not won this war, Elf."

"True but after your Prince dies tonight we will. I have also left a little surprise for him."

"You and a whole army could not kill this prince. Do not delude yourself! He is a proven warrior, not an assassin who comes in the night like you." says Kiree

"Take this bitch away we don't have much time." says Fica visibly irritated by Kiree's statement. Must everyone belittle his prowess in battle and speak of Remy's. One day they will all change their tunes when Remy lies beneath his dripping blade. That is if he doesn't die tonight.

They head towards the window where a helicopter hovers. The helicopter flies above the window and a rope ladder is lowered. Fica grabs the ladder and then Kiree.

"Come vampire wench we go to your fate." and they both swing into the helicopter as Commander Sauer and his men burst into the Queen's chambers. "I see your whelps have arrived. But it is much too late." The helicopter quickly gains altitude and is gone. Commander Sauer and his men slaughter the ogres who are left.

"Everyone must know the Queen has been taken. This is an act of outright war." signs Aster, one of the Queen's personal guards to Commander Sauer.

"No Aster, the Queen is safe. That was Kiree they have taken, my adopted daughter." Says Commander Sauer.

All grow quiet at this statement. They all know of Commander Sauer's love for this child who is not even of his flesh. Commander Sauer adopted her when her father died in battle. Taught her all he knew. It also allowed him to stay close to her mother. But that is another tale for another time.

"Then Milord we rescue her as we would rescue any of our brethren." signs Aster

"No Aster even though it hurts my heart to say it, we must not attempt a rescue. The prince will be beside himself as it is, when he is told the Queen has been taken."

They all look at him quizzically.

"But Milord it was Kiree who was taken." says Weol

"But only we know that. They think they have been successful and that thought should not be changed until the prince is upon his path of destiny. Do you all understand?" says Commander Sauer looking them all in the eye.

They all nod in unison except for Aster who signs agitatedly "But she is with child, Milord. She told me herself. This prince will burn the Alps down to get to his child. I have seen him in action. Honor is everything." Signs Aster.

"And that is exactly why he must think it's the Queen and not Kiree for now. Because he would give his life needlessly to save anyone, so much more rides on this situation. He must not know the truth yet. Do any of you doubt that I would give my life for Kiree? She is like a daughter to me. This is a trap and nothing more. They will not injure her she is they're only bargaining piece."

"I understand Milord." signs Aster tears in her eyes. "But if anything happens to my sword sister I will go to war myself and bring the Alps down upon their heads."

CHAPTER 10

"Pure evil is transparent"

REMY FINDS CLOTHES IN the walk-in closet that have been laid out for him by Kiree. How she did all that so quickly he will never know. She is just amazing. Remy has a feeling of being taken care of for the first time in his life. At the orphanage, the children were taught to be self-sufficient. Never to rely on anyone but themselves, independence was consistently rewarded by the leaders in the orphanage. It was by no means a loveless childhood some of his fondest memories came from that orphanage and the old man and woman who ran it. They were always there for him, and they always treated all the children as if they were family. None treated better or worse than the other. It was almost as if they all were truly a family. Remy stops in mid thought and chuckles to himself. Those two people were his parents, he is sure of it now. All the workers were warriors to protect him. It all makes sense now. They treated the children as family because they were and it was the perfect front to fool the elves. He openly wonders if any of those children were his brothers and sisters.

"My, My, My what a web we weave." he mutters to himself. "How many other lies had he been told to protect him from the elves" he wonders.

The clothes laid out for him are all black silk. A black silk Nehru collared suit and shirt. On the breast pocketed an embroidered red dragon the insignia of his clan. Black rubber soled shoes that seemed to have been fashioned for dressed battle. By instinct and routine, he dons his paper-thin black body armor beneath his clothes. The warrior masters made this body armor in Japan. It is strong enough to divert a sword or bullet, yet as light as paper. Remy wishes now that he had taken it with him to Malaysia. Maybe he could have saved himself a trip to the cryogenic tank. The armor was a gift to him by his sensei in Japan. Again, he finds so many coincidences as he remembers his training that summer in Japan. In his senior year in High School, he won an exchange student program to Japan. He was overjoyed. He had always wanted to go to Japan and study with the masters. He was to live with a family in Osaka. That family treated him like one of their own. Soon as he arrived, he registered into the Aikido dojo owned by his exchange family. At first, he thought the sensei did not like him. He would always push him harder than the other students. Always an extra session, always an extra move never acknowledgement of a deed well done. However, he never complained and excelled at combat. For some reason he loved it. Fighting had always been the only thing he could do well. To battle everyday seemed natural. Unlike the other students who came to class three times a week, he took lessons every day. Remy loved the feel of striking something, the power of out thinking an opponent and of course the joy of your opponent at your feet. He woke up at 5AM every single morning worked out before regular school and then would return to the Aikido school after doing his homework. It soon became routine and he would not miss it if for anything. Even when he had a fever and bad cough he went. The only time he would miss a class was at the sensei's command. All the time he spent in Japan he never lost a match. After a match, the sensei would push him to work out with him for another hour or two. Sensei would teach him weapons and strategy during that time. It was like he was preparing him for all out war. Remy felt honored because he was the only student learning these things from his Sensei. In his last two months in Japan, he fought a match every day. During his last match, before he was to enter the Air Force Academy, he beat his sensei's number one student. The student did not take it well and attacked Remy with a weapon. The sensei did not flinch. Remy disarmed the student in one smooth move and held the sword to his neck. "Will you yield?"

"Not to a gaijin. I will never yield. You are less than us. You are not warrior class. Losing to you means I am inferior. I deserve to die." Said the student defiantly.

"Then I yield." Said Remy dropping the blade and bowing. "You are the victor. I will not seriously injure one of my clan."

The class is in shock. A gaijin had more honor then the teacher's best pupil. This is unspeakable.

The student picks up the sword and bows before Remy and says "You are truly a great warrior. I have disgraced myself and our school by calling you gaijin and not a true warrior."

"We are all one in the way, my brothers. I am honored by knowing all of you. I will miss all of you." Says Remy bowing.

The class all bow in unison to Remy.

Sensei rises and ends class. Again as always, the other students were dismissed and the sensei requested he stay. This time his sensei said "I have a question for you my son?"

"Yes sensei."Remy answered from a bowed position feeling honored that Sensei had called him son.

"You have never once complained about being worked harder than the other students".

"No, sensei."

"You have never complained when students picked on you and called you names."

"No, sensei."

"Even now when you could have injured Hamichi with good reason you choose the path of honor. Did you not want revenge for the way you've been treated?"

"No, sensei."

"Why?" His sensei said looking directly into his eyes.

"Sensei, I never wanted to dishonor you or your home by quitting or doing something dishonorable."

"But you are Gaijin to them, and you know as well as I do that no one would have looked upon my house or I with dishonor if you complained or refused. In addition, you must admit you excel at battle. You honestly love it. A new move to you is like another meal to savor."

"I would have known sensei. You have taught me to respect everything that you teach me. I have learnt to treat everything new you teach me as a delicacy; something to savor and to slowly enjoy as I try to understand it."

"I am greatly honored that you say this. You are the best student I have ever taught."

"Sensei, I took the place of your son for one year I could do no less than he would have. It is the honorable thing to do."

Sensei turned his back looked up and sighed aloud. "You are more my son than my son. I will tell you something. My son could not wait to leave Japan and switch places with you. America was all he could talk about all that mattered to him was getting there. Once he got to America he disappeared from the exchange family. I honestly do not know where he is. Tsui never attended this school Remy. He thought the old ways of honor, were just that old. Yet you come to a country where you know no one and become all that I could wish in a son."

Remy sees tears well up in his sensei's eyes as he continues. "You Remy are my son in all but blood. I love you more than you will ever know as does my wife and my daughter. You have been diligent and humble in a world where these qualities are no longer revered. I would like to give you three gifts." He says walking towards his personal chest and pulls out three items wrapped in black silk.

"Here take theses as a token of my love for you."

Remy opens the first bundle and finds an exquisite short sword. The blade made of cold black steel about two and a half feet long sharp on both sides and a hilt that seemed to be made of one solid ruby. However, when he gripped the blade that he expected to be slick and cold it was warm and seemed to adhere to his hand. It felt magnificent almost like a true extension of his body. The second bundle held a paper-thin black matte suit with a hood and facemask. The last bundle had a piece of paper without any writing on it.

"This sword belonged to the Emperor of a great race, the protectors of the great races before man. It had a twin but it was broken in battle. You will one day forge its brother. This suit was constructed by a race called the dwarves. It is impervious to most conventional weapons. The scroll will come to life when the time is right. Always keep these gifts close to you. One day you will understand the importance of these items and then you will fulfill your destiny. I wish I could tell you more, but that is for another to do."

Remy is startled back to the present by a knock at the door. "Come in." He says closing the collar of his shirt.

In walk two ogres with battle axes. "Time to die, Prince."

Remy laughs aloud draws his blade and beheads the first with one stroke of his blade. The other ogre charges forward swinging his axe. Remy sidesteps and thrust his sword cleanly through his left armpit piercing his heart as Commander Sauer rushes in the room with the guard close behind. It is the first time Commander Sauer has witnessed an instantaneous progression to a feral state. He is shocked. Aside from a slight change in Remy's facial features, skin color and his scent, you would never know he was in a feral state. Remy pulls the sword out of the ogre and says. "Commander Sauer you smell of battle. What has happened?"

"The elves and ogres have captured the Queen. They used this event as cover to get into the building, Milord. It seems they thought to kill you as well."

"Killing me is not as easy as they think. So already they use me to hurt others. We must rescue her immediately." Replies Remy sheathing his sword and returning almost instantaneously to a normal state.

Commander Sauer takes a closer look at the sword and gasp. He keeps his composure and says "Milord that would be a strategic error. This is a long-term war. They captured her as a bargaining piece. She will be returned once we find out what they want and negotiate with them."

"I do not trust these elves and I do not negotiate. However, you are one of the few people on this earth I do trust, milord. So I shall heed your words for now." Says Remy

"The elves are a lot of things but they definitely are not stupid. They know they are not strong enough to start full out war."

"Still they will pay for this insolence in short order." Says Remy.

Commander Sauer is shocked by this man's presence. He feels every warrior in the room holding on to each of his words. He knows in his heart that all including him would follow this man to whatever end.

"Milord, I know I am being presumptuous, but where did you get that sword?"

"It was a gift from my Sensei in Japan, when I studied there. He told me this sword had a twin that was lost and that it belonged to the emperor of a great race and that it was part of my destiny. Why?"

Commander Sauer and all the guards fall immediately to their knees and chime together.

"To the death we will battle, for ours is the path of God."

Commander Sauer rises and says "Because milord, that sword belonged to our emperor Vincenzo. I have its twin in my quarters as a remembrance of him. What we have just recited was the mantra he would repeat before any event or battle. He always felt our path was the path of God, the way of the righteous and pure of spirit. A path he died for without hesitation."

"I see. Well then." Remy replies falling to his knee. He draws the blade once more and says, "To the death we will battle, for ours is the path of God."

There is a roar of voices as all the guards within earshot shout "To the death we will battle, for ours is the path of God." The shout reverberates throughout the building from floor to floor shaking the very foundations it stands on.

Great sadness can be seen in Commander Sauer's eyes as he remembers his best friend. Vincenzo was like a brother to him. He taught him all he knows. "Oh well" he says to himself. "Milord, it is not wise to show weakness at this time. You must go to the banquet and present yourself to the tribes. They must know the prince is made of steel. Steel forged in the blood of many peoples. They will not injure the Queen. She is their only protection against all out war. They took her to make you chase after them, so they could spring a trap. The people need you and the Queen knows that."

Remy looks around the room and sees bowed heads waiting for his word to rise. He sees the sadness in Commander Sauer's eyes and feels the weight of the world fall upon his shoulders. The words of his Sensei repeat in his mind "One day you will understand the importance of all these items and then you will fulfill your destiny."

Remy says, "Rise all we have a ball to attend and woe be the person who steps out of line tonight. Commander Sauer please have someone bring me the other sword it will have great shock value for all present."

"An excellent idea, Milord." Commander Sauer says signally for someone to fetch the sword.

"Oh and Commander Sauer bring something along to make an impact on the elves and the others at the ball" Commander Sauer smiles and says "Yes Milord, I will."

Naline's entourage moves towards their table, a table in the middle of the hall, close to the door of the kitchen, another subtle smack of disrespect. Elves sitting in the middle while the other clans, including humans, sit in the front near the Queen.

"They should learn to treat they're betters with respect." Thinks Naline to himself as he looks around the room at the rabble, it brings back memories of happier times, a time long ago when Vincenzo, Efisio and himself were all good friends. When they drank deep into the night and talked of the future. A time when Naline did believed in God. It seemed so long ago now. More like a dream then a memory. The war ended all that a war that began right after the death of Christ. Two millennia of peace brought to an end.

"When the great human prophet died, the world was changed forever. One god-dam human had changed the course of history forever. We knew he was special but how special we know now. His life changed the path of billions on this earth. It was then that they were approached by Lucifer with a plan to storm heaven after they defeated earth. Lucifer had long been casted out by God after he thought he was equal to him. If Vincenzo and Efisio had listened, God would have been defeated and they would rule now. With the Vampires and Dwarves by their side they would have been victorious. What a waste. But they would all pay under the dripping sword for choosing to follow God. Of all he missed Vincenzo, the only warrior to ever defeat him in battle and the only warrior that could push him to become feral. Oh yes, Vincenzo had taught him how to release his feral side spiritually. It is what made him the only true warrior elf. Only Vincenzo knew about this ability. The only drawback is the inability to teach it to any other elf. The truth was Vincenzo had no hatred for the elves, because he died for one.

After the last battle, an elven child eleven years old chose to follow the path of God, instead of his clan. Vincenzo protected the child from some elves who wanted to kill him. What Vincenzo did not know was ten handpicked shape-changers were waiting for him. Already weakened by the daylong battle he battled without stopping. Slaying all but three of the shape-changers protecting the child at all cost. Nonetheless, he had sustained dozens of wounds from which his life-blood flowed. He turned to the boy and said "Run, and save yourself." Just as a shape-changer rammed his sword into his abdomen, Vincenzo spun around pulling the blade free from his body and beheaded the shape-changer in the same motion. Another shape-changer tried to catch the boy, but Vincenzo threw one of his swords into the back of his head. As he fell the sword snapped in two. As Vincenzo did this, the third shape-changer impaled him on his blade. Vincenzo could have pulled out the blade and supped on the shape-changers blood healing himself. However, Vincenzo was not that selfish nor would he exact the power of his heritage if it meant feasting on a living being's blood. Because once you drink that steaming blood spurting from a body you may lose yourself into the madness and become a hunter for the rest of your days. Instead, he embraced the shape-changer impaling him on the same blade that protruded from his abdomen. The boy escaped, who he is or where he is no elf knows. Naline is brought back from his musings by the sound of the trumpets announcing the prince's entrance.

The ball seems packed with people as Remy and his entourage reach the door of the great hall. Remy is amazed by the size of the hall. It easily is as big as half a football field. The floor is made of exquisite gray and maroon marble tiles and the hall is illuminated by hundreds of crystal chandeliers. The food that is being served is fragrant and hot. Wine flows like a waterfall. Remy can see that the Vampire Clan had not wasted any expense for this gathering and so quickly. He looks around and sees dignitaries from many nations and from the clans. His senses tell him who everyone is. Everyone's scent is different and he is able to distinguish between all these scents very easily. This is quite new to him and is both confusing and exhilarating. The best is that there are elves masquerading as humans. They must have been placed in those positions very delicately. Extremely powerful positions. Killing any of them could lead to a full scaled conflict. He struggles to control himself when he smells the elves and ogres who are sitting together. He does not need to become feral now it could start a battle right here.

"Are you ready Milord?" says Commander Sauer "This is not the time to become feral, as well you know."

"Don't worry I have that covered. I am as ready as I will ever be. Let us get this over with; I'm not one for this type of thing."

"You sound more like vampire royalty all the time, my prince." replies Commander Sauer with a chuckle.

Trumpets blare again and everyone in the hall becomes quiet. "I now introduce to you, Prince Remy of the vampire clan."

There is a huge roar heard throughout the hall as Remy walks towards his table shaking hands along the way. He stops at the elven table, grabs Naline's hand and says quietly with a smile "If the Queen is not returned by the morrow I will personally behead you."

Naline tries to pull away but Remy holds him tighter looking directly into his eyes. All of a sudden, he knows all that the elf knows. All their plans and so much more it is his dwarven gift coming to the fore.

Surprised by Remy's raw strength Naline rips his hand away from Remy and says; "I don't know what you are talking about, boy? I expect to see the Queen come through that door at any moment."

"You do. Personally, I think you are a few ogres short at this table." Says Remy.

His personal guard and Commander Sauer laugh with great mirth at that statement.

"I find nothing amusing about that statement, boy." Says Naline

"You will. Believe me you will." Says Remy

Eji just glares at Remy hand on his hilt. Remy looks at Eji smiles ignoring Naline's reference to his age and says, "You are a powerful and great people. You should not be subservient to anyone. You should always be treated as an equal." Then looking directly into Naline's eyes he continues. "Not treated like a pet."

Naline is close to losing his temper for the first time in centuries. This prince reminds him of Vincenzo. Same manner, same sarcastic tone same arrogance. He would have to be careful with this one. The reports he received about this being have been quite inadequate, he has much more substance than he expected. Their intelligence in this matter leaves a lot to be desired. Maybe they do not know as much as they need to know. Naline thinks now they have been much too hasty. "I tried to warn those fools. But they would not listen to reason. But we are now at the point of no return." Outwardly he smiles and says "Milord, this is a ball, a time for merriment and fun not for battle. However, that will most definitely follow. There can be only one leader, only one clan at the helm of this planet. And I know nature will choose the most fit to live and to rule. I am sure your elven genes will make that clear soon enough, boy."

As Remy prepares to retort he hears a voice in his mind say. "You have much to learn young prince. Walk away before you begin a war over mere words. It is an old elven trick."

Remy turns to the Dwarven table where a young woman smiles at him and nods. More composed he turns to Naline bows and says, "Enjoy your evening. We will speak again."

As he walks away Naline sees the black blades and gasp as he realizes whose they are. "You are much more aren't you Remy."

The young woman rises as he approaches the dwarven table. She is dressed in a simple black gown with a string of diamonds around her neck. Her hair pulled back in a tight bun held by diamond-encrusted pins. As he gets nearer to her, he sees her eyes are the color of topaz and her skin the color of new turned earth. He thinks to himself these dwarves look nothing like the fairy tales. All the men at the table are stocky and muscular but none of them are disfigured or deformed. Again, he hears her voice in his mind. "Those descriptions of us were created by the elves to stop humans from communicating with us. Our roots began in Africa and Asia and many offshoots of our tribe still live there. Alas, most have lost the gifts given to us by God. There are not many of pure dwarven blood left, maybe a few thousand. We were a race the elves despised more than the vampires. We never allowed them a chance to control us in any way."

She then offers her hand, which Remy's grabs tenderly and kisses. "I am the Princess Gara, of the Dwarven clans. It is a pleasure to meet you Milord."

"No Milady the pleasure is all mine in more ways than one. You are breathtaking." Says Remy smiling.

"Thank you my, prince. You are quite handsome yourself." She replies blushing.

"You have spoken to me directly in my mind, so you also know of the elven stratagem concerning your people?"

"What stratagem are you referring to?" she answers puzzled.

"I assumed that if you spoke to me through the mind you could also read my thoughts."

"No milord. Our gift is very specific we usually can only mind-speak to other dwarves. Our power is really more in healing diseases of the mind and body. However, physical contact can sometimes create a link between two beings. Nonetheless, even amongst my people the ability to read a mind on contact is a very rare gift. I know your mother; I grew up with her. She too has that gift. Your dwarven blood is true. Soon you will spend time with the elders of our tribe and learn of your destiny. Now you must continue your rounds of the tables."

Remy just stares at this enchanting creature and smiles again "You are quite correct, milady. Please read my mind, see what the elves have planned, and alert your father. I will have warriors placed at your disposal as well as transport vehicles."

She holds his hand and concentrates for a few moments and her eyes open wide in horror.

Remy looks at her and says "Everything will be fine. Just inform your father and my people will do the rest. You must trust me."

"It's funny but I do trust you." She replies with a genuine smile."

He begins to walk away, but stops and says "Oh, and save me a dance."

As they walk away Commander Sauer says, "You are making quite an impression tonight. First, you piss off Naline then you speak to the one person who has never spoken more than two words to anyone at a function like this for centuries. I must warn you though the werewolf clan is a little more demonstrative in their greetings, especially for someone who belongs to they're clan."

"Commander Sauer, lean closer to me." Says Remy, who whispers something in his ear. Commander Sauer's eyes widen and he gestures for some guards to come forth. He speaks to them and they rush off quickly. Commander Sauer turns to Remy and nods his head.

The werewolf table is in full swing drinking, eating, dancing and shouting oblivious to all others in the room. When they see Remy they shout "To the prince of princes."

Remy feels a tingling in his spine and a warm feeling in his stomach. It is like coming home after a long journey. You just want to bury yourself in the memories and your family. For some reason he does a triple, flip right into the midst of the werewolves and starts giving out hearty hugs to all male and female alike. The whole hall stops and looks at this spectacle. They are like a bunch of cubs playing in a meadow.

"Welcome home brother." Says Warren, King of the werewolves embracing Remy. "As long as were- blood runs through your veins you will always be our brother."

"Thank you Milord." Remy says bowing.

"Oh and I must say it was worth the trip just to see you tell off Naline. He is quite perturbed."

"Not as perturbed as he will be, Milord."

"I like your spunk, lad. Does an old man's heart good."

"Excuse me, Milord "says Commander Sauer "We must reach your table so the festivities can go into full swing."

"Of course, Lord Sauer." says Remy and to King Warren "Milord we have much to discuss but I must fulfill my duties."

"Without question young prince and I have every ounce of confidence you will do just that." He turns to his contingent and waves his hand. They all sit immediately as if they were never raising hell at all. King Warren looks at Remy and shrugs his shoulders with a smirk playing on his lips.

Remy just laughs and heads towards his table. As he reaches his table and sits down, Naline asks to be acknowledged by all present.

"Now that the pageantry is over, I Naline of the Elven clan demand to be heard by the laws of God."

A hush falls over the hall with dwarves, werewolves, and vampires ready to slit his throat at his audacity to use God's name.

Naline feels their hatred and says "Well maybe not God's law. More like clan law."

"What is this nonsense, Naline?" says Commander Sauer.

"As you all know the law of the clans says one may challenge another for revenge."

"Revenge for what?" asks Commander Sauer

Eji gets up and says, "Revenge for my son's death."

"Your son was one of the trolls who attacked me?" says Remy calmly. "That is very interesting."

"Yes upon the orders of the Elven clan. You are a freak and deserve to die. If you did not have mixed blood you'd be dead already." Spits Eji.

"Actually, isn't that an open act of aggression against the vampire clan. There is a good deal of that going on lately." Says Commander Sauer

"They were sent on a diplomatic mission before the banquet and were attacked by the prince and his warriors. They were slain without a chance to defend themselves or to explain why they were here." says Naline

"Really? Is full armor and weapons the new olive branches of peace."

"They were there to discuss our arrangements for this banquet."

"Is that so? Then why were they in the Heme building and not the Haxe building. Everyone here knows this is the building you come to for parlays or discussions. That has been that way for centuries." Says Commander Sauer

"They apparently lost their way and were cut down by this adolescent boy who knows nothing of our culture or ways. It is a disgrace that you have named him prince."

"Well Naline that could possibly be." Says Remy getting up and walking towards the center of the room.

"Not probably, definitely and the death of Eji's son is the proof."

"I see. But proof of what?"

"That you are no better than the dung beneath my feet. You know nothing of our clans, nothing about our ways."

"That may be however, Eji, I do not know about this challenge of yours. I mean I did save and protect the life of Ejam with my own." Replies Remy smiling.

Eji almost faints on the spot. He knows the Laws of God and the clans. If Remy spared his daughter, he has no right to challenge. However, the elves never knew his son was actually his daughter. Before he can speak right on cue, Ejam walks into the hall with Lord Vaft. She is stunningly dressed in a gold gown low cut in the front and back. Her hair pulled back into two long braids with babies' breath as a crown. She smiles at the elven contingent and her father as she walks by towards Remy who just stares at her. Eji is surprised Naline is not surprised she is a woman, which means he knew all along. If he knew all along he just sent her to die. "You and I will dance one day Naline. You have wronged my clan for the last time. We have always been loyal to you." Eji thinks to himself.

Lord Vaft moves next to Remy and whispers something in his ear. Remy smiles and says, "I have an announcement to make."

The hall becomes quiet and Remy walks up to Ejam. She looks at him and whispers in his ear "I know it will not last forever. But, I am yours for now. I love you."

Remy looks at her and whispers back 'How could you be so sure? We do not even know each other."

"There is much you need to learn Milord. Love does not require time to begin it just requires tending to grow. I've loved you from the moment you spared my life. Nevertheless, you are a prince Milord, soon to be an emperor. There are many things you don't know yet, I am satisfied with what I can have."

They both turn around hand in hand. "I am claiming Remy as my Mate." Says Ejam. The hall erupts.

"This is blasphemy." Says Naline "A troll cannot mate with royalty they are our slaves." Naline realizes his mistake too late. He has admitted what has not been verbally acknowledged since the creation of the troll race.

"I am glad you have spoken the truth, Naline." Says Ejam smiling.

"Now while all the races are present." says Remy. "Know the vampire and troll clans are allies against whoever chooses to go against the word of God. This is a day of rejoicing. It is the first day of freedom for a proud people and the beginning of a lasting alliance between the clans."

The hall erupts into cheers. Even the vampire clan did not know the trolls were slaves. They thought them equal allies to the elves. Many animosities fall by the wayside as they cheer. Commander Sauer thinks to himself. "The elves are taking this too lightly. Something is amiss."

Eji rises and request to be heard, he waits until the cheers die down and says "Milord, I know you think you are doing the right thing. However, we are in bondage by force also. My people may be dying as we speak. The elves kept us in caverns with poison gas bombs lining every inch of our living quarters. And after the women and children are dead they will have the ogres and a new race the fairies cut the rest of us down. I must implore you daughter to not claim Remy as your mate to save our people."

Ejam steps forward to her father grabs his hands looking into his eyes and says "Our people are safe, father. Lord Sauer and Lord Vaft took care of that. While these snakes were here a small force of vampire aided trolls helped our people escape into the Alps where ten transports sent by the vampire nation picked them up. I spoke to clans-keeper, Tyds, myself and told him of my plan. He accepted and now our people are free. He even was able to gather those who were held as body slaves to the elves. They will reach Canada within the hour escorted by vampire clans' gun-ships."

The vampire council is shocked. None of them had been consulted about this decision.

The council head Tagom says with a smile. "This prince may

just be who they say he is. Not one vampire has so much as gone to the bathroom without permission from the council since Emperor Vincenzo died."

"Be careful what you wish for." says Dastor, second elder. "They may soon have no need for us at all."

"These young bucks may be impetuous, Dastor, but they are not disrespectful. Honor is back. Chivalry and all that go with it. They saved an enslaved race and we all can take the credit for it."

"And we have gained some powerful allies as well." Replies Dastor aloud. "As always your wisdom shines forth." To himself "This could destroy all my plans. I need time to think after this ball."

Naline is beside himself with rage. "This is an open act of war against the elven clans. We will retaliate." The elven guard surrounds him for protection.

"Ah Naline." Says Remy

"Lord Naline to you whelp." Says one of Naline's guards drawing his weapon.

The hall falls silent; all hands are moved to weapons. The vampire guards have drawn their weapons and are moving towards the elven guard.

Before any, one can slit the elven guard's throat Remy says, "Hold all of you. Sheath your weapons. We are an honorable tribe and will not fight during a festive time. That is the Law of God, the law which the elven contingent has bantered about like a piece of trash."

"Who are you to speak of the Laws of God? You are but a pubescent boy compared to most of the people in this room. Look around you child. These are the first clans of God. You are a mutt, the worst of all these great races. You are not even a half-breed. You're a no breed." Shouts Naline

"Touchy, touchy." Says Remy as Commander Sauer hands him a sack. Remy reaches into the sack, pulls out an ogre head, and tosses it onto the elf table. "When I say that the elven contingent has bantered the word and Law of God I do not say it lightly.

This is the head of an Ogre who attempted an open attack on this building against me personally. They invaded the building during the festivities in an open act of defiance of God's laws.

Naline thinks to himself "Again you over step your bounds Fica. No wonder Remy knew everything. You will pay this time Fica."

"Naline you have twice this evening referred to the Laws of God, but let me ask you do you believe in God?"

"All of you know the answer to that question." Replies Naline

"Please remind us, Naline. You see I am a just pubescent boy who knows nothing and I'm sure everyone here would like to hear it personally from your own lips." Says Remy.

"I don't believe in God and all of you know that. We did rebel against him."

"So why use his name? Why act like you believe in his laws or the laws of the clan?"

"He turned his back on us. We were his favorites. The elves not the creations we made for him like man .Us."

"God never turned his back on your clans. And the door is ever open for you to return to him. He is a forgiving creator." Says Commander Sauer

"You don't know that. We cannot trust God's word. We are the first of the first. We are your betters. We are his better."

"That's all I needed to hear. Thank you, Naline." Says Remy.

"What are you thanking me for, fool?"

"You make this so easy, Naline. You and your clan are so full of hate. You just won't accept that you and your clan are all part of the fabric of existence. You see yourselves as everyone betters and even though your clans' blood flows through my veins, I must choose the many over the few." Remy says to Naline and then he turns to the gathering and shouts "Now I ask all of you. Will you follow me to right wrongs done to others?"

They all shout "Yes."

"Will you help me feed and clothe the poor of all races and bring peace to God's earth?"

"Yes Milord. Yes, Milord."

Remy turns looking directly at Naline and says, "There is your answer, Elf."

"You forget to quickly that we have your Queen." spits Naline as hush rolls over the hall "That's right we have the Queen."

Commander Sauer starts laughing aloud and is soon joined in his jollity by the Queen's guard and Remy.

"You find this a laughing matter. I said we have your Queen." shouts Naline

Commander Sauer hits a switch and the Queen's face appears on the overhead screen behind Remy's head so he cannot see her.

"My people I am safe. However, the elves have taken Kiree who posed in my stead. I am at the blessing of the births. I will join you soon." The transmission ends. The clans now all look at Naline.

"You never could be trusted Naline. You know the laws of God. No military action during a festive time." Says King Warren. "You have made a travesty of this sacred gathering."

"So what of their involvement in the trolls escape, does that not break the law as well?"

"I think not Lord Naline "says Lord Vaft "We only sent a medical team and civilian pilots. No weapons at all until the transports were met over the Atlantic by our gun-ships well out of Switzerland. The Trolls freed themselves. After we contacted them they just packed what they could and left. There was no resistance at all. For some reason not many warriors were about anyway."

"That is true," says Naline smiling. "They were sent on another mission."

"Yes, I know Naline. But the Dwarven village is already evacuated. So call your troops and tell them to return home! Before they do not return home at all." says Remy smiling.

"What the hell are you talking about?"

"I am talking about the order to slaughter woman and children by the fairies you created in the werewolf and dwarf camp."

"How did you know?" asks Naline

"Let's call it an old family secret and leave it at that."

"You are an abomination."

"Why thank you. Compliments are always well accepted."

"Do not worry, boy. You will not be so smug a year from now. You all will not be so full of yourselves then."

"Maybe and maybe not, Naline, But it is time for you to say goodnight."

"Are you dismissing me like some mongrel?" Says Naline infuriated.

"Well it's always good to know one self, mongrel. Now leave while you still can. There are a few tribes here who would like to string you and your people up about now."

Naline looks around the room and feels the hate being generated by the other tribes' eyes. He now realizes just how dangerous this one being is. Within minutes, Remy has exposed most of the subterfuge his tribe has put into place over the last century. Naline now understands this is truly a formidable enemy.

"You are right, Vincenzo. Once again you have made the other tribes unite against us. The difference this time is that we are ready to battle to the end for supremacy of this planet. So we will take our leave." Naline says as he waves his men back.

"The name is Remy not Vincenzo, Naline and I owe you personally for what you did to my grandfather. Remember that. One day I will raise your head in celebration, you can count on that." Remy says smiling.

Naline stares at him and then signals his contingent to leave and says "Some elves were trained by the best for combat; you would do well to remember that."

Naline thinks to himself "Fica and I will have a long chat when I get back. This Robon is nothing like he said."

Eji walks over to Remy with his daughter and says "She is all I have left and I thought she was gone. I was willing to risk all for a chance to battle you."

"My Lord you were only doing what you thought was right with the information you had. The elves have held your people in bondage so long you could only see what they let you see."

"My daughter has chosen wisely. You are an extraordinary young man. I thank you for freeing my people." Says Eji

"No Milord. You must thank Lord Vaft and the whole clan. I did nothing."

"Come father I want you to meet Lord Vaft and Commander Sauer. You will excuse us, my love?"

"Of course, please mingle. These are your people now." Remy says watching Lord Eji being greeted with the respect his station deserves. It gives him a great feeling accomplishment. But Ejam saying "My Love" is a whole different feeling itself. One he thinks he could come to like very much.

The hall begins to buzz with conversation as everyone breaks down into groups. The Dwarven contingent walks towards Remy.

"Milord." King Hozeer says bowing with Princess Gara by his side. "We have just met and already my people owe you a blood debt. You have saved many women and children with your swift actions. We are grateful."

"It was my duty to preserve life, Milord. I would give mine happily to save another's. It is an honor just to serve." Remy says with a bow.

This mere boy's demeanor and humility astonish King Hozeer. "He must be the one." he thinks to himself, however outwardly says. "Milord, I have heard you wish to visit your parents and converse with our elders. It would be our pleasure if you would accompany us on our journey back."

"It would be my pleasure, Milord". Answers Remy. "But, for now let us return to the merriment. This is a ball after all." And he takes Princess Gara's hand. "You owe me a dance, Milady."

"We all owe you much more than that, my prince. Far more than you'll ever know." She says staring into his eyes, which seems so young and full of spark. "Much more."

Remy swings her onto the floor and they dance as Princess Gara used to dance when she was a child. The joy on her face is clear to see and her father smiles for the first time at a function since Vincenzo died. The hall erupts into merriment. All the tribes present begin enjoying themselves for the first time in centuries. "Thank you God, for giving us another." he says looking to the sky. "I don't know why we deserve it, but thank you all the same. I will protect him with my life. He is special and by sending him to us you have made me understand how special you think we are."

CHAPTER 11

"The knife it seems cuts both ways."

NALINE IS FURIOUS AS he gets into the plane at the airport. In reality he is actually surprised they are letting him leave in one piece at all. So many reasons to kill him, for once in a long time he needs to thank God for his laws. They have saved his life. "That piece of trash Remy spoke to me as if I were a peasant. He does not have the mannerism of ordinary person. Remy smells and acts like one used to welding power and influence. I must admit his royal genes are true." He thinks to himself. "Remy is so much like Vincenzo; I even called him by his name. Fica is a fool if he thinks he can combat this being by himself. Remy is a warrior true, not some impostor. With the training he will receive Remy may be a better warrior than Vincenzo. He is definitely the real deal. The stories he had heard from the others were not exaggerated. In person Remy is a much more impressive specimen and his grip was like a vise, much like my first sword master who had wrist of iron. His scent was off though. You could clearly smell all the tribes on him. He is truly the one."

Naline looks up and sees Torm looking at him.

"Interesting specimen, that Remy, quite handsome and well built to boot. I think had my daughter met him first maybe she would have made a wiser choice." Torm turns away from Naline and looks out the window. He then turns back and says "Of course, I must admit, Naline, you were right and we of the council were wrong."

"Old friend, the council voted on this decision and I accept whatever fate comes of it." replies Naline

"This is not a time of accepting fate. We must find a way to have Remy mate with one of our royal family. It will give us time to prepare for the final conflict for the ownership of this planet. If he has mated with one of us the Laws of God are clear. They cannot declare war against us. However, since we don't care about God's Law we can. Plus we might be lucky and have his life-mate." answers Torm.

"Now how are we going to accomplish that? We stole their Queen or who we thought was their Queen. I knew that Fica's plan had some risks, but this is a total disaster. Even when the council decided to attack the dwarven village I did not agree. I should have spoken up. We will not get that opportunity again. Remy knows of the temples so he will systematically shut them down. Not only are most of our covert actions known to the world, Remy will never have faith in anyone with an Elven scent. No one will be able approach him with his werewolf senses."

"True, quite true Naline. Nonetheless, we need to formulate a way to have this happen. Our survival may depend on it. Remy may be young chronologically, but he is wise beyond his years. He is truly a powerful speaker. He had the crowd eating out of his hand and he only known his heritage for few days. What an emperor he would make. I must say I almost cheered for him."

"That I must admit he is something to behold in person."

"We must return the girl."

"Return the girl? Are you mad? The only reason they let us out of there alive was that we had the girl. We need her as a bargaining chip or it's quite possible they will bring the Alps down on our heads."

"Naline, I am surprised at you. Remy would only want the return of the girl and nothing more. He is a man of honor. He knows nothing of pure hatred. If it were us, they would already be buried, girl and all. Plus, he could have killed us and still went and retrieved the girl. He is a better statesman then you give him credit for being. He was rallying all the forces to his cause and he is actually really good at it. That is what makes him more dangerous than any other threat to our plans we have ever had."

"That may be true; however I still will not relinquish the girl yet. She may have another purpose."

"Don't let your anger cloud your judgment we are too close to victory as you said. Do not become infected with the same foolishness the rest of the council has been. We need one clear thinking person on the council."

Naline looks at Torm and wonders "All these years Torm, you always challenged me about any decision. You have never agreed with my plans for patience and stealth. You are always aggressive, always on the offensive. Something is amiss."

Outwardly, Naline says, "You have the right of it but I still will keep her awhile."

"As you wish, Naline."

"Well, we could try your daughter again and infuse her with a dwarven scent. Have her skin darkened and her eye color changed to look more like a dwarf."

"Alas, that is out of the question now."

"Why, its' not difficult to do? It would cause her no pain."

"My daughter mated with Fica yesterday, destroying any chance of a union because she is pregnant with his child."

"Pregnant with his child! How could you know so quickly?"

"Right after the council meeting my daughter was filled with lust for Fica and the thought of mating with a vampire was so abominable to her that she mated with him. I of course had my spies watching them. Unfortunately, they did not contact me in time to prevent it. My personal physician examined her and noted that she was with child. Fica has been dealt with for that and for underestimating Robon."

"I am glad to hear you have begun to rein in your wild dog.

He has been personally responsible for bringing Robon into this situation from the beginning had he killed him before he knew his birth right, this would all be conjecture. His thought of killing Robon himself is ridiculous. He is to full of himself and does not think of the clan first."

Torm looks at him and sucks his teeth slightly "Number one he is not my dog and I am personally offended my daughter chose to mate with him. However, he is one of our best warriors and trackers. Ave will tame him over time, together with the twelve hours he is now, spending in the iron maiden will not kill Fica, but it should teach him a lesson or two. Nevertheless, placing blame on anyone is a poor way of fixing the problem."

"So you think I blame Fica for this mess. No you are wrong. I blame myself for allowing our clan to make some of the decisions they have made in the last year without protesting."

"A pity the council would never name you emperor instead of council leader. You have always made the correct decisions for our clan. I see that now."

"Our clan believes in no kings or emperors only decisions by the few who represent the many. I believe in our ways and want no more."

"Well said. Excuse my speaking aloud what I think."

"I think we are really at a great disadvantage now. Your daughter is the last of pure royal blood. It will be impossible to block pure bred elven pheromones."

"No there is another way. It is a little roundabout but it could work. This vampire named Kiree who took the place of the Queen is also pregnant. However, she is pregnant with Remy's child. Her mother is your lover. Is she not?" Torm says looking at Naline.

Naline's eyes widen and he says "You're kidding aren't you? How could you know so soon that Kiree is pregnant? Her mother is not my lover she is a spy who I use."

"I am not without my own spies and recourses. I just don't lay with the enemy." Says Torm tacitly.

"What do you mean by that?" Says Naline visibly upset.

"I meant no disrespect. I was just pointing out that you have already sacrificed your body for the cause. I know you loathed her touch. How could you not. Isn't she just a vampire?"

"Vampires are vermin. I spit upon them."

"Then your speech about letting prejudices fall by the wayside was just a bunch of words. A way to offer up Princess Ave to mate with a vampire against her will. I would think that you would do no less for the cause, especially since Dresa has done so much for us as it is."

Naline composes himself quickly. Torm is not one to play with. "You are right, Torm. I have and will do whatever is needed for the cause. However, under the circumstances I think it will be difficult to get to Dresa. By now, they know that she was the one who let us in for the attack. She might be beheaded at this time."

Torm smiles and waves his hand. Within minutes, Dresa is ushered in chains.

"Remove those chains at once!" shouts Naline as he moves towards her. "She is a loyal citizen of the Elves."

Dresa eyes start to sparkle as they remove her chains. She knew Naline could not be part of this. She rushes into his arms and says "I knew you were not part of this, Milord."

"No, of course not." Replies Naline looking at Torm, who enjoys his discomfort.

"Milady, much has happened this night. Your daughter is in the Alps." Says Torm

"My daughter is where?" she replies. Dresa was not present at the ball because Torm's men had taken her prisoner. Torm planned to use her against Naline by telling the counsel he was fraternizing with the enemy. However, what is unfolding now was so much better.

"She is in the Alps because she masqueraded as the Queen, which means the vampires were aware of our plan to attack." Says Naline looking at her.

Dresa understands this is a very important moment and gives great thought to her answer.

"They did not know. The Queen just did not want to meet the prince yet." Dresa says

"Why?" asks Torm

"I'm not sure. But she has evaded him since he arrived."

"That could only mean one thing, Torm." Says Naline

"She thinks he is her life-mate." Replies Torm

"Why would that matter?" asks Dresa

"Do not underestimate Sariel and her brother Sauer. They are excellent strategists. They know if Sariel is his life-mate, he would not mate with Ejam. Also he would not have impregnated your daughter, Kiree." Says Naline.

"My daughter is impregnated with his child?" states Dresa

"Yes, she is." Replies Torm.

"Then she must be returned as soon as possible. If the Prince finds out he will thwart all your plans by attacking you to get his child." Replies Dresa.

Torm just looks at Naline with a smug smile playing on his lips.

"It is your daughter we speak of here." Says Naline "We have a plan. We would like her to return home after a mind trap has been implanted in her mind. The same type of traps we have used to enslave dwarves in the past. Remy obviously has their ability to read minds. I realize that now, that is how he knew of the attack on the dwarven encampment. He also must know many of our other superficial plans, nonetheless, the deeper recesses of my mind are locked at all times with traps. He did not push very hard or he would be dead. When your daughter returns a dwarf will have to check if her mind has been tampered with and then Remy or some high ranking dwarf will belong to us. To use as we wish."

"My daughter will not willingly allow you to place that trap and if she knows you tampered with her mind she'll kill herself before she gets near the prince." Answers Dresa.

"Oh, this we know. We need you to convince her nothing is

wrong." Says Torm "You must get her willingly to allow one of our half-breeds to enter her mind to place the trap." He eyes her curiously and continues "We can trust you, right"

Dresa stiffens from this statement and thinks to herself "How do you trust someone who has betrayed her own people". She has played both sides for so long; she is sometimes not sure what side she is really on. Her statements now may mean life or death for both her daughter and herself. She laughs to herself. Her child is everything she has no choice, but to continue the game as it is. "Milord as always I belong to the elven people."

"We will see if that is true."

The elven guards come and take Kiree from her cell. She knows by now they know she is not the queen however they treat her like royalty nonetheless. She is sure it is because of the child growing within her. They want the child for their hideous experiments. This will not happen because she is willing to die first. First chance she gets she will get a weapon and take as many of them with her as she can. They walk through several tunnels and finally a door is held open for her to walk through. Inside the room are Naline, Torm and a bloodied beaten form spiked to a wooden circle. Closer inspection makes her gasp. It is her mother. Traitor or no she is still her mother.

"You will all die at his hands for this and the many other atrocities you have committed. I guarantee it." Says Kiree with very little emotion.

Naline looks at her and smiles. "This one is not easily intimidated." He thinks to himself and to her he says "She's not dead yet little one. Close, but not quite dead. You can prevent her death with your actions."

"I will not allow you to have my child. No matter whom you have nailed up there. The prince would understand what I do and why. You know as well as I do you cannot drug me or take the fetus out of me to grow. In both cases the child would die. So I'm sure you also know that if I had a weapon now half of the warriors in this room would be dead."

Torm laughs aloud and says "We want no bastard children, especially a bastard child with vampiric blood."

"So what do you want, in exchange for my mother's life?"

"Straight to the point, just like a vampire. What we want is to extract some information directly from your mind." Replies Naline.

"I know nothing vital to the vampiric forces. You would waste your time."

"We will be the judge of that my dear.' Says Torm "So what will it be? Do we continue to torture your mother or do you allow us to check your mind."

Kiree looks at them and then her mother. She bites her lip and says "I will consent as long as she is freed immediately and given medical attention."

"So be it." Says Naline clapping his hands. Two ogres come in and remove her from the wooden torture circle and carry her away. "I hope you live up to your word"

"I am a vampire, we always live up to our word. I can only hope you live up to yours." Kiree says as Princess Ave walks into the room to even Naline's surprise.

"I guess I do not know everything about you, Torm. I never knew you had mated with a dwarf and to pawn your daughter off as a purebred, very interesting indeed." Naline thinks to himself.

"Ave, my dear." says Torm "I would like you to meet Kiree." The look exchanged between these two young women would ignite a blaze. Deep inbred hatred wells to the surface. These young women are not politicians in any form of the word. They are warriors trained from birth and what they have been taught to kill stands before them at this moment.

"Father, I don't think I can do this. I can't merge with this filth without feeling dirty after." Ave spits like a cat.

"It will be no picnic for me either, bitch. If you want some of me we can do this at sword point. Believe me your perfumed ass would be dead in moments." Replies Kiree with equal venom.

"Enough." Shouts Naline "we have made a bargain with this vampire and it shall be honored, Princess Ave. You have already gone against the counsel once and gone unpunished. It will not happen a second time."

Ave looks at her father who nods his head and says bowing to Kiree "Please allow me to apologize for my behavior. You are a guest and should be treated as such." Kiree is taken aback by her answer and is speechless at first.

"Let's get this over with. What do I need to do?" says Kiree

"Well first, please sit here." Says Ave pointing to a chair in the middle of the floor. Kiree sits in the chair with Ave behind her. "Now just relax. As I penetrate your thoughts you will feel some disorientation." Ave places her hands on both of Kiree's parietal areas near the temples and closes her eyes concentrating. To Kiree it feels like the beginning of a roller coaster ride very slow and deliberate. Suddenly the ride picks up speed and she is whirled through her memories. However, something is not right. She feels nothing taken more akin to something being left in her mind, she is not sure. It is over in what seems an instant. Ave releases her head and falls back being caught by her father. She is pale and diaphoretic and totally spent it seems.

"How long has it been?" asks Kiree looking around the room getting her bearings back.

"You have been under about three hours." Says Naline

"Three hours, it seemed like a few moments."

"Is it done, Ave." asks Naline

"It is done." Ave says drinking some wine. "She may go now."

"What of my mother?"

"We will release her in time. If we released her now the vampire nation would put her to death. You know that don't you. She is a traitor to her own people. They would never take her back. You on the other hand may return home. After a couple of months, we can release your mother to her fate. For now, she needs to heal." Says

143

Torm looking her directly in the eye. "There is transport waiting for you as we speak."

"I have your word no further harm will come to her?"

"You have my word." replies Naline. "Please escort the young lady to the ship." Two guards step up and escort her out of the room.

As Ave and Kiree leave Torm and Naline alone, Torm says "Obviously, we both have some secrets that do not need to be shared with rest of the council."

"Obviously, actually keeping Ave's origin a secret has given you quite an advantage in the council. I mean you probably know what's going to happen before it does."

"I have never used my daughter in that way. She is strong willed and has a mind of her own as you can clearly see."

"What of her mother?"

"She was killed in battle not long after her birth. She was my life-mate you know. A very rare mixture."

"Why keep it a secret. Ave would have been accepted without question by the council."

"But she would not have been treated as a princess."

"I see your point. No one will know. I give my word."

"What of Dresa?" says Torm.

"Dresa has outlived her usefulness. However, I will keep my word for now. It will take her at least three weeks in a cryogenic tank to heal. She is after all not an elf and will not heal as quickly as we do." Naline says with a chuckle.

"Don't you think she will wake up in a vengeful mood? I mean you did torture her for real. Even though you knew everything you asked her."

"It had to be convincing to all who viewed the interrogation, plus she received what any traitor deserves. She cannot be trusted by anyone. A person who turns away from their blood is a fool. You cannot run from yourself. No matter where you turn you are there. When she wakes she will be mind wiped and I will make her a personal body slave. She does have one good use after all."

CHAPTER 12

"When the wind blows, it is the
inflexible that will be blown away"

REMY STANDS AT THE door as all the guests exit the hall, wishing all whom have attended a personal goodnight. At his side stands Ejam as if it was what she was born to do. Her beauty and majestic presence make her fit perfectly into the role of his wife. "I'm starting to think just like Commander Sauer. That's a bad sign." He says to himself. From the moment, he had seen Ejam walking up the aisle at the beginning of ball Remy could simply not keep his eyes off of her. He watched her every move. The way she spoke, the way she walked, the way she smiled, and the way she danced. It was as if she were free to be herself for the very first time. Such unbridled glee was a joy to see. As the last guest leaves, he turns to her the two of them alone for the first time. She looks directly into his eyes with such intensity he feels like he is about to melt. He begins to perspire heavily and his knees actually feel like they are buckling. She steps forward and wipes his brow with a smirk playing on her lips. "Come along my love we have much to speak about." Ejam says kissing him lightly on the lips. "Much to speak about."

He leads her to his quarters and feels a twinge of uneasiness because Kiree's scent is still there. Was he a monster to just make love to another woman so soon and in the same bed. Ejam wakes him from his musings with a passionate kiss. A kiss so full of need and desire he is addled by its strength. They part and he asks "What did you mean by saying our time together would not be long? You are the second woman this night who has told me that."

"There is much you need to learn about being a person of rank. First you do not belong to someone you belong to everyone and no one at the same time. Your station in life requires that you unite many different races together in an effort to save a world from a foe that is unrelenting and uncaring. I know your enemy better than anyone. They are wicked and have no compassion. They will kill anyone and everyone in their way."

"What does that have to do with you and I?"

"A night with you may be more than a woman could expect. Loving you can be a tragic curse. But it is one, I gladly accept." She hugs him as if she were holding on for dear life. He feels the warmth of her tears flow down his cheeks.

"Why do you weep, milady?"

"These are tears of joy, Milord. My people are free. I am able to be a woman again and I am in love with a good man. You know nothing about me except that I tried to kill you. Yet you allowed me to claim you as my mate in public."

"You were doing what you were ordered to do. In fact you were doing what you thought was right."

"Now look at that. You have turned around the whole situation and made it sound like I've done nothing wrong. We have been taught to hate vampires from birth. My clan has killed many, yet you have helped free my people and now accept them as part of your clans. Believe me when I say the vampires would have let us die without batting an eyelash if you did not exist. Plus I chose you to be my mate not because of obligation or to create some royal union. I love you."

"But I do exist. Helping people is what life is about. I have been taught to think that way all my life. I do not know any other way.

Your people were held in bondage and miss informed, the only ones to blame here are the elves."

"I have never been with a male. My father would not allow it. You will be my first and my last. I will not mate with another. That is of course until I find my life-mate."

"That is one thing I don't understand. I mean I guess you are not my life-mate. But will I stop loving you when one of us finds their life-mate or is it torture on the person who has not."

"It is the way God made the first tribes. It is actually both gift and curse. You are complete when you find your mate and utterly empty if you lose them. The Queen's life-mate was Vincenzo, what a lonely life she must have. To be fulfilled so completely and then have it ripped away. She is a strong woman. Very few people find a second life-mate in their lifetime. Even knowing that you have a life-mate out there does not make loving you any less unique than it is. I know you will love me relentlessly and that is something no woman could want more. No pretenses, no empty platitudes to fill the moment, just pure honesty in its simplest form and that makes me love you more than ever."

They kiss again and Remy leads her to the bedroom with thoughts of Kiree no longer in his head. They begin the age-old ritual of getting to know one another in every way possible. Soon they are completely spent falling asleep in one another's arms.

Ejam wakes up to the sound of the wind around her. As she focuses, she sees Remy completely naked enacting some sort of martial arts kata. She is a warrior herself, but is taken aback by the sheer force of this man. His muscles are like corded steel, his movements quicker than the eye can pick up easily. Watching him this way seems to arouse her more than before. It is almost as if the acts of violence amplify her passion. He crouches and spins as if he were a ballerina. However, that has to be impossible; he weighs nearly two hundred and fifty pounds and is at least six foot three inches tall.

Yet he lands like a butterfly on a flower barely disturbing its surface. If not for the gust of wind created by his movements, she would have never heard him.

Remy is caught deeply in an imaginary battle with twenty warriors with weapons of all types. He attacks two ripping their throats out and somersaults back disemboweling two others, four down and sixteen to go. Three warriors charge forward spears lowered, he pirouettes under the spears and attacks their legs splintering bone with a leg whip. He then launches himself into four others. Using various hand techniques, he crushes their windpipes. The rest of his attackers enclose him in a circle. What fools he says to himself finally drawing his double swords. He launches into a spring leg form and cuts down six of his attackers. The last three decide to rush him. Remy lowers his blades and waits. As the first reaches him, he pulls one of the swords up into his groin. In the same motion, he spins and beheads the attacker from the rear with the other. The last assailant had already committed to a frontal attack to his own chagrin. Remy hits him with a roundhouse kick knocking him back. Remy is upon him before he can defend himself slashing him from the right shoulder through his waist. With all of his assailants' either dead or incapacitated he shakes the blood from his blades and resheathes them in one motion. He is suddenly aware that Ejam is watching him and turns towards her.

"How long have you been watching?"

"About ten minutes. I must say I have never seen anyone quite like you, Milord. Your speed belies your bulk and your power belies your size. I have seen eight foot ogres who you would have crushed with a hand strike."

Remy sits in lotus position and beckons her over to sit in front of him. She quickly complies. She notices that he is erect and slides his member smoothly into her. She gasps loudly and stays still just enjoying the feeling. She wraps her legs around his waist pulling him closer. She opens her eyes and looks deeply into Remy's eyes.

"I would never hurt you, milady. I have been instructed to trust no one, but I always follow my heart. It has failed me very little in my lifetime. You have shared with me all that has transpired in your life and I have shared nothing with you. Nonetheless, listen to me now. I was born an orphan. I have never known who my parents were until now. I spent many occasions alone and basically tried not to get emotionally attached to anyone."

"You mean you have never loved anyone."

"I loved a woman once. Her name was Renchi she was my sensei's daughter. She was my hope and my dreams. I gave as much to her as she gave to me. She and her family were killed soon after I left Japan. I have always blamed myself for her death and the death of her family." Tears begin to fall as he continues looking directly into her eyes.

"I know now who killed them. It was the elves. They have killed everything that has been precious to me. They will not kill you, I swear it." She brings her mouth down hard on his and kisses him deeply as they climax together thinking "So much pain and such little love this world can create".

The next day they are on a plane heading to Canada with the dwarven contingent. They are greeted with sparkling snow upon their arrival. That morning before embarking Remy had married Ejamine in a hasty ceremony. Commander Sauer thought it would be a good idea not to travel together without being married. Remy cannot help, but think Commander Sauer just wanted to solidify the alliance more than anything else. Remy knows he loves Ejam, but he wonders if it is her pheromones, trolls were bred to be love toys and their pheromones are quite strong. Any man or woman would swear they were in love. No there is something else that gnaws at his heart, he just cannot get that dream out of his mind and hearing the Queen's voice almost drove him mad with passion for a woman he hasn't even met yet. All he has read about life-mates comes to mind when he recalls her voice. Kiree had told him he could mate with whomever he wanted, but, he was married now and would honor his bond with Ejamine. During the flight he had read most of the both books given to him by Commander Sauer. The idea that no child was a bastard was the best idea he had heard from the laws of the tribes. Many of the other laws were written for the survival of the tribe. A maimed or weak warrior was of no need to a tribe trying to perpetuate its existence and was done away with to prevent another tribesman from being injured or to be killed. The Elves had enlisted all of the other clans against the dwarves, werewolves, and vampires marking them as demons and devils, as far away from God as possible. When in reality they were probably the closest to God of all.

They soon come to a smooth landing on an airstrip in the middle of what seems to be nowhere. Remy experiences a strange feeling of warmth in his abdomen. He has not returned to his homeland in fifteen years. Canada was his home. He was born here and brought up here. The clean fresh air is like a perfume and the snow like a spring shower. He stands outside the plane for a moment just reveling in the feeling. His eyes close with the snow landing lightly on his head and his face.

"Home" he says quietly to himself. He opens his eyes and sees all of the people from the orphanage waiting for him. His face lights up and he rushes forth like a child greeting all with a hug and tears. As he reaches the woman and man, he knows to be his parents he bows before them and says, "I have come home at last. I hope I have lived up to your expectations for me."

Treya reaches down, pulls her son to her, and replies, "We have had no expectations, and you are our son nothing else truly matters. What I hope is you can forgive us for lying to you all those years, my son. Believe we did what we thought was best for you and the survival of the clans." She kisses his face gently and gestures to his father.

Dewa has aged greatly, however is still in good physical shape for a man many centuries old. His hair is as completely gray as his eyes. He looks at his son with tears flowing. "Welcome home son. I have missed you more than you can imagine. Many nights your mother restrained me from coming to get you. Especially all the times you were injured so badly. Remy, we have placed an incredible burden upon your shoulders. Which, I am sorry to say is going to get heavier as time goes by. Nevertheless, you have made your mother and I proud. We have followed all your movements and you have always conducted yourself with dignity and honor. We could ask no more than that."

They embrace and hold one another as if they would never let go. Ejamine has watched all of this transpire and is amazed by the primal energy being emanated into the air. It is almost like a drug. A sense of belonging and well-being seems to flow through her. After all the hate and pain she has experienced in her lifetime, this is like a cleansing of her soul. Many clans living together in peace, no slavery, no violence, and no prejudice, incredible, how it revitalizes ones spirit. She thinks to herself "God is good." Even though the elves did not believe in God, her people had worshipped him in secret. They prayed to him daily for deliverance from their bondage. A deliverance, which was shaped by an act of violence transformed into an act of mercy, which now has become an act of love. Yes, she says again "God is good."

Remy glances over to Ejamine and brings her over to meet his parents. "This is my wife, Ejamine. This is my mother and father, Dewa and Treva."

"I am honored to meet you, Lord and Lady." Ejamine says curtseying

"And we you." Says Treva kissing Ejamine's cheek and embracing her. "She is beautiful, my son."

Ejamine blushes, she is not used to female complements being lauded upon her. Remember Ejamine had been considered a male since birth. This is all a new world to her in many ways. She has much to learn about being a woman and about accepting compliments.

"She is also quite shy it seems." Notices Treva "I recognize many things may be going through your mind, my dear, nonetheless, we accept you for who you are. The tribes before you compiled of many races and we are bonded to each other in every way. Prejudice does not reside here. Our home is much like we hope the world will become one day, a place where there is a place for everyone. Any of your clan is welcome here as is anyone who chooses to live in peace. The rest of your clan has been set up in an abandoned mining town about sixty miles from here. They of course have a team of the clans' engineers working with them to make it a home. You may visit while you are here." Ejamine is shocked by the frankness and power of this frail looking woman. She is only a little over five feet with skin the color of ruddy clay. Her eyes are the color of wheat and seem to impart warmth and understanding. Nonetheless, her posture indicates so much more beneath the surface.

"I thank you all for what you have done for my people

"I can only try to be the best I can for my husband. His road has been and will be filled with challenges and disappointments. I wish to only be there for him while I can. I promise he will face no challenge or danger alone, milady."

"My son has made a wise and lucky choice with you and I truly believe that in my heart."

Ejamine finds herself overcome with joy. Such acceptance has been a foreign concept to her for so long. She begins to cry and hold Treva tightly. Treva holds her as if she was a child again and soothes her.

"I should not cry so easily. I am a warrior of the Smit clan. It is not becoming, milady."

"While you are a warrior, my dear, you are also a woman. Showing emotion is not a sign of weakness, it is instead a sign of great strength. They are a symbol of a person with a heart and soul. Remember love is always more powerful than hate even though it may not seem that way at times."

Dewa pulls Remy to the side leaving the women to talk and says "You my son have done more for the trolls than anyone could imagine. I must admit while we knew they were treated harshly, none of us knew they were enslaved."

"Father." The word seems to hang in the air for Remy. It is a word he has never used in this context all his life. All the same it feels so right and makes him feel more at home than any time in his life. "I have done what is right, not what is popular." Answers Remy looking directly into his father's eyes.

"That is precisely why it is so out of the ordinary. No politics no games just real concern for someone else's well being. Most things accomplished on this planet have a payoff. From all the reports I have received you have never chosen that road. You always made your decision with your heart. I hope that was one of the things you learned here."

"Father, all I have learned about life and how to treat other beings I learned here and in Japan. I owe who I am to my upbringing and the training I have received.'

"Vampires have always played the protector of the races because it was their perceived destiny. No one has ever said we wanted to be the defender for everyone. However, with you it is different. You actually seem to have a vested interest in everyone's welfare on this planet."

"Why not? We all live here. What the elves did to my wife's people was a travesty; no one should ever be treated as property. From what I have learned of the elves, they care for no one but themselves. They thirst for power and dominion over all on this planet. They actually think it is their birthright and keeping people in slavery is an acceptable way of life. I shall not allow that to happen, to anyone. While I still have breath in my body, they will always have an enemy to deal with. When the time comes I will personally behead Naline for all the crimes he has committed against the people of this earth and against my family." Remy can feel his anger begin to surface as he speaks to his father. The pure anger of feeling all alone in this world. The anger of watching beings with no worries generates despair and grief for beings that don't even have enough food to eat. He swore to himself as a child that he would make a difference and by God as his witness, he will make a difference for those who have no voice.

"And so you shall young warrior. It is your destiny." Remy hears in his mind. He spins looking for the person responsible. "But don't hate so vehemently, there is good in everything including the elves. We will spend a lot of time together soon. You have much to learn about the truth of all of our origins. For now know my name is Juzef. Calm yourself, hate and anger are all consuming and are beneath you. These emotions can become your downfall. You must learn to focus on the good and less on the bad. I leave you to your family. Enjoy them. You deserve it."

"Remy, are you all right?" asks Dewa looking concerned.

Remy realizes that he had been engrossed with Juzef and not paying attention to his father. "I am sorry father; Juzef was mind speaking to me about my bad temper."

Dewa laughs and replies, "So he has already started to teach. You must be exceptional indeed."

"What does that mean father?"

"It means that you are worthy of special attention. Juzef trained all the warriors of God."

"Who are the warriors of God?"

"Juzef will explain during your teaching. For now, let us just enjoy this moment. It is so good to have you home my son." Says Dewa embracing his son with tears streaming down his face.

Dewa and Treva lay in each other's arms after Remy's coming home celebration. Treva traces his lips with her fingers and says, "I know what the council has requested, but I do not agree."

Dewa exhales noisily and replies, "What they ask is not forever. They only asked that Remy be placed on the path before we tell him anything."

"I know but my dream keeps reoccurring. Remy already has suffered enough for several lifetimes."

"I am sure Juzef will come to Remy tonight. Once he is on the path the council will allow us to tell him."

Treva sits up and says, "I don't see what they are trying to gain. My son is home and he has a right to know and they deserve know about him."

Dewa sits up as well and encircles his arms around her from the back. "You more than I should know the dwarven council is more in tune with God then the rest of us. They have stated those are his wishes."

"I understand that. I just have a premonition that he will not meet them before something happens to one of them. You know my premonitions are never wrong."

"That is true. After he has been with Juzef I will go to the council myself and ask."

"That will have to do for now. My son deserves to meet his siblings as soon as possible. Council or no council. My children were told to hide from their brother and that does not sit well with me at all. Our bloodlines have given much for the cause. When is it enough?"

"When God says so, my love. When God says so. Your son is as close to an archangel as anyone can be and like all angels he has to make a choice to follow him. You and my children are my life. You are all that matter to me. I do my part but all of you come first."

Treva turns and holds his face and says "How is the pain today?"

"It is bearable." Dewa answers

"You know I could take it away."

"Yes, and I would forget who I am and who you are. The pain is worth the risk."

"Soon my love, I will not have a choice. The blocks that the council put in place are starting to erode. Those blocks cannot be placed again."

"I understand the risk, milady. However, it took me so long to find you. Maybe the power of our life-mate bond will help me know I love you."

"Well you know it could be exciting getting to know each other again." Answers Treva

"Yes, that's true. But, for now let us dance the dance of life and forget the moment and become lost in one another.

CHAPTER 13

"Truth has a way of becoming a burden."

VINCENZO AWAKENS AND HEARS the voice of Juzef calling him out to the glade. He looks down on his wife and kisses her forehead lightly not meaning to make her stir. Remy never knew he could love someone as powerfully and as rapidly as he has this woman. Almost like magic. Maybe it was magic. Was not all the tribes' part of nature's magic? Ejam just rolls over with a smile on her lips. So peaceful, so content, Remy imagines her whole life has been wrought with fear and pain. Living a life that was a lie and succeeding. Her father's best warrior, his right hand so to say. One day he knew, he would have to test her mettle. In the mean time he is amazed by this awe-inspiring woman he has married. Yet with all the happiness he feels, there is hollowness within him that he cannot explain, that hollowness is created by the woman in his dream, a woman who looks just like Kiree's twin. Since becoming prince he had studied a great deal about life-mates and now he was sure in his soul that woman is his life-mate.

Remy sighs as he puts on his clothes and says to himself "To keep Ejam happy I would gladly suffer the hollowness."

"Young one your path is to meet your life-mate and to join with her. As it is written is as it shall be. Realize now that you are a child of destiny. More so than any being on this earth. You are but a puppet on the stage of life, but unlike a true puppet you do not know your role as of yet and you must accept the burden. Now come. We have much to speak about." Remy hears in his mind from the Juzef. Remy completes putting his clothes on and reaches for his weapons and hears.

"You will not need them where you are going, however bring the parchment that was given to you by my brother years ago."

"Efisio was your brother, Milord? Remy asks in shock.

"Yes, and I grieve the death of both his family and him every day. But, as you will learn we are all God's children and have a portion to play in the final conflict that approaches so quickly. Now come boy, would you keep an old man waiting in the cold?' Juzef says.

Remy puts on his parka and steps out into what seems like a blizzard. Juzef stands before him and beckons him to follow. They walk straight into the woods for about ten or twelve miles without stopping without a word spoken between them. They soon reach a huge oak tree, easily twenty to twenty-five feet in diameter and the height of a six-story building. Juzef touches the base and the enormous roots rise up and reveal a tunnel. Juzef leads Remy deep into the bowels of the earth. Remy hears the roots close above and expects to be shrouded in darkness. Yet the tunnel walls seemed to be luminescent. The tunnel is cool initially and then becomes sweltering. It seems they have been walking for hours. Remy perspires profusely and removes all his clothes except for his pants and boots. The dwarven master is not even breaking a sweat. They soon reach a cavern with a stream of molten lava flowing through it. "This is incredible." Remy thinks to himself as he surveys the cavern. There are trees and grass teems across the ground. The cavern has to be as large as some of the small villages he had seen in Asia. The cavern is illuminated by thousands of brilliant colorful fungi growing on the ceiling. Remy is breathless. "Man in a million years could never create such majesty and splendor".

The Juzef bends down before the lava stream and scoops out

some of the lava in his hands. Remy just stands there speechless. The lava looks hot enough to melt a solid steel pillar on contact. The Juzef sniffs the lava and lets it spill from his hands. "Rich with metals this lava is. This is the earth mother's milk. All dwarves know this is what sustains this world and keeps it from freezing. If the earth had no inner warmth the sun could never provide enough heat to stop this planet from becoming a giant ice ball. The earth mother should be loved and respected for she sustains all life on this planet with her bounty. If you didn't believe in God, one moment in this cavern would change your mind forever." He then sits cross-legged by the stream and gestures for Remy to join him. Remy sits beside him and says, "Milord, if you think I can do what you have just done then you are gravely mistaken."

The Juzef laughs aloud and replies, "You have dwarven blood surging through your veins, boy. And that blood is pure, not deluded. What we can do you can do. It's a matter of concentration. But, that is not what I brought you here for. I have brought you to the womb of the earth to tell you the history of the many peoples who inhabit this planet. I have heard that Martin has given you an abbreviated version. However, now I will give you a full-length version without omission. First let me tell you your real name. You were born Remiel named after one of the seven archangels. This archangel was known as the mercy or compassion of God. You exemplify too many that God has compassion and mercy for those that have stayed faithful. The prophecy is about keeping the faith in the direst of times. Preaching and keeping his word even if it meant eminent death. Many of the tribes have died for his word and I am sure many more will join them. The incredible part is that we know as his servants we will have everlasting life after we leave this plane of existence. That my boy is our ultimate weapon, death leads to eternal life with him. You know how the first four tribes came to be and how the elves created the other life forms. Now I will tell you the story of a very special child. After God gave man intelligence and the ability to choose, the Elves went totally berserk. As far as they were concerned

God had stolen their ultimate creation. You know the story of Adam and Eve. It was Lucifer who found this much more distasteful then the elves. He tricked these newly created beings to go against the father's words forcing them out of paradise to his domain. Let know one fool you, the earth is his domain for now. The elves enlisted several of God's celestial angels to fight against God and they tried to dam us all by making us eat their flesh. One of the angels was the fallen one named Lucifer. The elves did not know that it was Lucifer who had tricked them into joining him in the battle for heaven and into having them eat the flesh of the humans. Of course, it was his idea to share this flesh with the tribes. The vampires were foolish enough to partake not knowing what they were eating or the consequences of eating it. Lucifer hoped that would turn the vampires to his cause but their faith would not waver even though they knew they were damned forever in God's eyes. The memory of the valiance they displayed in the face of being hated and hunted by humankind. There was a major celestial battle, which resulted in the rebel angels being defeated. God banished them to the netherworld and they became parodies of celestial angels. They became wraiths, all that is except for Lucifer who remained his malevolent self. But he too was now physically banished from earth. He still holds spiritual sway and continues his spiritual battle via influences, but he is cut off from making personal physical attacks.".

"Milord that is the name of the beings that the trolls said had been enlisted by the elves".

The dwarven master's brow furrows and he snickers. "They will never learn. The Elves have once again enlisted the fallen. Nonetheless, I'm sure none of the wraiths are on this plane of existence yet; this knowledge can be used as a weapon against them. Believe me when I say an Elf is a pure trickster, a master of illusion and deceit. They of cause had the prince of lies as a teacher. This could all be a lie, but I doubt that. They are so hungry for retribution they just don't care about the consequences of their actions."

"So you do not think that a wraith exist on this plane yet, Milord?"

"If one did, the first person they would come for is you. They must destroy the child of the prophecy before you realize you're potential. Plus, there would be a tremendous energy flux that all the spiritual beings of this world would feel. Do not worry young Lord, God foresaw this entire happening. It is why you exist. God's celestial angels have the gift of all the tribes and more. It is how angels could move through humans to give them hope and the word of God. They would take the shape of the most beautiful of humans to speak to them. The two gifts that God took from the wraiths were shape changing and the ability to regenerate. So they can be killed. However, they are God's greatest warriors and are not easy to kill."

"How many wraiths are there?" asks Remy

"There are six that were banished to six different parts of the Netherworld unable to contact one another. Lucifer tried to create duplicate of God's seven archangels to lead his demon armies. Three of them were killed during the battle. The Elves plan is to attempt to help each of the survivors to re-enter this realm, because God gave his favorite children the elves power to reach into other realms to create life in this realm. For some reason God was more wary of the Vampires then the Elves to join Lucifer's cause. He trusted the elves too much and gave them many special powers he could not revoke, God-like powers. Nevertheless, time and inbreeding have decreased the number of elves with these special powers. God you will learn gives all life the benefit of doubt, God believes in the good of all creatures and allows them choices."

"And the celestial angels who rebelled had a choice?"

"Of course they had a choice. Angels were given choice by God that is why Lucifer and his minions were able to go against his word. There was no such thing as a wraith before the non-fallen rebelled against God and the clans. God could have had them wiped out, but chose not to. Everyone and everything is worth loving and nurturing."

"But what of Lucifer?"

"My, son, Lucifer was God's favorite until he thought he was better than God. He was known as the angel of light. Lucifer chose to rebel against God and take over heaven. Lucifer created his own fate and God even gave him a choice. That is how the first fallen were created. The archangels threw the fallen from heaven but they were not wraiths. They were demons, incubus and succubus who followed Lucifer."

"How many elves do you think are left, who can unlock the magical wards, Milord?"

"There are probably about three or four older elves that have the power to transverse dimensions and unlock the magical wards between this realm and the netherworld. One of them is Naline and probably two or three of the pureblood council. I am sure they have already built a Temporal Sanctuary."

"What is a Temporal Sanctuary?"

"It is a place where the elves can bring all the wraiths temporally close to this realm. If I am right they will only be able to free two or three."

"If that is all it takes, why haven't they released the wraiths sooner?"

"Because they must wait for the next galactic energy nexus to release them, God was no fool. A galactic energy nexus only happens every ten years. There are two parts to the nexus the winter and summer. The winter nexus is much stronger than the summer nexus. This plays right into our hands. The winter nexus just past and the summer nexus is not for six months. That gives us time to train you and prepare our defenses. I am sure they did not plan to release the wraiths for at least another ten years, when the power of the winter nexus would be at its peak. But your existence forces them to move faster. To fast I think."

"Why do you say to fast, Milord?"

"To fast because the elves wanted to attempt a takeover without the wraiths. Releasing the wraiths is a very dangerous gamble. Once the wraiths have wreaked havoc on this realm, they will turn on God and try to conquer the celestial plane. If they succeed the elves will either be enslaved or butchered. Lucifer is a heartless and ruthless warrior, who would kill anyone on this realm to get revenge for what God did to him. By taking away the trolls and alerting the other races to their enslavement you accelerated everything for the elves. Naline must be livid. He has always preached patience and hates to do anything in haste. The next nexus will happen during the lunar eclipse six months from now. In the mean time they will confer with the wraiths over the temporal distance for advice in the sanctuary."

"Milord, Will it be the wraiths alone or will they be bringing they're minions from the netherworld?"

"I must say for a novice at magic and battle you sure ask a lot of pertinent questions. I can see why Sauer was so high on you."

"You know Commander Sauer, Milord?"

"Know him? My boy, I trained him. He was one of my best students, who I turned over to the Emperor Vincenzo to complete his training. But, as to your question, that is one of the things that are in our favor. The elves only have the power to bring one life form from each dimension at a time. As you must have surmised the wraiths have gained total dominion over their respective realms and have hordes of warriors waiting to rush across the dimensional wall. What I don't know is if God took away their power to transverse realms from this plane of existence. I know they cannot bring themselves here but can they help others across. This realm would be destroyed in a matter of hours not days, especially with Lucifer leading them."

"This is the same Lucifer that is in the bible and that God has instructed us to avoid at all cost."

"One and the same, I'm glad you asked that question, because it brings me back to my original story, the story of a very, very special child. Lucifer my son as I said earlier was God's favorite celestial angel and his greatest general. He taught most of us the art of war, including myself, Vincenzo and Naline. But he never taught a pupil everything and gave each pupil a special attack to use in battle. For

Vincenzo it was the spinning sword. For Naline I do not know and for me it was the penetrating arrow technique".

"He taught Naline. I thought the elves were not warriors, Milord?

"That, my son is a great fallacy. Every tribe has a group of warriors. Lucifer or one of the other celestial angels trained the best. Naline is a true warrior. He also was Vincenzo's and my friend. That is until his race made the decision to take over this realm. Blood you see is always thicker than water. The friendship he had with Vincenzo is the reason he still lives today. Vincenzo could not bring himself to kill his blood brother. They were raised and trained together. They spent more time with each other than their own tribes."

"Then how could he hate vampires so deeply."

"Because he must, his elders declared war on every living thing on this planet and they declared war on God. Naline did not have a choice in the matter. But don't think his past would prevent him from striking down anyone who threatens the Elven master plan."

"Yet, I have Elven genes, Royal Elven genes at that. Will I turn on the other races at the order of the Elven council?" Remy says looking down into his hands.

"You my son are banded to all of God's first races, you more than all of us have a choice of path. Much like Jesus did. You are only held by the rules of God if you wish to be. God gave all intelligent beings the ability to choose a path. The Elves no longer listen to God's words. They have made a choice. They want to try and replace him."

"But maybe some of the Elves still believe in God. Maybe they only go along because they feel they have no other choice."

"This may be true. Yet, they were all given that choice when the celestial war ended, three choices to be exact. One, to be executed, Two, to live in exile, and the last was to choose the path of God and return to the clans. None chose the first or the last. That offer still stands for any elf that has had a change of heart. As a person of faith you know that all one has to do is give your heart to God in earnest to be saved. However, you will soon learn that the elves think of themselves as a superior race to all including God. They will never pray to God again."

"I see. They see their cause as righteous. So anything they do to win is acceptable." Says Remy.

"Naline's motto has always been at all cost."

"Is there any chance for peace? No chance for reconciliation?"

"Remy you are amazing, they have tried to kill you at least three times and still you persist, a very admirable quality indeed. But it is pretty evident your elven genes mean absolutely nothing to them. Only your death will suffice."

"Yet I still wonder Milord."

Juzef smiles and remembers those same words coming from Vincenzo before the war. "Many of us have had the same feeling of wonder, my son, many of us. Nevertheless, the elves have not shown the slightest need to be part of the clans or to be ruled by the laws of God."

"Since we are speaking of genes, can weapon and battle techniques be inherited in your genes?"

"I doubt that. Why do you ask?"

"Because Commander Sauer told me that he observed me using the spinning sword technique of Vincenzo's in battle against the shape changers."

"This is most interesting and you never saw that technique before?"

"No, Milord, most of the techniques I know I learned from your brother."

Juzef gets up and paces back and forth in deep thought. Then as if he has an idea stops and hands Remy his bow and quiver of arrows and says, "Fire an arrow into the cavern wall to your left."

"As you will, Milord." Remy notches an arrow and fires with speed Juzef has never seen before. Remy could have easily notched four or five arrows within the same time and fired. The arrow hits the wall and shatters it, leaving an opening into the next cavern.

"Fascinating!" exclaims Juzef. "Simply fascinating! You know my technique without learning it. Your body just knew what to do. This will be quite helpful in your training, quite helpful indeed. These are exciting times." Juzef seems giddy. "Maybe you even know Lucifer's and Naline special attacks.

"Milord is something wrong?"

"Oh no, my boy. You are everything God said you would be and probably a lot more. Anyway please sit down and I will continue the story." Remy hands Juzef back his bow and quiver of arrows and sits down. Juzef looks at his weapons like it were the first time and lays them down beside him stroking the bow tenderly.

"Now where was I. Oh yes, the child I spoke of was named Jesus. The three kings at his birth were Naline, Vincenzo and I. We were to protect the child against any harm. We gathered the apostles to stay by his side night and day. They were warriors, but they were also scholars and the writing of the New Testament began. The elves were still furious at God for taking humans away from them and giving them the freedom to choose. What was worst is that God had allowed the humans to give birth to a pureblood. That pure blood was Jesus, a child of light and great courage. Not born to be a warrior, but born to be a teacher of the people. To teach them the ways of God and the part they played in this realm. He gave his life to end their sin. Sin created when God took the first humans Adam and Eve into his garden. Once again Lucifer had a hand in their separation from God and the humans being a very young race began to worship different Gods. The elves then infiltrated as many religions as possible, a very old elven trick. You saw an example when you were in Indonesia. By setting up false temples that engaged in ritual sacrifice, they were able to talk the congregations into giving their infants to the church and so the elves got humans to do exactly what they wanted. It is amazing how gullible humans can be." Juzef pauses and reaches into his sack and pulls out a bottle of wine with two wooden goblets along with some bread and cheese. He pours the wine and shares out portions of food for Remy and himself. After a quick meal in silence Juzef continues.

"The elves placed a traitor within the apostles. Can you guest who that was?"

"According to the bible it was Judas."

"That's exactly who it was and Pontius Pilate?"

"An elf, Milord, it's all clear except how could they get to Jesus if God had him surrounded by protectors?"

"Good question. God told us to let just the human apostles protect Jesus. God needed to know if the humans were mature enough to choose the path of peace and love and like every other tribe in existence the humans let him down. Yet, Lucifer was the closest to Jesus. He walked with Jesus for forty days asking him not to give his life in vain. That God's plans were ridiculous. He preached to Jesus of being better than the humans. He implored Jesus to allow him to conquer them in his name. But, Jesus was pure of spirit and could not be swayed. Jesus was unlike any celestial he was the embodiment of God in the flesh. The rest is chronicled well in the bible." Juzef pours another goblet of wine for them both and continues. "Lucifer lost his mind with grief after Jesus died. It was at that point that he promised to use all humans to go against God's word and started having them worship him. He could not believe that God could allow his own son to die. It was soon after that he interested five other celestial angels in his cause including his younger brother and sister. They joined the elves and prepared for battle to the death with God and his legions."

"Milord, I don't mean to be blasphemous, but I must ask why God did not foresee all this happening?"

"That is where you are wrong. God knew that someday Lucifer's ambition would lead to destruction. He knew that Jesus needed to die and rise again to start the spiritual growth of human beings. Revelations speaks of Lucifer's return to power on this realm. The bible is a book of history and of the future to come. All of these tragedies hurt God more than you can believe. Alas, he teaches life is a struggle to find yourself and to find your place in the scheme of life. God's plan is always to plant a seed of hope that will grow in the darkest hour. That seed of hope is now you."

"Why me, Milord?" says Remy draining his goblet.

"For that matter, why not you? God gives us all a burden we can usually carry and ever so often he asks one of us to go above and beyond for the greater good. You must accept that this is an honor not a curse. No one will tell you it will be easy. But, you must achieve peace within yourself before you achieve peace for all of us. You are of pure royal blood from all the first four tribes. That makes you as close to a celestial angel as anyone could be. The key is the prophecy indicates the chosen one must mate with one of the other tribes and not humans. You have mated with a troll, yet I do not think that is the tribe God had in mind. Nonetheless, your genes hold the knowledge of countless battles and techniques. All you need is the training to allow it to spring forth. Training I will give you. Come, we must head back. We have already been gone two days. I still need to explain the book written before God inspired the bible to be written by human hands. We will return in a week to begin your training in earnest."

"But it feels as if we have only been here a few hours." says Remy.

"Remy do you think I could have told you the whole story of creation in a few hours. The wine and cheese I gave you was enhanced. It allowed you to stay awake and I gave you more wine as you began to nod. You have great strength and endurance. But you will need much more to battle Lucifer, much more."

"I am prepared to do what it takes, Milord."

"I know that young one or else we would not be here. Now give me the parchment."

Remy hands Juzef the parchment and watches as he dips it in the lava. The lava burns words into the parchment without destroying it. Juzef picks up the parchment and tears begin to roll down his face.

"Is there something wrong?" asks Remy puzzled.

"Not a thing young one. It seems my brother held you in great regard. He writes he showed you most of the techniques and I will not have to teach you very much physically. You were his best pupil. He thought of you as the son he never really had. He gave you his own personal dwarven armor to honor you. The sword he gave you was Vincenzo's, but it is his ceremonial blade not made for battle. I will help you forge your double blades during your training. My brother knew the elves were close to him and his family. His son turned out to be a traitor and gave the elves his location. It should have broken my brother's heart, but he writes that to train you and spend time with you was well worth the risk. He asks that you only do one thing."

"What is that, Milord?"

"Find his daughter and return her to me."

"His daughter lives? How is that possible? I ripped that country apart. Used every contact I had. Where is she?"

"My brother mind wiped her and sent her to Spain right after you left along with her mother. The villa is in Madrid. But this must be a trap."

"Trap or no that man was the only father I knew until I found out about my real father. If his last wish was for me to save his daughter then so be it. It's probably just another test anyway."

"Well let's hurry back. You must finish this quest before we finish your training."

"Everything I do, Milord is training."

"Oh hell no! You're joking? Right." Says Ejam looking around the room. Remy has assembled his family to tell them of his plans to go to Spain and bring back Juzef's niece. Ejam is less than pleased.

"No, I'm not joking. I owe my sensei at least that much. I will take six warriors with me and even now our intelligence network is locating her. It will basically be a pick up operation." Answers Remy

"This is a trap. I know the way they think and how they do things. They just want you dead and I will not allow that. I will die first." The passion in her voice catches everyone present by surprise including Remy. A silence falls over the room and then Remy's mother turns to Ejam and looks into her eyes and says, "You will refrain from questioning the prince immediately. What you discuss with him in private is your own concern. But what is said in public is another thing. There is always to be a united front, always. Never question his decisions again."

The force in her voice overwhelms Ejam almost as if she heard it directly into her mind.

"You did hear it directly in your mind. That is my gift and I would never reprimand you in public. But heed my words well. Remember he has to answer to the Dwarven, Vampiric and Werewolf councils at all times. They have agreed this is another test just for him, a test of honor and payment of a debt. We are much different than the Elves; life is not as cheaply spent. Now retract your statements with dignity and honor. Everyone will understand a newlywed being upset her husband may be in danger."

"Thank you milady." Ejam says through the link and aloud she says, "Please forgive my outburst. I have only been a wife for a short time. Emotions are high and my tongue a little too loose. Please continue Milord."

"As I was saying, this has been already discussed with the councils of the clans and they agree I must undertake this endeavor. The Spanish government has agreed to assist us with the operation. Which means the Elven spies in that government know we're coming they just don't know when. Which is exactly what I want, I leave within the next two hours and our intelligence group will contact me in the air. No plan is flawless; nonetheless, this is the most prudent. There is one more aspect to this situation. Juzef's niece has most of the Elven spies' names and positions locked in her mind. Her father placed them there for safekeeping. May God protect her until we can find her and bring her back."

"Ejam stop pacing." Says Remy sitting on their bed watching her pace back and forth.

"What would you have me do? Be a quiet obedient wife. Well

I'm a warrior first and a wife second. I love you more than I can explain. This is driving me crazy" she exclaims and tears start to flow. Remy just reaches his hand out and pulls her onto his lap and cradles her like a child. "Hush my love. I love you too."

"Oh, Remy, I am so ashamed. A warrior should not be blubbering like a lovesick high school girl. Maybe I am not worthy of you." Remy gently puts his fingers on her chin and turns her head so he can look in her eyes.

"Ejam, there is nothing wrong with feeling the way you do. We are all slaves of destiny nothing more and nothing less. What we share at this moment is beautiful. Nevertheless, we are at war and I will not hide in the shadows while other beings fight my battles. As a warrior and a leader of warriors you must understand that."

She kisses him hard on his lips and grabs him tight to her and says, "I understand my love."

"Good." Remy says with a sigh of relief.

"That's why I'm coming with you. You should have the best warriors at your disposal. Especially one who knows the elves battle strategies." Ejam answers standing up and looking at him with a devilish smile playing on her lips.

"Well I guess you've made your point. What if I say no." replies Remy Leaning back on the bed.

"Then I will follow you and act as back-up. One way or another I'm going to be there. So we can do this the easy way or the hard way." She replies smiling again. Remy burst out into laughter.

Consternated she looks at him and says, "What's so dam funny?"

"You are incredible. No matter what I say you're going to do what you want to. As your husband I may feel one way, but as your prince…"

She leaps on top of him before he can finish his sentence and kisses him again and he feels himself responding to her touch.

Catching his breath he says, "I would be honored that you joined me. We have about forty-five minutes before the briefing."

"I know. Let's not waste it." Ejam says smiling.

CHAPTER 14

*"Shadows can be more dangerous
than the real thing."*

NALINE SMILES TO HIMSELF as he walks through the corridor leading to the inner chambers of the temporal sanctuary. It took his people close to three centuries to complete this magnificent structure buried beneath the Alps. The gateway leading to the inner chambers is made of solid marble. The building itself looks like a French cathedral. Like a place where a God of some kind is worshipped. Yet no crosses or idols will be found here. The elves believe in no one or nothing but themselves.

"How ironic that God's greatest warrior is now bonded to the elves in more ways than one the warrior who taught Naline to fight and lead, God's favorite celestial angel. He used to be the angel of music and light. But when humans were created he rebelled against the God because he felt the humans were fabricated by one of God's lesser beings and when God breathe sentience into them he could no longer control himself. Lucifer was demoted from favorite to enemy. Like the elves he has learned that the title of "favorite" is fleeting when you choose not to worship him anymore. He was cast out thrown out of heaven with all who were loyal to him. He lost his power of song and light. His sentence was to live in perpetual darkness. You call that a forgiving God. Naline begins the painstaking process of unlocking the spiritual wards, which keeps everything in and out of the sanctuary. This is important because any energy flux of that magnitude would be felt by the spiritual beings on this planet and would need to be investigated. Something the elves could not afford at this point, especially, after the folly at the banquet. Even he had lost his composure and allowed his anger to best his judgment. Remy has so much more substance than he could have imagined. All the reports from Fica were totally incorrect. This being has shown great resilience and an aptitude for survival. God did not lie through his prophets; Remy was not a story to scare children. He was real and now they're whole timetable was accelerated, maybe too fast. But the commitment has been made and the path chosen.

The door to the sanctuary is made of solid steel three feet thick. The whole structure is laced with solid steel to help conduct the energy needed for its purpose. A loud creak is heard as the door opens. He quickly creates a vortex the pulls all the spiritual energy back into the sanctuary. Naline steps in and the door slams behind him. The smell of freshly cut lemons hits him square in the face. This is the smell that comes from the other realms. Until you enter them of course. Before him are eight windows into eight realms. Just like looking at eight television screens.

As he walks forward he hears a gruff voice calling out to him.

"I have been waiting for you."

"I know, milord, I was detained."

"When will you release me, Naline? The summer solstice approaches within six months."

Naline turns to the voice and says "When the time is right, Milord."

The voice belongs to Lucifer, once God's favorite celestial angel God's greatest warrior and leader. That is until he betrayed God by claiming he was just as powerful. God kicked him out of heaven into a realm he could rule, hell. But he also gave him the ability to manipulate humans and to walk the earth after Adam and Eve fell out of his grace. He sent his son Jesus to die for those pitiful beings sins, sins he helped promote and create. Then God allowed him to be killed by those miscreants and then he sided with the Elves in rebellion against God. For hjs transgressions he is now banished in another dimension, a dimension like hell that he has conquered and controls completely, a dimension that he cannot leave to get back to earth and that God will pay for. Lucifer stands six foot five inches tall and weighs close to three hundred pounds. He is three hundred pounds of pure sinewy muscle, his biceps the size of an oak tree's branches and his thighs the size of its trunks. Not a speck of hair on his body and eyes with feral yellow irises. Another gift from God when he stripped him of his angelic form and he became the demon he had always feared.

"I asked you a direct question Naline. I don't expect riddles in return. Joining your cause has cost my compatriots and me more than we bargained for. The least you can do is give me a straight answer."

"Soon, Milord, at the next solstice, I am first trying to find your brother and sister."

"I do not need them to conquer your world. You know that very well. All I require is my hordes from this plane to be successful." Says Lucifer.

"And that Milord is exactly what I can't do. I will be able to free you when the next energy nexus reaches its peak in about six months. But I must find your brother and sister to assist you. I will have two others from the council help me. As you know God only granted some of us the power to bring life forms across the dimensions only one at a time."

"My brethren and I will suffice. Why do I smell fear upon you? What has happened since last we spoke?" replies Lucifer sitting on his throne being handed a cup of wine by a slave girl, who then steps behind him and begins massaging his shoulders.

Naline looks at Lucifer and exhales noisily. He knew he was

worried about Remy, but he did not know he feared him. Yet if a wraith or celestial angel smelled fear it was real.

"There is a new player in the game."

"The child of the prophecy has reached maturity. Didn't I tell you to kill him? God's poor try at creating an earthly celestial angel with all the bloods of the first tribes. What a joke. I will crush him in battle. He is no match for me." Replies Lucifer emptying his goblet in one gulp and holding it out to be refilled by the girl behind him.

"He is being trained by Juzef, the dwarven war master as we speak. He has already handily defeated many of the warriors we have created and he is pure." explains Naline pacing back and forth.

"What do you mean pure I am sure he has lain with a woman or with a man depending on his preference?"

"No, I mean the blood that flows in his veins is pure. He has the blood of all the royal families running through his veins. He seems to have the magic of all the tribes. You know as well as I that any one of old blood holds no angst against anyone. He doesn't hate anyone or anything. He is pure in action and in thought."

"Can he be corrupted?" says Lucifer leaning forward.

"I don't think so. He worked for his company almost for free bringing medicine and building a hospital for the people in Indonesia. All attempts were made to bribe him with money, women and power. None were successful."

"So his only weakness is using his loved ones to get at him much like Vincenzo."

"He is much like Vincenzo. I even called him Vincenzo at the ball." Says Naline

"That Naline is blasphemous. Vincenzo was the greatest warrior I have ever trained. When we battled that last time he could have beheaded me. But instead he said "I cannot kill someone I love as much as you. You have been a great teacher and a good friend." He then used the hilt of his sword to knock me unconscious. When I woke I was here. Letting me live is probably why God let him die. God could only make one Vincenzo."

"Evidently Milord, he has made another. Direct attacks I fear will not be successful."

"What did you say?" says Lucifer standing.

"I said direct attacks would not be successful. Why, milord?"

"I think I know an easier way to fight this man."

"How, milord?"

"I will bestow you with enough power to free my sister before the nexus. She can begin while we wait for the full nexus." Lucifer sees Naline's eyes light up at the mention of his sister and says "You must push that aside. You know my sister. You were but a plaything to her. I know you felt deeply about her. Nonetheless, she has been banished a long time and her appetites are much larger than yours could ever be. If you know what I mean."

"Milord you ask too much. I could not bear to see her with another. There must be another way. There must be." The anguish in his voice is almost tangible.

"This is war Naline. When it's over and if she wants you then you can do what you want. But for now free her and send her out to find him. You know as well as I if he can deny her, he's really special."

"Yes, Milord, but if he does touch her I will kill him myself."

"I see the scent of fear is gone. That's good. Now listen to me very closely."

"The nexus on your plane past by a month ago, but here the nexus comes tomorrow. You must find my sister by then. At that time I will give you the power you need to free her. Heed my words Naline. My sister does not continence weakness; if you have a chance at all of having her you must remain strong at all times. Should she smell weakness upon you, she will loathe you. Do you understand?" says Lucifer staring at him.

"I understand, Milord." Naline replies

"Good, now go find my sister." Naline turns and leaves. As soon as he is gone, Torm steps from the shadows.

"Good day, Milord." Torm says bowing to Lucifer

"I guess you heard all that transpired. Naline allows a woman to make him weak. And to think I trained him. Yet he is a wonderful vessel for destruction, but enough about Naline. He at least can control his minions." Lucifer says looking directly at Torm.

"Milord, I had no idea she would bed Fica and become pregnant."

"I warned you she was head strong and that her hatred for vampires would make her do things we all would regret."

"Yes, you did Milord. But we left a trap in Kiree's mind for Remy. He will be incapacitated within the week or sooner. That you can be sure of and with his inability to lead them it will be our final victory."

"You must be joking. Do you think the other clans are idiots? He has a brother and a sister. Neither has shown the aptitude he has for violence; however they do have the proper blood. Plus the girl has a child in her womb. With Juzef's training anything is possible. What we need to do is turn the prophecy to our advantage. Once again God left a loophole so either side can triumph. Remy is not the child of the prophecy. Remy will be the father of the child of the prophecy. You see Remy is as close to a celestial angel as one can get without being one and what God wanted was for a celestial angel to mate with a wraith so that all the bloodlines are covered the blood of the first four tribes and the two celestial beings mingling to create another like his son Jesus."

"Another being like Jesus, what are you talking about, Milord?"

"None of you knew the truth. Jesus had the blood of all the tribes including celestial angel blood. He was perfect or as perfect as one could be without being a God. But he was a child of peace until he died for the humans sins. I knew this and tried to sway him before that happened. It did not work and your tribe killed him without knowing who or what he truly was. Then I fell into God's trap the second time and rebelled with your brethren against him allowing him to create the second celestial being the wraiths. Jesus was not a warrior until he died for those fools sins. Remy is a warrior from birth, he is the sword of God. You do understand that the second coming is not a peaceful being in any way." says Lucifer popping a grape in his mouth.

"So killing Remy will not end the prophecy?"

"It may or it may not. But turning him to our side will definitely destroy the prophecy or at least bend it our way and we will control an infant that is close to God. My sister has no idea of her role. When she was a celestial angel she could not bear children. But now as a wraith she can, she just doesn't know it. She of course will be as promiscuous as always, letting her hunger for the flesh outweigh her common sense. And of course, this Remy is handsome and dashing. God would not have created him any other way. My sister will not only lust after him, but she will fall in love with him."

"Why will she fall in love with him Milord? She has had thousands of lovers over the centuries. She has been Venus, Aphrodite, Cleopatra, and many more. How could any being possibly make her love him?" says Torm

"My sister has only met one person who was pure of heart and she loved him more than you could know. In fact, when that being was killed, she chose to follow my cause to the death. You see my dear sister was Mary Magdalene and she loved Jesus more than life itself. It is why she hates God so much and exactly why she will fall in love with Remy."

"Milord, no offense, but I think we are forgetting that Remy has to also agree."

"Oh don't you worry. What my sister wants she usually gets one way or another. The only one she did not have was Jesus. She will not be denied twice that you can be assured of."

"How do we get them to meet, milord?"

"I will leave that to you. Naline would never allow them to meet he is too blinded by her charms. But I suggest using someone he cares about to make him come to meet her. The best scenario would be if my sister were his life mate. Nevertheless, this must happen and soon, because if he meets his true life mate before, then all my planning is for naught."

"How do you know he hasn't, Milord?"

"Are you an idiot? He made love to two women in the same night. Neither is his life-mate. Plus when he meets his life-mate it will be felt throughout the spiritual plane. I will know and God will know. Anyway, I am tired of talking. There is a battle here that needs my attention. Make sure this is done as quickly as possible or I will wring your neck myself when I return to that realm."

CHAPTER 15

"One man's truth, is another man's lie"

DASTOR LOOKS OUT THE window of his limousine at the Spanish countryside. It took him no time at all to make the decision to speak to the clans in Europe and Asia. Remy's presense has changed everything. Dastor had planned to place the prince of Europe and Asia upon the throne by getting him to wed the queen. He had cultivated a relationship with the council of the Europe and Asia clans. He actually sat on both using the information from each to suit his needs. So it had been for centuries. He was just bidding his time, waiting for just the right moment. Of course neither council knew he was on both councils. Now this upstart was going to ruin everything. Well Remy was not emperor yet, but if he wed Sariel he would be. He must implore the prince of Europe and Asia to request her hand to become emperor and lead them against the elves. He could not stand by and let these fools allow a half-breed to rule the vampire nation. Only those of pure blood were fit to rule. The North American and South American council have so easily accepted Remy as part of the prophecy. They were all fools and now they would pay for their foolishness. "My plans have been in place to crush the elves since the last war. God was a fool. They all should be dead." Thinks Dastor to himself.

The sun is just breaking over the hills as the car rides over the mountains. The sunbeams against the morning dew seem to create a prism effect. Spectacular splashes of colors seem to slide across the horizon as the sun begins to climb. The car quickly approaches a huge ranch surrounded by a seven-foot wall made out of stone. The workmanship is exquisite; it looks as if each stone was lovingly placed in its spot because they had. The vampires had used humans to build it by had as penance for hunting them. When it was completed they were all drained dry. Dastor has not been here in years, even though it was his place of birth. The car comes to a halt in front of a beautiful palatial ranch styled home all one level. There are guards posted all along the perimeter. He is searched when he gets out of the car and again when he gets to the entrance. He is lead through a maze of hallways by three guards. They finally reach the library where two more guards stand at the door. One of the guards excuses himself and goes inside the room. He returns and leads Dastor into the study. The room itself is incredible. The stained glass dome is arrayed with the likenesses of many of the vampire royalty who ruled over the centuries. All the walls and the floor are pure mahogany polished to an immaculate sheen. The room much like a conservatory looks out of place in this one level flat structure. That is until you begin to notice that only artificial light is coming from the ceiling and you realize you are underground. Standing in the center of this majestic room is a tall thin figure with shoulder length black hair held in a ponytail by a silver clasp. He has a moustache and goatee with gray penetrating eyes that seem to burrow into your very being. He is dressed in pure black leather with a dirk at his waist. On the hilt of the dirk is a blood red ruby that seems to wink at you. Much like the ruby handles of Vincenzo's blades. In a deep melodious voice with a hint of a Spanish accent he says, "Welcome to my home Milord. I must apologize about all the security and for any inconvenience I have caused you during your journey. However, these are troubling times and one can never be too careful."

"I was taken care of quite well, Milord." Says Dastor bowing with accordance to Castilian etiquette.

The man smiles noting the formal gesture and replies "It seems some of us still remember the old ways."

"Many of us actually do, Milord."

"Well, where are my manners. My name of course is Prince Dauthi of the Vampire Clans of Europe and Asia." He says bowing.

"It is my pleasure to finally meet you Milord."

"Please sit." Dauthi says gesturing to two chairs in the center of the room. "It would seem that you are held in great regard by the council here in Europe and Asia."

"It is an honor for you to say so, milord."

"Well to me it seems more like spying and playing one against another."

'Not at all Milord. I am loyal to the vampiric world cause."

"Really, the two clans have a very different thought process about what is the vampiric world cause."

"I think that all that is needed is clear leadership speaking in one voice."

"One voice you say. How would that happen?"

"With a joining of the two clans through marriage."

"Do you presume to dictate who I will wed?"

"Not at all Milord." Says Dastor bowing again.

Dauthi smirks and says "Would you like something to drink?"

"Whatever you have will be fine." Replies Dastor thinking he has finally made his point.

Dauthi calls over one of his servants and they quickly get two goblet of wine from the bar. "This Dastor is a hunter's brew, a true hunter's brew."

Dastor takes the goblet and sips the contents. He becomes immediately lightheaded and starts to breathe at a rapid rate. It feels as if his heart will jump out of his chest He begins to perspire heavily and falls to his knees from his chair.

Dauthi just looks at him with a smile on his lips. Then he says "I warned you it was a hunter's brew. Potent isn't it. I will drink nothing else."

Dastor composes himself and says "This is pure human blood."

"Yes, pure human blood with a couple of herbs in it. Of course it is fresh from last night's hunt. No synthetic blood for a true hunter."

"But the treaty, Milord?" replies Dastor

"The treaty states we cannot hunt humans in their cities. It says nothing about hunting them in the woods, mountains or seas. We do not break the treaty, but we do not honor it either. It goes back to that statement you made about the vampiric world view and how each clan sees the world." Dauthi says rising from his seat with a snarl. "We are what we are. Nothing more and nothing less, humans are our food. We have a right to eat and survive. As all the creatures God has created."

"You are right, Milord. I have brought you news."

Dauthi sits back down and stares at Dastor and answers with pursed lips. "What news?"

"There is a new player in the game, a very dangerous player, Milord."

"Only vampires are dangerous, old man. It is why God did not give us the powers he gave the Elves. Where the elves have tried and failed, we would have succeeded. God fears only us."

"The new player has royal blood from all the tribes including vampire, milord."

"That is a wives tale told to children to scare them. You can't honestly expect me to believe an elf would actually lay with a vampire and have a child. The child would die a horrible death, a death that could have been prevented. No vampire or elf would willingly risk that."

"Nonetheless, it is true Milord. I have brought the blood test results and a drop of his blood to be tested by your own scientists. He is a reality not a myth."

Dauthi becomes immediately agitated and throws his goblet across the room. All the servants present begin to tremble. "If this is true all my plans are for naught. He must either join me or die."

"Milord, he would never agree to vampires ruling the world. He has already married a troll."

"That is nauseating. They are sub-humans created by the elves. They are the second set of God's children and they are the unblessed. He is no true vampire. He is nothing more than a dog. A dog I will personally kill."

"Sire, he has already killed trolls, ogres, shape-changers and humans."

"How many could he have killed?" Dauthi says laughing aloud. "1."

"No Milord, he has killed four shape changers, two ogres, six trolls and hundreds of humans."

"So he is a true hunter. It must be Commander Sauer who is taking him down the path of peace between the clans. Had we wiped out the elves at the beginning, we would never have had that toxin that prevents us from having children created. We by now could possibly outnumber all the races on the earth. The warriors in my clans are aching for battle."

"My lord. There is a better way." Says Dastor

"What is that?"

"As I said earlier we could unite the clans. You could ask for Sariel's hand in marriage and unite all the clans again. She could not deny you. Yours is the appropriate bloodline."

"That is true. But I deny her. I will not accept Vincenzo's leftovers as mine. Plus I am not in the business of marrying my own family."

"But my lord it the easiest way to prevent Remy from becoming emperor and to keep the bloodlines pure."

"You really do not know my history prior to becoming prince of these clans do you?"

"Milord, I do not understand?"

"Never mind it does not really matter. If the North and South American clans accept him they are fools and deserve to die. Where is Remy now?"

"He will soon be here in Spain. Where I do not know?"

"That is a small thing. This is my country, everything that

happens here I know about. My clan will hunt again. His head will adorn my gate and I shall devour his heart while he watches."

"Milord that could start a war between the vampire clans, we need both clans united to defeat the elves. A war would undo all that was planned."

"I know." Says Dauthi as he cuts off Dastor's head. "But I have no need for traitors around me. You cannot play both sides against the middle and not be found out sooner or later. When you betray your blood, you will betray anything or anyone. Clean up this mess and I will see to this mutt."

"Why you choose to come here by commercial means eludes me, my love." Says Ejam looking out the window at Madrid as they prepare to land.

"Well I am thinking of this as our honeymoon." He says with a chuckle. Ejam punches him in the shoulder playfully and kisses him fully on the lips.

"So we will have time to lay on the beach and bask in the sun." she replies with a smirk, knowing full well any dreams of anything like that are just that dreams.

Remy cups her face in his hands enjoying the supple softness of her face and smiles again and says "If I could give you that I would. But now it's not mine to give, nothing is mine to give anymore. You deserve all those things and so much more, my love."

Ejam sees the pain in his eyes and is sorry she was so thoughtless in her use of words. Remy was a man who would have little if no joy in his lifetime. Only a life of duty and servitude to the masses of this realm was his fate. What a brat she could be at times, her tongue was her sharpest weapon. Sharper than any sword could ever be, God, he deserved so much more. A woman who truly understood his position in life a woman who knew her place at all times. A woman she would have to learn to be if she meant to keep this man. She says aloud "Oh, my love. I did not mean what I said or the way it was said. I merely thought to make a joke to see you laugh. You have barely spoken a word since we left New York."

"I have many things on my mind at the moment, many things. One of them is how do I act when we find Renchi. I cannot diminish what she had meant to me at one time in my life. Yet you know when the mind wipe has been cleared she will remember being in love with me. It will be awkward."

"Do you still love her?" Ejam says plainly

He pauses and grabs her hands gently and replies "No I do not love her I love you, Ejam and I will not betray our marriage vows by lying with another."

"I know that, Milord. You have said this to me at least a hundred times since you found out Renchi was alive."

"No you do not understand. I need you to believe this in your heart and soul. Not because I said it but because you believe it is true." He says holding her hands tighter.

"But I do believe you, Remy. I believe everything you say is true. You are not a liar. You pride yourself on your honesty. However, you have read what a life-mate is and I am not your life-mate. There is so much more that you must come to grips with. It is not you that I worry about, it is who you are. You are meant for more than one bed, my love. It is your fate until you meet your life-mate to bed whoever the councils decide you should. Power resides in heirs to the throne, you have four thrones to make a claim to, and each one is a merciless taskmaster. Each one waiting to swallow you whole and make you what it wishes. You equate sex with love, which is very romantic. However, while we all hope to have sex with the one we love, the one we have sex with may not love you at all. You are not a woman and cannot truly understand the power we feel when a man needs you. In addition, how inadequate you feel when he does not. I have witnessed women use it and I thought them whores. How wrong I truly was. Until I felt your need for me, I did not truly understand myself. When I think of us I am complete and have no worries. Woman may not think they are equal to men at most times. Nonetheless, we are superior. We can actually use your need to our own advantage and you would never know. It is a weapon we wield and wield well. To own a man in the bedroom maybe even better than owning his throne, yet even I know it is no use against the masses. You do not belong to me exclusively. You belong to this realm. So yes, I believe you. Nevertheless, it is a promise I do not and cannot expect you to keep. Because it is a promise you're not in a position to make. We are together now and I will always love you. And that is enough for me now." She says caressing his face.

"I see." says Remy "We are landing." His face goes blank for a moment.

Ejam is shocked at his curt response. He releases her hands and signals for the guard to prepare for battle. While the plane coasts to a landing two warriors walk into the pilot's cabin and two warriors walk to the back exit. Ejam looks out the window and sees about thirty to forty warriors on the runway. From their scent, she determines they are vampires and she breathes a sigh of relief. Yet, she looks at Remy in wonder as he straps on his blades.

"Prepare yourselves for battle." Remy says

"My love what is happening? They have the scent of vampires. Why are you telling us to prepare for battle?"

"Because they are not of our clan, their scent is completely different and utterly wild. They have the scent of pure human blood upon them."

"You can discern the difference between synthetic and real human blood. That's impossible even for a werewolf." Says Ejamine strapping on her weapons.

"Believe me it's true. They are here to kill us. Take the passengers to the back of the plane and have them disembark from there."

The warriors move quickly to do his bidding. From outside the plane Dauthi shouts "Vampire prince, I hope you are not using humans to cover your escape. No one worthy of the title vampire prince would run away."

Remy smiles a smile unlike any Ejam has ever seen. It was as if danger filled him and fulfilled him. As if it were the only lover he craved or needed. It scares her a little to see that gleam in his eye.

"Now let's see to these traitor vampires." Remy says as he descends the stairs onto the runway. Outside the vampires stand in a defensive posture around the plane. All the warriors are suntanned with long braids or ponytails. They are all dressed in dark crimson, the color of congealed blood and they all have the scent of pure blood seeping from their pores. Dauthi stands at the head of them dressed as they are except for a cloak with a ruby clasp holding it. Remy measures him and rates him a warrior true. He was not a foppish nobleman he was a true warrior.

Dauthi says "Remy, welcome to Spain. I am Dauthi, vampire prince of the clans of Europe and Asia.

"Good day, Prince Dauthi. I have no intention of running from my brethren. Those are just humans being moved out of the way." Replies Remy with a large smile and a slight bow according to etiquette.

Dauthi is taken aback by the gesture and says "I see. What brings you to my land?"

Remy measures him with a look and smiles again saying "I am on a honeymoon of sorts."

Surveying the situation, he wishes he had left Ejam at home. They were outnumbered approximately five to one. Outlandish odds, yet he felt deep within himself he had already won this battle. They all lay before him with their throats lying open. It was like rapture to him, battle is pure rapture.

"A honeymoon, how interesting, sources close to you reported to me that you were here in search of someone." Replies Dauthi laughing aloud.

"Someone who is close to me told you this?" Says Remy "I guess we share associates then and well we should as kinsmen."

"Kinsmen it is then. Well we no longer share that associate anymore. You see traitors sicken me. If you are a traitor to your clan, then you are a traitor to yourself. No one can outrun his or her blood. Do you agree?"

"Without a doubt, all traitors deserve to die. It is the only coin they should be paid for their actions."

"I'm glad you feel that way." Dauthi says gesturing for one of his warriors to hand him a black bag. "Here is what is left of your associate." Dauthi throws the bag to Remy, who catches it with one hand and reaches into the bag pulling out Dastor's head in one movement. All the warriors with Remy gasp aloud. Remy is not surprised at all. He expected the council to prevent his ascendance to the throne. He just did not know what lengths they would go to prevent it. Prophecy or no prophecy he was still not purebred.

"He came to me and told me all about you. He did in an effort to gain favor with the clans here in Europe and Asia. He also offered me the hand of the Queen in exchange for an alliance. The moment he finished his tale I relieved him of his head."

"The Queen is a very independent woman. I am sure the council would try but in the end she would do as she pleased. I guess Dastor got what he deserved." Answers Remy.

The warriors with Remy are stunned by his response. How could Remy, think so little of a vampire that has served the cause all his life? Several of the warriors begin to step away from Remy creating the air of non-allegiance. Remy notices this and chuckles to himself.

"We of little faith." He thinks to himself.

Dauthi also notices this turn of events and he says. "I see your warriors find the old ways distasteful. In the old days, acts of treason were not taken so lightly. All of you step away from your prince, and choose a being that came to me with traitorous thoughts and actions. What fools you really are. Shame on all of you for questioning your prince's loyalty, your clan has become quite weak in a short time. No discipline I would wager is the reason. If you were my men, I would drink you dry myself. Now I have a question for you, Remy."

"What's your question?"

"Do you believe in God and abide by his laws?"

"Yes I do Dauthi." Remy answers purposely leaving out his title.
"Then you are my enemy."

"Because I believe in God I am your enemy. We do not even know one another."

"That is true Remy. However, your mere presence offends me. You are an abomination and must be destroyed, you are after all part elf add to that that God is our sworn enemy and I think you can see my point."

"If that is how you feel, then release the others and I will battle you one and all by myself." Says Remy with a smirk playing on his lips."

Dauthi notices the change in Remy's demeanor and cannot understand his nonchalant attitude. It is as if he and his warriors were no more than a slight annoyance. He thinks a different tact is required. "Spoken like a true vampire. You have more substance than I expected. You really do not know much about the clans or their history. You do what you do because you genuinely think it is right. No Remy I do not think I will battle you at this time."

"Then explain the show of force and the veiled threats?" Remy replies.

"To let you know how easily you can be killed. To place a little fear in your heart, the same fear that most vampires feel everyday living in the human world. However, I must admit that I feel no fear emanating from you."

"Then what is your point, Dauthi?" says Remy confused.

"My point is that you don't know the whole story of vampires. You only know what you have been told by Commander Sauer and the book of etiquette. There is so much more to us than that. There is an older book you need to read, a book of our true history. Do you dare face the truth?" says Dauthi smiling.

Ejamine can no longer control herself and says "Don't listen to him, Milord. He sounds just like an Elf."

Dauthi's stare silences her immediately. "You have no right to speak in this arena. This is between princes and has nothing to do with lesser beings. I thought the Elves had taught you manners and to be seen and not heard. At least you have a place. Stay in it." Replies Dauthi

Turning back to Remy he continues "We and the Elves are brothers born from the same seed. So much like Cain and Abel in the bible, always fighting each other over petty things and I believe it is time the fighting came to an end. We should bring the Alps down upon their heads before they can unleash the pain and suffering they are planning to inflict on the world."

"So you mean to exterminate the Elves like they were vermin." Says Remy

"They are vermin. We are the superior race, the race that was born to rule this realm. Your existence means the end of the first four tribes, the rest are blinded by their faith in God and the prophecy that they do not see their own end. We are Gods chosen, Dwarves, vampires, elves, celestial angels and werewolves. Nevertheless, we have fallen out of favor since the humans were created. All of us have been touched by the magic of God, it flows through our veins, and we are one with mother earth. With end of the clans, the earth magic will be gone forever no longer a threat to God's existence."

One of the vampire guards with Remy asks "How did you come to such a state? Why would God want us all eliminated? We are his healers and warriors."

"Another fool who speaks out of turn, is there no respect anymore? Anyway to answer your question, if all the first tribes are eliminated God will have no need for warriors or healers. God wants us out of the way."

"What proof do you have of this? God has a path for us all." Remy asks as he looks at the warriors around him. They all to a man are beginning to take heed to Dauthi's words and Dauthi knows it.

"What proof you ask? Well I have the deaths of thousands of vampire, werewolf and dwarven children to start with. All killed by God's new favorite child, the Humans. Until we created sanctuaries and began to fight back we were being slaughtered. Now we have become the hunter instead of the hunted."

"So you blame God, for the humans' propensity to kill whatever they don't understand." replies Remy

"That is where you are wrong. We do not blame God for that. We blame the Elves for creating them. Before humans were created we sustained ourselves on the blood of many beasts. We did not require the blood of humans to survive any blood would do. However, just like the biblical Adam and Eve, Elves and Vampires strayed from the path. Soon after the humans and had been thrown out of Eden the elves had a celebration. They let the other tribes know they had created the humans from nothing and God had taken them to his bosom. They were celebrating their fall from grace. Werewolves and Dwarves refused to go to the celebration believing the Elves had gone mad. Mad because they were trying to create not just life in God's name, but judgment of those beings was the domain that belonged to God. You would ask do not the trolls, ogres and shape changers hold the same regard with God. Unfortunately they do not because they are the unblessed. They never truly accepted the Lord as their king. Humans began as unblessed you know, but God chose to bless them anyway and have them take on his own image. The vampires were foolish and joined in the celebration and enjoyed the feast immensely. The food so tender and so sweet the blood wine so rich and hearty, like no other fare they had ever partaken of. They enjoyed it so much they made orders for the blood and meat of that animal to be sent to all the vampire clans. Within a short time, we all found out that the blood of beast no longer sustained us. No one could figure out why. However, the Elves were becoming rich on this new animals meat and blood. Finally, our scientist tested the new blood and meat and found out it came from humans. The elves had tricked us again. To piss off God who had breathed intelligence into man, they introduced a chemically enhanced human flesh and blood into our diet. Now we are addicted for life. Of course, many of us went rogue and hunted humans to survive. The humans retaliated by trying to annihilate all the werewolves, dwarves, and vampires in Europe and Asia. In North America and South America, the clans choose to sign treaties and they created synthetic blood. The Clans of the Poles and Africa soon joined the clans in North America and South America. This led to the signing of the treaty with the humans. We only signed the treaty because the clans were outnumbered by the humans at that time. Not long after the treaty was signed, the war with elves began. All vampires joined Vincenzo and followed him into battle against the Elves and their followers. We were of course victorious. Vincenzo did not heed our warning and followed God's instructions to give the Elves a choice regarding their fate. The tribes of Europe and Asia did not agree and chose to break off from God's laws. It was then we realized that we were expendable to God. We had served our purpose. The elves had been punished by God for killing Jesus and were now easy to control. So now both of his favorite beings were flourishing. Believe me when I say it is all part of a grand plan. We have chosen to become the hunters and have waited for the day we can avenge our brethren, the day when we finally can get our vengeance against the Elves and God alike."

"I cannot allow that." says Remy "So if we are to battle now. Let's go, if not I have things to do."

Dauthi laughs aloud as do his warriors. "Just like that, you really are quite brave or just insane. Either way I have said what I wanted to say to you. Here" Dauthi throws a large leather bond book at him, which Remy catches with great care. Dauthi notices this and says "You are not a fool that much I can see. Read the book and make up your own mind. If you agree with what I have told you, you know where to find me."

"And if I still don't agree." Replies Remy

With a raise eyebrow of surprise Dauthi says "You need to know what happened before you can make a decision of such finality. God wants us gone."

"Dauthi, isn't that what the Jews thought when Christ was born and died. Look at the bible, there is an old and a new testament. In the old God did everything through laws and rules. That is how the clans think about God. They think of just the laws and rules. But God thought better of all of us and he sent his son Jesus to teach us love is the way. I am sure you have not read the New Testament and I am sure you were affected by the savior's death much differently than his disciples. In olden days you needed to reach God directly, now as the New Testament says we reach God through his son. All Jesus ever preach was love of God and love of one another."

Dauthi stares at Remy and says to himself "Could it possibly be. Is this the one? He is so young, so unworldly. God it seems always has a sense of humor." Outwardly he says with a crooked smile "The the next time we meet one of us will probably not walk away. With the coming of war, only one vampire pack can lead and rule this realm. Good day, Prince Remy, do not let them use you overmuch. You deserve better. I can tell from this meeting that there is so much more to you than any of us may know. Your own warriors lack honor and loyalty to their prince. They are so easily swayed by the unknown, watch your back with them." Dauthi says bowing.

Remy bows in return just a little lower to show respect and says "Good Day, Prince Dauthi. May God walk with you?"

"I'd rather walk alone." Dauthi says with a smirk playing on his lips and he gestures for his warriors to leave.

"Milord." asks one of the warriors. "What was that all about?"

"Oh you still think of me as your Lord. Are all this clans warriors swayed so easily by words? If so your weakness is apparent and can be used against you in battle. Learn to follow your commander's lead and make no assumptions, it may cost you more than your own life. And that was a lesson of old ways for me." Says Remy smiling.

Ejam is not smiling and says "I told you we should have not taken a commercial flight, Milord."

"But it was worth it Ejam, I have learned much this day. It is part of my own special education. I now have a better understanding of my vampiric roots and why there is so much hate. The killing of children can change anyone. Once I have read this book, I am sure I will know much more."

"To read that book is blasphemy, Milord. It speaks of a death God. "Says one of the warriors "It speaks of the vampires right to hunt where they want and who they want."

"Interesting, you know of course every book ever written has a counter book, every angel a demon and every God a devil. It is the balance of the cosmos. Attaining knowledge about something is not a crime nor is it blasphemy. A zealot is dangerous because he becomes ignorant to both sides of coin. He chooses to believe the way someone else thinks is dangerous and learns to hate. After awhile only the hate remains and you can't even remember why you hate a person, a place or a thing. The best way to defeat an enemy is to know your enemy. Everything he cherishes and everything he hates and why."

"Milord, we don't know any better. All we have ever had to sustain us is hate."

"Then perhaps it is time to learn to live for the sake of living to learn to be sustained by love. A love for God and all around you, Jesus teaches us to love our brethren. It is the hand of Lucifer and his minions that drives a stake between us all. No, forbearance and bigotry are not the paths God has tried aspired us to. We all have a place in the scheme of things. Finding that place may be the most arduous and long personal journey anyone can undertake. Do not fear the challenge. Embrace it. It will make the journey sweeter and more fulfilling. Tomorrow is promised to none of us. Zealots are of no use to the world. They are blind to everything including why they became a zealot. Have clarity of purpose and keep your eyes, your mind and your heart open. It takes more effort to do this; nevertheless, it is worth the extra devotion. Remember in the end a place in God's kingdom has been promised to us. That place comes after service to him with our all including our lives. It is clear that you shun one book but you do not read the book of books. Your hate would be tempered if you read the New Testament of the bible and experienced Jesus' love and sacrifice first hand. I know you lived the Old Testament but it is time to embrace the New Testament and what it stands for. Realize we are like the dinosaurs and may have outlived our original purpose. It is time to find a new one that is more in line with what Jesus preached."

The warriors and Ejam are astounded by his words; he sounds more like a prophet than a warrior. Especially, the warriors who suddenly hear Vincenzo's voice coming from Remy's lips, they bow before him with tears running down their faces. How could they ever doubt their prince? Dauthi was right maybe this being was to good for them.

"Please forgive us Milord. How could we have doubted your loyalty? We deserve no less than death at your hands." They say in unison placing their weapons on the ground in front of them and exposing their necks.

"Oh yes we have come all this way so I can kill you all. Like I said in New York, do you all have a death wish? I just spoke to you of brotherly love, do you think I do not practice it? Get up. We must find Efisio's daughter and return her in one piece to her Uncle. That is our quest and we will fulfill it. Enough nonsense for one day, there will certainly be enough bloodshed for all before this is all over no need to sacrifice yourselves now. Come we have people to meet." Remy pauses for a moment and then turns to Ejamine.

"That includes you. Let's go." Ejam is shaken by the power in his voice as well as the tone. A tone that indicates clearly that he will no longer tolerates her loose tongue.

She replies "Yes, my prince."

They soon reach the market in Aranjuez, a town not to far outside of Madrid. Ejam watches Remy as he seems to glide through the town. Remy speaks to the people in fluent Spanish without the hint of an English accent, almost as if he were born here in Spain. Ejam notices he takes times to give the poor money and to touch and offered them a smile. As he walks along he takes a crying child from one of the women and shushes him to sleep. The woman astonished thanks him profusely. He smiles his infectious smile and kisses her on the forehead, at the same time giving her money. Children are all of a sudden everywhere around him. He takes time to greet each one and give them his full attention. Soon all of the townspeople begin to gather around him and speak to him and touch him. The warriors try to stand between him and the crowd and he signals to them it is all right. Young and old come. He orders the warriors give the people their money. They now realize why he had told them to bring several thousands of dollars apiece. The towns people start to set up tables in the center of town and they bring food and drink.

Amazing is not the word for what has transpired thinks Ejamine, she now knows deep in her being that Remy can never just belong to one person, he was made to be shared.

She is awakened from her daze by Remy's voice. "Ejam, this is Ernesto. He has the information we need. He also has told me there is a sect of priest who has been taking children away from this town. You know what that means." The look in Remy's eyes is of pure disgust.

"Yes, I know what that means." She replies.

"I have instructed Portin to contact Commander Sauer and have a strike team brought in. They should reach here within the hour. I will not stand by while children are harmed and I hope it's the same team that was in Indonesia." Remy says as he holds a little girl on his lap and almost as if he were another person he says with a wide smile. "This is Ernesto's daughter Carmen. Beautiful isn't she."

"Yes, she is Milord. She certainly is." Ejamine says smiling at the child who smiles back. What a puzzle this man is that she has married, she thinks to herself. His face reverted from repugnance to kindness in seconds and his tone totally changed when he spoke of Ernesto's daughter.

Remy gets up and smoothes down the little girl's hair and says in Spanish, "I have to go now little one. Nevertheless, I will be back. Soon there will be a lot of men and women here. Do not worry they are my friends. They will protect you until I return." She smiles at him and hugs him around his waist burying her face in his stomach and says "I know." she then runs over to her father who smiles at Remy nodding his head in thanks as his daughter hands him the money Remy gave her.

"Gracias, Senor. This town is alive again. May God walk with you?" An old woman says after watching Remy with the child. "That child has not spoken a year since her older brother was taken. Bless you."

"Give your thanks to the almighty. He should be your armor and your shield at all times. He will bring all comfort when needed. You need only ask him." Remy says taking her hands.

Looking at him lovingly she replies "I now know prayers are answered and that renews my faith in God. You have renewed the whole town's faith with your presence." She says kissing his hands. She then smiles an old wry smile and walks to her son and her daughter and turns back to say. "Do not let them use you much, you deserve better. Look in your own house for Lucifer's hand first. He is the prince of lies and we are all weak in some way. Bless you my son."

Remy swears he sees wings appear at her back with a rose hued glow as she makes this last statement. He blinks and she has joined her family and is gone. "Blessed be your name Lord God. I will heed your warning."

After eating and some goodbyes, Remy and his men get on the horses the townspeople gave them for their journey and start out of town.

"Ernesto says the oriental woman and her daughter live at a hacienda about two kilometers out of town." Says Remy on horseback. "The countryside is picturesque in the moonlight. A slight breeze cools you as you ride and the stars seem to wink down at you from the heavens. It is miraculous how God seems to paint each horizon differently. How the land seems to merge into the sky and become one in an abundance of colors that can be experienced but not explained. How wondrous you are Lord. We have so many daily gifts given to us that we ignored. I now understand once a man twice a child. As a man you are too concerned with things of no true importance, but as a child and as an elder you experience the world. You do not try to explain it you just enjoy it." thinks Remy looking about.

"My Prince, how did you know you needed the money you gave to the townspeople?" asks Ejamine riding beside him.

"I didn't know for sure. I have just seen so many countries that are impoverished, that it has become second nature to try and provide for the people less fortunate them myself. I unfortunately have experienced poverty first hand. These people are no different than any of us, they were just born under different circumstances." He answers stopping his horse and looking at her he continues "Ejam, what good is it to have the power to help people and you don't use it every chance you get. I did not ask for the burdens placed upon me, but I accept them nonetheless. It is what Jesus would do and what he did for his brief lifespan. Those burdens are not as heavy as some of the burdens I have seen many poor people carry every day. Hunger, pestilence, and disease are much greater burdens then I will ever carry. Some have told me I sound like a priest or a prophet and if that is so then so be it. The world needs a lot more Jesus and a lot less hate."

There is a small explosion and then a plume of light on the horizon behind them. Remy chuckles and says "I guess Commander Sauer wasn't far behind me. I knew he would not leave me alone for long. He probably was right behind us all the way over the Atlantic. Come we have a ways to go. Another reason, my dear that it did not matter how we flew here."

Ejam just looks at him shocked an says "How could you know that?"

Remy smiles and says "One of my gifts is reading minds on contact. I now know that power has a mind of its own. When Commander Sauer embraced me when we left I knew he had four gunships fueled and ready to follow us to our destination. Which mean that Dauthi was outnumbered immensely, he just did not know it."

They soon arrive at the hacienda. It is a plain looking stucco structure, desert beige with a red roof and a well in the center of the courtyard. Goats and chickens walk freely about and several horses are drinking noisily from a trough. Remy looks around and thinks to himself "This is a good home. A quiet life, a life he could never even dream of now." He is roused from his musings by a dog's bark, a very familiar dog's bark. He jumps from the saddle and a black Akita runs straight at him. He kneels and the dog licks his face. "How you doing boy? I missed you too."

An older woman comes into the courtyard to see what the commotion is and stops dead in her tracks looking at Remy. He gets up slowly and looks back at her across the courtyard. Recognition clearly lights up her face and they move towards one another and lock in a hearty embrace. She holds him tightly and weeps openly. Stepping back she says "Let me look at you. My God, you have grown. My little Remy is all grownup, excuse an old woman's tears, it is sometimes the only thing we have left."

"How are you, Milady?" says Remy not letting her go.

"I am fine now. We have been safe and have lived well in secret."

"I am sorry I was not there......."

"You were not supposed to be my son. By now, you know the whole story. I am sure Juzef has placed you upon the path of your destiny or you would not be here."

Remy leans back and looks into her eyes as she says "She is in the kitchen making dinner. She knows nothing of her true past, but upon seeing your face all those memories will return. To protect her I had to lie about her father's death and who caused it."

"Then maybe it would be unfair to shatter this dream. It is beautiful here. The elves do not know you're alive and they would never find you. Perhaps it is better if she does not see my face and remember."

"It is time, Remy. We all must serve God in our own way.

My Efisio must not have died for nothing. His death must have a purpose a reason. You are our son in all but flesh, not like that demon child I bore from my lions. Go to her, it is her destiny." Again Ejamine just soaks up this emotional scene and almost gets caught up in it. That is until she remembers why she and her fellow warriors are there. She signals the other warriors to set up a perimeter and to contact Commander Sauer's troops for extraction. Now this part she is comfortable with.

Remy heads into the house where the smell of garlic and butter is everywhere. He walks into the kitchen and Renchi's back is to him. He gazes at her admiring her long black hair and enjoying her fresh smell.

"Mother dinner is almost ready." Renchi says as she turns and sees Remy. Her mind explodes into a million thoughts at one time. Renchi is besieged by all her memories at once and faints. She awakens with her head in Remy's lap and her mother kneeling over her with a cool cloth.

"Renchi, I hope you can forgive your father and me. We had no choice; your brother had told the Elves where we were and where they could find Remy. We had to protect both of you."

Renchi jumps up visibly angry pushing Remy aside and says "I would have fought for his life, mother. I would have chased those elves into hell."

Renchi's mother looks at her and in a very composed manner rises and replies "That was not your father's wish. His wish was for you to live and as his daughter you should respect his wishes." Her mother says sternly staring directly into Renchi's eyes.

Renchi quickly composes herself realizing it must have been twice as difficult for her mother. To live a lie, lose your husband and your son must have been dreadful, not to mention the loss of face just for not being truthful.

"I apologize, mother. I spoke without thinking." Moreover, to Remy she says coldly "Why are you here?"

At first, Remy is bowled over by her response, but then he

realizes maybe a cold welcome will make the situation easier to manage.

"I asked you a question? Why are you here?"

"I am here to bring you and your mother to your Uncle. It was your father's last wish. I could do no less." Remy says bowing. At that same instant Ejamine walks into the kitchen.

"What rights have you to speak of my father? It is because of you my father is dead. Did you think I would just take you back into my arms and forgive you for that?" Shouts Renchi

Remy just stays bowed and says "If it is of any consolation, I personally killed all involved except for your brother who escaped me in the Alps, I to grieve for him. He was also like a father to me."

Renchi moves forward as if she is going to hit Remy. Ejamine is between them instantly, grabbing her hands she spits "Over my dead body will you strike the Prince of Princes'."

The two women look at each other with murder in their eyes. Remy's sees this and intervenes quickly.

"Ejamine let her go. All of this has been quite a shock for her. She has been living a ghost existence for years. She needs understanding not violence."

Ejamine releases her and steps by his side. Remy can see that she is seething. In retrospect, Remy was actually quite surprised by Ejamine's speed and strength. Renchi is an accomplished warrior.

"Renchi, honorable Mamason this is my wife Ejamine."

Ejamine bows as does Renchi's mother, however, Renchi does not. Renchi just totally ignores what Remy has said and says. "What does she mean you are the Prince of Princes?"

Before Remy can answer, Renchi's mother says "First, you will show some manners and acknowledge his wife. Have you forgotten how you were brought up?"

"I apologize. I am not myself. Congratulations."

"Now I will explain who Remy is" says Samilo. "He is a Prince to dwarf, werewolf, elf and vampire empires. He has all the bloods of the first tribes flowing through his veins and since I know you did not forget your lessons as a child, you know what that means. Your father and I were charged with his training in the ways of battle. We never knew we would come to love him as a son. It of course was our duty, but it was more of a pleasure then a chore."

Renchi just stands with her mouth open looking at Remy. So many emotions are brought to the surface at once. Her love for Remy her love for her father, her brother's betrayal, and so many other things. She turns and runs out the back door.

Remy clicks on his COM and says "Our pickup has left the barn; make sure there are no wolves in the barnyard."

"We are on it, my prince." Replies Postin "She has just run into our line of sight."

"Good. Do not approach her. I'll be there soon." He turns to her mother and says, "Even if I have to drag her back we must leave soon. The elves also have their own spies. There were several in town, I am sure they did not know I could smell them. Please get her and we must leave."

"I understand. But this is a thing for you to do." Samilo says caressing his cheek. "There are things you must say to her and things she must say to you." She pauses and leans close to him. "Your wife is beautiful and very protective. I approve." She whispers in his ear smiling.

"I am glad you approve." He says kissing her on the forehead and heading off after Renchi.

Samilo turns to Ejam and says "Tea, dear?"

Befuddled Ejam replies "I apologize, but I do not think I have time."

"Oh dear, there is always time for tea. Plus I would like to get to know you a bit. You are married to my adopted son." Samilo says with a huge smile that lights up the room.

Ejam smiles back and says "A little honey please?"

Remy finds Renchi sitting beneath a huge tree overlooking the ranch. From where she sits, you can see the whole valley. Such a breath taking view, fig trees as far as the eye can see vineyards to his left and a lake to his right. A scene that is so beautiful and so romantic. He approaches her slowly after surveying the area.

"Why did you have to come? I was happy with my life. I had no worries and no fears." Renchi says with her back to him stopping him in his tracks with her words.

"I am doing my duty to the clans and the memory of your father. I can do no less."

"So it is true. I am not the reason you are here. You are more like my father than you think. Remember how you professed you were different. How you would never be like him."

"That may be true, Renchi, but life has a way of changing you. However, now is not the time to discuss it? You may have been safe here for a while. Nonetheless, the elves know where you are. You and your mother must come with me." Suddenly Remy smells a familiar scent and draws his blades spinning towards it.

"Vincenzo's blades, huh. Even with those I doubt if you can protect her any better than I can. After all, I am her fiancé." Dauthi says with a smile. Renchi gets up and kisses him fully on the lips as much for show as for feeling.

Remy laughs aloud and sheaths his blade. "Touché, Prince Dauthi."

"Prince Dauthi?" says Renchi

"She does know you are a vampire prince, does she not?"

Renchi looks at Dauthi in disbelief. "You are not Don Martinez's son, you lie to me too? What is with you men?" She says stepping away from Dauthi.

Dauthi just smiles and looks back at Remy and replies "You truly are a formidable..." he hesitates then continues "Is it ally or enemy at this point."

"Dauthi I understand your hatred for the tribes. You feel betrayed by them and I can also understand your displeasure with God. However, I am neither your ally nor your enemy. I am a pawn, as you well know. I have much to learn about all my heritages. In addition, I have not had a chance to read the book you gave me. I am sure it is the counterpoint to the human bible. Inspired I am sure by the same power that tried to conquer the world in his name ever since he was kicked out of heaven. I believe in God whole heartedly but I was taught by her father not to formulate an opinion until I have all the facts." Remy says.

"To be truthful I admire your refreshing optimism. But I have been jaded by what has transpired in my lifetime as you know. Watching the tribes hunted down almost to extinction can change a man."

"True, but you are still a man who can learn from the past and formulate a new future. God gave sentient beings a choice. It was and is one his greatest gifts to us. His greatest gift was Jesus and you know that better than I." Says Remy.

"You make an excellent point, Prince Remy."

Dauthi turns to Renchi and says "Renchi, I could not tell you who I was. You had been mind wiped and I knew that."

"So you have known who I was from the start. Why did you not tell me?" Answers Renchi.

"I was afraid any reference to Vampires would clear your mind and make you forget me. A selfish thought I know. But when it comes to you, my heart gives me no other choice. I love you with my whole being.

You must forgive me." Dauthi says as he takes her hands in his. Remy is no fool he notices her muscles relax and sees the longing in her eyes. She loves this man. Dauthi continues, "If you chose to leave with Prince Remy, I will understand. To be quite honest, I can protect you, but not as well as he can." Dauthi looks at Remy and weakly smiles. Dauthi is a proud man. Nevertheless; like a good leader and warrior he seems to understand his limitations. He is also a man who is deeply in love. Remy bows in respect.

"Remy was sent by my Uncle to bring us back to him. I love you Dauthi and nothing can change that. Nevertheless, I must honor my father's last wish. It is my duty." Renchi replies tears streaming down her face. Dauthi gently wipes her cheeks and holds her close to him.

Remy says "I will wait inside. You deserve some time alone. I must say I am sorry for any sorrow I have caused either of you."

Remy turns to leave and Dauthi grabs his shoulder. "Prince Remy." Dauthi says "I must be a fool, but I must say what is in my heart. I love this woman more than life itself. I beg of you not to let any harm befall her until I see her again."

"Prince Dauthi, you are my blood, my kin and probably much more. You are always welcome in my home as well as all the vampire, troll, dwarf and werewolf homes on this planet. You are a great warrior. We are in need of great warriors. I know we have differences, but who does not. The greater good should always come first for a warrior, always."

"That is true, my brother. You sound more like Vincenzo every time I hear you speak." Dauthi replies as Commander Sauer and his men approach. "Come with me to the tree, Prince Remy."

Commander Sauer stops in his tracks as he notices Dauthi's warriors surrounding Dauthi and Remy near the tree. Commander Sauer does not know what to do. He has sworn an oath to protect the Prince at all cost. However, what Dauthi does now is ceremonial. Commander Sauer cannot intervene and save face. Remy is alone on this one.

"Please kneel with me and give me your dagger."

Remy hands him his dagger and kneels.

Commander Sauer says to himself "Is he insane? Dauthi will kill him for sure. This has all been a trick to assassinate Remy. Nonetheless, before he can act Dauthi hands Remy his blade and kneels with him.

"My father had one teaching in life that has always stuck with me. He said, "When you are in the company of greatness, you must acknowledge it. My father could have been emperor but he knew that was not his path and I now know that is not the path of my family. You my Lord are a better being than I have met in centuries and I pledge my life to you." Dauthi says slitting his wrist with Remy's blade and raising it above his head.

"I accept you as my blood brother nothing more and nothing less. We are kin, not royalty and subject." Remy then slices his wrist with Dauthi's blade and presses it against Dauthi's wrist. All Dauthi knows Remy knows, but it is not the same for Dauthi. Their souls touch, yet all Dauthi receives is a blank sheet from Remy's mind. As if there were a great wall between Dauthi's mind and Remy's. They do bond on a feral level. Dauthi feels Remy's strength and knows a slight tinge of fear. He has never felt fear before, always sure of his abilities and prowess. Nonetheless, after not being able to see what is in Remy's soul and mind he wants no part of him as an enemy. All the warriors of both clans erupted into shouts.

"The clans are one again. The clans are one again."

All the years of hatred seem to flow away. Cousins turn to cousins and embrace one another. Commander Sauer is shocked. He falls to his knees and begins to pray to God. "My Lord, we are greatly blessed by him. You have united warring brothers and sisters once again. Not through death, but through the hope of life please hear an old tired man's pleas, let this be a great beginning and not the beginning of the end. Amen."

Commander Sauer walks over and bows before the two princes.

Dauthi takes one look at him, embraces him roughly, and says, "So many wasted centuries, father."

Remy is shocked as well as most of Dauthi's warriors.

"Dauthi, it was God's will. As it is now, what I have witnessed has warmed an old man's heart. I have always loved you and prayed for the day you would realize no matter what our differences that our family bonds are what truly mattered."

Dauthi steps back from his father more composed and says "I have pledged allegiance to the clans and Prince Remy, not yet to God. He must show us a little more before our faith in him is renewed."

"Fair enough." Says Commander Sauer to his son's surprise

Dauthi stares at his father in shock and says "Did you just say fair enough? No argument, I mean are you really my father?"

"Since meeting Remy I am not the same embittered man I was. He has a way of changing you without trying. A way of transforming you into what you should be, exciting but terrifying all at once, much like his predecessor Vincenzo."

"Yes, father he is much like him, but he is also much like Michael the archangel…"

Commander Sauer cuts him off looking at Remy and then back to him. He grabs Dauthi by his shoulder and walks a little away from the group and says "He has not been brought up in the clans. He has been brought up with humans to him Michael is a deity the ultimate embodiment of an angel. He is not yet ready to have himself mentioned in the same breath as the angels."

"But father he even has the scent of a celestial angel. We all remember the teachings and God said his chosen warrior would return to lead us against evil. My spies have told me Lucifer is part of the elves' plans. He would make a wasteland of this planet and then march into heaven after God. Remy has to be the one. He is the warrior prophet."

"I see your point. Nevertheless, Remy has only begun to learn how to live amongst us and to abide by the rules of God and clan. If he is the second coming of a Michael then so be it. Yet if he is not, it does not diminish who he is."

"Agreed father, it is time you and your warriors left."

"True, but we have a task to finish. We only destroyed the elven temple's engines. We must finish the job." Says Commander Sauer

"Allow me father. My warriors need a little exercise." Replies Dauthi with a smile. Commander Sauer looks at him with pride. His son has returned to his side God could not give him a better gift. He embraces him again and says "Raise our banner high as you expunge those devils from this world. The house of the hound lives again."

"I will father. See you soon." Says Dauthi signaling his men to leave.

From the house runs a little girl shouting "Mommy, Grandma

says we are going on a trip." Renchi grabs her up and kisses her looking at Remy. He looks back and she nods her head in the affirmative. The little girl looks at him with his own eyes and says "Mommy who is that? He is crying."

The tears run like water and the pain of not having a life of his own finally hits him dead in the chest. He will never live a normal existence and will probably die in the upcoming battle. But this little girl is so beautiful so full of life, a true reason to end this conflict.

"That is your father, Remiella. Go to him and greet him properly."

She jumps from her mother's hands and at a full run jumps into his and says "Grandma always said you would come. She told me never to say anything to mommy. You see I can keep a secret."

Samilo looks at him with tears in her eyes and bows. Remy bows back and squeezes his daughter tight and says "I have a daughter and she is so pretty. You look so much like your mother. God is good."

CHAPTER 16

"All that is in the light is not good and
all that is in darkness is not evil"

THE TRUMPET SOUNDS AS the council is called to order. All the leaders of the clans are present, much like the day when Vincenzo called them together to propose war against Lucifer and the elves. The only difference is that he is not present like so many others who died. Vincenzo died because someone from the clans told the elves where to find him and they used his greatest weakness against him. Vincenzo could never let an innocent be injured or killed. To this day, no one has been able to find that child to find out what really happened. Vincenzo's escort had been held up by other shape changers cutting him off for their trap. Warren the Werewolf King remembers that day as if it were yesterday. A day that should have been filled with rejoicing was filled with great sorrow. Warren feels his heart pumping again; hope springs anew with this new young Prince. God is good. He kept his promise and all the people of this planet will get a second chance at redemption. Warren never had a doubt in his mind.

Everyone is soon seated and Juzef stands up in the center of the council and says, "My brethren we have reached the crossroads. What we have waited for has arrived in the guise of Prince Remy. All of you have met him and wondered at his warmth and easygoing manner. You have all heard of his exploits in battle and seen his political cunning in person at the banquet in his honor. What I have to say today runs deeper then all these things. I have witnessed for myself that he has all the gifts of the first tribes and more. My brother taught him the ways of battle and war. The humans taught him about medicine and the use of machinery. His genes hold all of our secrets our strengths and of course our weaknesses. Life has sharpened him to a keen sharp edge, maybe a little too sharp. The fact he exists has forced the elven council's hands. They must now accelerate their timetable. Their element of surprise has been lost. I am sure you all can feel it on the spiritual plane. There are great rumblings. The elves think that their sanctuary keeps the dwarven counsel from feeling their contacts with the other planes of existence, but we know they have been in contact with Lucifer. Though war has not been declared, we must at least vote if they will be allowed at any of our functions after what happened at the ball. Raise your hand if you agree that we should ban them from all further functions."

Everyone in the room raises their hands almost in unison.

"Then it is agreed the Elves and their allies will not be allowed to attend any functions." Says Juzef.

"My Lords." Says King Warren. "We must also take into account that all the other tribes connected to the elves could be in slavery just like the trolls, I mean think about what they did to us?"

"You make a good point, King Warren." Answers Juzef.

Lord Tagom stands and says "While I hear what you have said, King Warren, I have to counsel great care in that thought process. The ogres and shape changers were created just for war. Not like the troll and human who had several tasks to perform. They only know war and I am sure have been chomping at the bit to create one. There is always a possibility they are slaves, but that is not how Grener the Ogre King and Sep the Shape Changer commander acted during the banquet. They quickly stood in front of Naline to protect him."

"While that may be true, I am only stating that we should keep it in mind." Replies Warren.

"Lord Tagom, where is Lord Dastor?" asks Juzef.

"He should be coming along presently. He told me he had business in Europe and would meet us here later." Replies Lord Tagom

"That is strange. What type of business would he have in Europe?" asks Lord Cratis of the vampire council. "I have never truly trusted Lord Dastor; he truly loved the hunting of humans and the draining of their blood."

"I can see your point, but he has worked with the vampiric council without incident for centuries and has promised us he gave up those ways." Says Lord Tagom

"You my friend are like my blood brother. If you say it is so, then it is." Replies Lord Cratis.

"Then let us discuss the plans for Prince Remy. Now that we have established that he is part of the prophesy we must create a strategy to prepare ourselves for impending war."

King Hozeer rises to speak "While we all know that Remy is the perfect instrument for God, we also know there are two others with the right blood."

Lord Krodert from the South American vampire tribes rises to be recognized. "Yes, this is true but neither of them can lead us in battle. Neither of them has Remy's presence. Yes, the blood is true however; their battle prowess does not exist. A warrior is what we need now, not philosophers. You all know as well as I, that God said Lucifer will lead them. Remy is our best chance to defeat Lucifer. That is the plain truth."

"He has done much for my tribe in a short time. His quick thinking prevent the death of thousands of my people." says King Hozeer "But we may be asking a little much from this young man."

"I do not agree. I have spent some time with Remy and he seems capable of doing whatever is needed. Or at least he would try. Only God could say if he is to be defeated or if he is to be victorious." Replies Juzef.

"We all must remember that the elves do have at least three pure bloods left. All of them have the power to bring a wraith across into this realm. This means three wraiths to battle. Lucifer of course is the most powerful, but I'm sure Daniel and Jakob will still be formidable warriors." Says Lord Krodert.

"Then having more than one being with the right bloodlines is a boon." Says Lord Tagom.

"With that I must agree." Says Lord Cratis.

"Then we must decide on a course of action. The survival of this world will depend on it." Replies Warren.

"There is only one course of action and we all know it, all out war with the elves. I will take both his brother and sister and train them the best I can. But as I said previously Remy is already a skilled warrior with all the gifts of the first tribes while his brother and sister seem to only have one or two gifts." Says Juzef.

"If it comes to that they will have to do. And we must be covert in our actions. We will build our forces and strengthen our strongholds. However, no overt actions at this present time. There is still six months to the nexus." Says Lord Krodert

There is a loud murmur of agreement throughout the room. A messenger enters the room and asks to be recognized. He wears the colors of the European and Asian tribes.

"Forgive this intrusion my, Lords. However, I bring joyous news. Prince Dauthi and Prince Remy have become blood brothers. The tribes are one again." The room burst forth in shouts. Juzef just smiles and says to himself "He is a wonder. Nevertheless, will it last? His greatest tests are at hand. Way before he battles Lucifer, he has to battle himself."

"There is more Milord." Says the messenger.

"Quiet everyone. There is more to the message." Says Juzef.

"Lord Dastor was a traitor and was dealt with by Prince Dauthi himself. He was planning to marry the Queen to Prince Dauthi in return for power."

"How could this be?" exclaims Lord Krodert.

"It is why we always must be careful." Says King Warren "Lucifer evil has no bounds and can reach into anyone's heart, anyone's."

It seems Ejam and Renchi have become fast friends. I guess living a cloaked existence gives them a feeling of simpatico thinks Remy to himself smiling. That is good because he really does love both women. What all have forgotten except Samilo is that Remy had planned to marry Renchi after he graduated school. Closing his eyes he reaches back for the memories of that day.

"Master, I must ask you a boon." Remy said bowing before Efisio
"Yes, my son. What is it you wish to ask?"
"I know I leave for the academy in a week, however, I would like to ask if Renchi can be my wife when I return."
"Well, my son. That will be up to Renchi. I am her father but not her keeper. While we live in Japan and I adhere to the customs here, you will understand one day that we adhere to a different set of customs."
"You have always said that Sensei. Would you explain a little further please?"
"You my son are far from an orphan. You belong to the first clans of this earth. It is not the time for all to be explained to you. But know you are meant for incredible deeds."
"Another question, Sensei?"
"Yes., my son."
"Why have you always trained me with two short swords instead of the katana?"
"Because while you are proficient with the katana, you needed to master the double short swords because they will one day be your weapon of choice. Enough of this talk, go find Renchi, my son." He said smiling.

That night Remy went to Renchi and said "Come walk with me in the garden."

With a smile that seemed to light up the room, she replied, "It would be my honor."

It was a beautiful august night and the view from atop the mountain was breathtaking. They walked and talked of so many things and they soon arrived at the school. She took my hand and led me inside locking the door behind her. We sat across from each other looking directly into each other's eyes for the first time alone.

"Renchi, I have asked your father for your hand in marriage. He told me I must ask you."

"My father is wise not to make a decision for me. I am not an easy daughter for him in Japan. I bring too many of the old ways from where we use to live."

"I had thought you were brought up in Japan."

"No, we came to Japan five years ago. It is what angered my brother more than anything else did. He enjoyed living in the United States. It was all he could talk about from the time we arrived."

"So that is why he wanted so badly to be in the exchange program."

"Probably, but tonight is not about the past or about my brother. It is about us."

She says caressing his brow bringing to the surface feelings that Remy had never felt before. The love they made that night transcended anyone he had ever been with. They made love every day before he left. That was nine years ago. Remy now realizes Efisio and his family were part of the Mongolian dwarf tribe. The child was gestated in three months. They never told him, once again to protect him. So no one could use his loved ones against him.

Remiella is lying on his chest as if she had always been there. He is just enjoying her rhythmic breathing and the puffs of sweet air emitting from her small perfect lips. She is so at peace as she sleeps. He remembers how happy she had been to finally meet him. No, anger no questions just unconditional love of a child for a parent. The strange part is how easily everyone around him has taken it has taken it. Commander Sauer actually playing with Remiella and making jokes with her. Ejam and Renchi both were beaming over her as if she were the most precious thing in both their lives. Renchi had told him she had no remorse. It was not his fault those two months after he had left her brother had betrayed them. Full of child she had told her father she would stand and fight. That night is all she can remember because he placed blocks in her mind and made his wife promise to leave and not tell him where they had gone. It was not until she had some time to think that he now realizes why her father did what he did. She had never understood why her mother had asked her to name the child Remiella until now. Renchi had thanked him for Remiella. Remy smoothes her black curly hair away from her beautiful little face and kisses her brow and thinks, "No, thank all of you for what you have done for me."

Kiree lands near the dwarven camp and is met at the plane by Remy's brother Dane. As she walks out of the plane her head begins to whirl and she feel nauseous. She falls to her knees and almost passes out in the snow. Dane reaches out to her and his touch sends both of them reeling.

Breathlessly he says" Who are you, milady. I feel like I have known you all my life."

"My name is Kiree." She replies staring into his eyes as he helps her up.

"Kiree, what a beautiful name for such an extraordinarily beautiful woman, Are you all right?"Dane says wrapping her in a warm woolen blanket.

"I am now. What is your name?"

"My name is Dane. I am part of the tribes here and you are surely welcome."

"Welcome indeed." They are afraid to let go of each other's hands. Hoping the feeling of completeness will not end. It is as if they are the only people on earth.

Smiling Treva intercedes "Folks we will surely freeze to death if we let you two continue stand out here in this weather."

"I am sorry mother. Please we have a car waiting." Dane says looking directly into her eyes.

"A car you say? Waiting, oh I am sorry. I just cannot focus." Kiree says staring back into his eyes.

"Ok, listen up. I know meeting your life-mate is a great event, but neither of you will be leaving each other anytime soon." Treva says separating them "Now get in the car." She says laughing.

Both of them come back to reality as their contact breaks and ashamed they get into the car.

Once inside they entwine their fingers again and feel complete.

"Are you all right, my dear? They did not torture you at all did they?" Treva asks

'No Milady. They only asked me some questions. They did however torture my mother."

"I am sorry that happened to you and to her. It must have been hard for you to witness that."

"It was difficult to see what they had done to her. But I know the Prince will enact vengeance upon them soon enough."

"How are you feeling?"

Well Milady, I must say I have never felt this good in all my life." Kiree replies looking at Dane who can't take his eyes off her.

"I bet. Don't worry we will be at the compound soon and you two can get to know each other better?"

"That would be wonderful mother." Replies Dane

"This might be one of the worst cases of life-mating I have ever witnessed." Says Treva

"There must be something augmenting this mating. I know. Kiree are you pregnant by chance."

"Yes, Milady." She answers embarrassed to say so in front of Dane.

"Do we know the father, my dear? It is a joy that there will be another strong child for the tribes. You know we hold no rancor against anyone carrying a child. You know our ways never an orphan always a child of the clan."

"The father is Prince Remy, Milady."

"The prince, I see."

"Does that change anything, Dane?"

"No, mother is right any child is a gift to the clan, Kiree, I could not care more for you." Says Dane smiling

"So it does not matter that I carry a child for the prince."

"We will raise it together in love, our love." He replies kissing her deeply.

"Well that keeps everything in the family. Alright like I said we will be at the compound soon." Says Treva to herself turning to the driver."You better step on it or this back seat will be in flames.

"Treva, this is highly unusual. Both my sons are involved with this woman. One is the father of her child and the other is her life mate."

"Oh give it a break, dear. You know the tribes accept all children and this child's bloodlines are true."

Smiling Dewa says "You are really enjoying this aren't you."

"A grandchild is a grandchild. I am sure there are others I haven't met yet and they will all be welcome. The council has controlled our every thought and move because of our bloodlines. This proves those bloodlines have a life of their own. God is in control as always."

"I love you."

"You better. I know the rules of the tribe but you are my man. Got it." she says smirking

"I would not want anyone else." He suddenly falls forward with an ear piercing scream.

"I knew those blocks were becoming weaker." Treva says grabbing his head and concentrating. Into the room rushes five of the dwarven guard.

"What has happened, Milady?"

"Quickly we must get him to the elders' pavilion. We don't have much time." They pick him up and rush towards the pavilion as others call the elders. Everyone is assembled by the time he is placed on the ceremonial table. After a quick evaluation Juzef says "You must choose now, he does not have much time. You know we have to mind wipe him completely this time, we no longer can hold the blocks in place. The serum his father created is true but he will lose any gift he had from each clan, elf or vampire. The only thing is we have no idea if he will remember anything. He will be just a blank sheet. He will remember none of us."

"Just save him. I knew this day was coming. I am prepared."

"Alright, come let us do this as one." They all surround him and begin humming.

Dewa begins to convulse and the dwarven guard hold him down. Soon it is done and the elders fall back into chairs exhausted.

Dewa stirs and sits up. Treva is quickly by his side. "How are you?"

"I feel like I have been awakened from a dream, milady. Where am I?"

"You are amongst friends."

"I think I should know you, but I cannot remember."

"Well I guess that will give you time to get to know all of us better."

"I would like that dear lady. I would like that very much."

"So would I." Says Treva tears in her eyes.

"Have I wronged you good lady. I did not mean to upset you."

"I am not upset. I am relieved that you are well."

"Was I ill or injured?"

"In a way, My Lord, In a way."

"Dewa, I am Juzef. I am the eldest elder of this tribe." Juzef says extending his hand.

Dewa takes his hand and has information placed in his mind about the tribes by Juzef.

"Now please take Lady Treva's hand."

"Is that her name? Treva it rolls off my tongue so well." Dewa says taking her hand and all of a sudden he needs her more than anything in the world. His eyes widen and his breath comes in short gulps. It's almost like drowning in a person. "Milady, I don't know you, but I love you. Touching you makes me feel complete. Where ever I have been I thank you from returning me from the brink.""

Treva embraces him tightly tears streaming down her face feeling the life mate link as strong as ever and just keeps saying "Thank you, God."

After they have left the elders of the council look at Juzef with stern glances.

"They have given so much for the cause. I don't regret gifting them this."

"You know you have broken our code. You cannot mind wipe a person and then give them made up memories. They must relearn on their own." Says Grewen the second elder.

"Furthermore, you can't make them fake life mating. It is unfair and cruel."

Juzef begins to laugh aloud.

"What are you laughing about?" asks Werth the third elder.

"All I gave him were memories of the camp and the tribe. I guessed that God would not be cruel and as always he proved me right."

"Are you saying they life mated even after the mind wipe." Says Grewen "That is impossible."

"That's why God makes the impossible possible. Enough we should be grateful we did not lose him. It would not do for Remy to have another thing to worry about."

"You are right. Thanks be to God."

"But what of Kiree and her child?" says Juzef

"The child will of course be protected and the blood taken to see if we can create a serum that will prevent others from becoming mad and dying."

"These times are both exciting and perilous. You know if the elves can they will try to steal that child."

"That is true. But there is another." Says Werth smiling.

"He is right Efisio's daughter also gave birth to a child for Remy. The reports say it is a female." Replies Juzef

"So the Lord has created many avenues for the prophecy to be fulfilled." Says Grewen.

"You all know revelation is at hand. While it may not be the time for Jesus to return, it is time for the Lord to pave the way for his entrance. To battle Lucifer will be bad enough. The final confrontation comes quickly." Replies Werth

"But we will be ready brethren. For we have followed his word and protected his people. All we need do is to continue to believe in him and heaven waits. Just not quite yet." Says Juzef

"Well come brothers. Let us retire it has been a long spring and winter approaches quickly without a fall."

CHAPTER 17

"And there came before my face another spirit,
as it were a woman in the form she had"

NALINE HAD NOT KNOWN Ene was a fallen angel until Lucifer educated him about that fact much later. Naline was told that without those demons controlling her she would want nothing to with him. Naline thought her to be one of the humans his people had created. He hated the fact that he was unable to personally feel her celestial aura and that he had actually copulated with the demons within her and not her truly. Nonetheless, this did not change how he felt for her or the desire he had for her. But Lucifer was right in her right mind without the demons she would not continence any show of weakness from him or any other male. She like Lucifer had been angry at Jesus for not praying to God to send his angels to protect. All of the fallen would have rallied to his cry from hell and from heaven. However, Jesus had accepted that he was the Lamb of God and was to die for the humans' redemption from the curse of sin. By giving his life in such away he opened the door for the humans at death to heaven. All they need do was to accept him into their lives completely and their name was in the book of books. All of the first tribes had their names in the book of books in the beginning. They all were blindly following God and were about only his business. That was until the elves decided they were greater than even God and their names were forever removed from the book of books until they asked for his forgiveness. Had they not created life for him? Had they not proven to be his greatest creations? But he turned his gaze from them to the pitiful creature they created. "Made in his image, what a joke". Naline thought to himself. The angels and the elves were made in his image and God had cast out his most beautiful creations. God cast out Lucifer who was the most beautiful of all and he allowed Jesus to bind him to this world. For it is written that Jesus was sent to hell upon his death and defeated Lucifer and took the keys to hell taking upon him all of mankind's sins. Lucifer soon came to the elves with a plan. He spoke of all the fallen angels at his beck and call. He spoke of defeating first God's favorite child and the other first tribes before marching on heaven itself. God in anger allowed the other tribes to defeat us both. Vincenzo was the driving force of our defeat. He followed God's word to the letter. He even helped Gabriel and Michael to banish Lucifer and his followers to another plane of existence. Vincenzo was God's greatest general on earth. But Vincenzo was no more and this pup, Remy would soon learn to respect his elders. Naline enters the chamber as the ritual begins. Before Naline, Torm, Tre and Werg the last great Elven elders is Lucifer conjuring a wicked spell. Lucifer draws runes in the earth and consecrates them with a maiden's blood. Soon it is as if time is going backwards in his world. Instead of dawn to dusk it is dusk till dawn until he has forced time back to the nexus. Great beads of sweat roll off his body and his muscles are pulled taunt as he holds sway over time.

"Naline it is time I will only be able to hold this for a few moments. When I bring my sister through you three must pluck her from this plane and bring her to yours."

"My lord, I can do that alone."

"You are so full of yourself, Naline. Just do as I say without question or she will die horribly. All of you will be required. It is the power of the unholy trinity that will allow my sister to return to your plane of existence."

Naline snaps his mouth shut at the thought of harm coming to her. Lucifer smiles to himself and thinks "You really are a fool. This will also teach me if God has placed any other blocks or traps in the way. My sister is actually my guinea pig." Lucifer thinks to himself aloud he says "Be ready she is coming." The temple is a blaze with activity. Staff members are running back and forth as quickly as possible. Today a wraith will be brought through to this plane. All the seals on the temple have been double checked and all hope that the coming will not be felt strongly across the spiritual plane. The amount of spiritual energy used will be enormous. Like a birth when a woman's membranes burst and the child flows into the world. With its first cry shrill and loud that fills the room and lets everyone near know they have arrived. Naline is the most unnerved. From the moment Lucifer had told Naline that he could turn back time in his realm to the nexus and free his sister Naline has not eaten or slept. Ene, short for the fallen angel Enepsigos, had been a myriad of women with a myriad of names over the existence of time. She was one of the fallen angels spoken about in the book of Solomon in the Old Testament of the bible. Ene was not always a fallen angel. She had been a general of the Hellenic Angelic host. One of its greatest warriors, but she chose to follow Lucifer after his fall from grace and in so doing was possessed by demons who enjoyed perverting her. She had carried many names during her existence on earth. The name that carried the most meaning for Naline was Mary Magdalene the most important female disciple of Jesus. Naline knew full well that Jesus had cast out the demons that had held sway over her after her fall from grace. He cleansed her body and her soul and in so doing created a bond that could never be broken. She had been Naline's mistress up until the time she had met Jesus. How he hated Jesus for that and that was the main reason he assisted the humans to kill him. None of the first tribes knew of God's plans of allowing his son to die for mankind's sins. But the angelic host did know those plans and some who disagreed became the fallen and chose to follow Lucifer. Lucifer had convinced them that God once again was placing man above angel. They did not realize that Jesus was the most obedient of sons and only would do his father's will.

Materializing before him is the form of a woman. A form Naline can never forget. He begins to concentrate with the others to bring her across into this plane. After mere moments Naline realizes he could have never brought her across himself. His pride once again could have led all to ruin.

Lucifer shouts "I will push her towards your plane as you pull. It should be enough to get her through." There is a great flash and Ene is kneeling before them completely naked. The priestesses quickly cover her with an emerald green gown and place on her feet satin green slippers. Ene stands regally and her essence fills the chamber. She has long straight raven black hair and a slight almond shape to her light brown eyes. Her skin is the color of cream with a hint of sun kissed cinnamon. She is small breasted with an athletic medium build. She stands about five foot nine inches tall.

"Why have you brought me here Naline?" she says pushing the priestesses aside.

"It was not his doing." Says Lucifer behind her in his deep malevolent voice. He has already settled into his throne and is sipping from a goblet of wine looking at her.

"You brought me to this plane. That is impossible. You are not even on this plane"

"As you know my dear sister I am quite resourceful when I need be. I brought you to my plane and the elves plucked you to theirs. But what does that matter. You are free."

"Free to do what, Lucifer. I was given forgiveness for my discretions against the Most High. I fell on my knees and prayed to him in my dimension and I know he has forgiven me."

"Really? You think he would forgive a wraith who stormed heaven and who has slain celestials and humans alike for the cause."

"Of course I do. You know as well as I that if you had not been so vain and incapable of being forgiven that he would have forgiven you as well."

"I do not want his forgiveness. I want his and Jesus' head on a pike. "Lucifer feels his temper taking over and takes a deep breath. He had not expected Ene to have renewed her vows with God. He thought she would still hate him for what he put Jesus through. He must use a different tact.

"Lucifer, all you have to do is let him into your heart. Remember how it was before humankind."

"Yes I do. We were his favorites. We were all he needed. Then the elves decided to create humankind and God breathe life into them in his own image." Says Lucifer aloud, but to himself "Something that they will pay for all of eternity. They will be tortured by his minions a hundred times and then again. Their screams will be music to his ears."

"Yes, but you know as well as I nothing happens without his blessing. The humans already existed in God's mind in a likeness akin to him. It was the elves that chose to create them as a food source going against God's wishes and then you tricked them into disobeying God, Jesus was sent to die for their sins."

"Believe me Ene; I know the story quite well. But the Lord has done it again."

The elves are astonished that Lucifer is not beside himself with anger at Ene's reaction. Naline is livid at her statements. She should be banished back to the domain she came from. To ask forgiveness from that charlatan was ludicrous. How could he have loved such a weak minded fool?

"What has the Lord done again?" Ene asks with a twinkle in her eye Lucifer knows all too well. She was of course a woman with certain needs.

"He has created another one step below Jesus. A being whom has the blood of all tribes running through his veins a celestial on earth."

"You lie. You are the prince of lies. You talked me into going to war against my God for the love of a man I was not destined to have. But you made it sound as if he would be mine all that time I followed him. You whispered in my ears day and night that one day we would be together and you lied to get me to join your war. Well I fought your war and killed a countless amount of innocents. I will not do so again, Lucifer. Not again."

"Have I once made a comment about war? Naline, Torm, Werg did I say anything about war?"

"No Milord." They say in unison.

"Then what do you speak of Lucifer?"

"I just bear information you can act on yourself nothing more and nothing less." Lucifer answers with joy in his heart. He feels her softening and he hopes the three idiots don't blow it by exploding.

"I have learnt to live peacefully on my plane. I have ministered to the sick and injured. I have preached the good Lord's word. I have done all this and I have asked for no tribute. I have used none of my God given powers in battle or to create a following. You have obviously taken a different route. Again I beseech you Lucifer. Reach your hand out to him and he will take it."

Lucifer's eyes started to glow and his breath becomes short, but he holds fast to reason and takes another sip of his wine before answering. He also feels the elves change of attitude about her and feels the pure hatred that now is present in the room. What wonderful pawns they were in this game.

"Again I must refuse. I am not ready to bow before our father. I am the wayward child. I am the demon seed. However, I enjoy those mantles at present. If you don't believe me use your spiritual power yourself and feel this newcomer's presence. Find out for yourself if I lie."

"I will." Says Ene moving her consciousness to the spiritual plane where she is met full faced by Remy's aura. She is shocked at the purity of his spirit. He is without a doubt the closest to Jesus as a man than any spirit she has ever felt. Except she knows he felt her presence. Ene quickly shuts down her consciousness, but finds Remy still there with his hands out towards her beckoning. She again forces herself to return to the present, however, no one has ever pulled her back to the spiritual realm. This indeed was a powerful man.

Lucifer smiles to himself. He too could feel Remy's aura even on his plane. This was not a being to be trifled with God had done his work well as always. Though Lucifer knows it could not have been done, he wishes the elves had killed him while he thought of himself as human. But this might play out much better and of course so much more fun.

"You are right this time, Lucifer." She replies still shaken by the contact with Remy. "But he will never bow to the will of you or your accomplices here. He is pure of mind, body and spirit an innocent in all ways."

"Why must you always think in that manner about me? He has already sworn to protect all including the humans. In fact, he has already made the elves in this room regret not killing him while they had the chance. Is that not right gentlemen?"

"Absolutely, I truly cannot wait till he lies under my dripping sword. He has insulted us and killed many of our loyal subjects and he will pay with his life prophecy or no prophecy." Spits Naline.

"Oh please Naline. This is not a willing sacrifice like the poor human carpenter that was born in Bethlehem. Not a teacher, healer and peaceful being. This being holds within him the power of destruction given to the arch angels. Do not delude yourselves. This is no ordinary adversary. Even you brother would have difficulty with this one. Do you remember when Jesus died on the cross and he spent three days wreaking havoc on hell. Finally throwing you about like a rag doll. It was amazing how our father allowed him to become his greatest warrior to atone for mankind's sins. Yet that calm, peaceful loving man turned your realm upside down and stole the keys to your gates. Is that why you hate God so much? Was it because he allowed Jesus to sin in his name and best you in combat."

Lucifer is seething now. His nostrils flaring his eyes coal black his chest heaving with hate for God and for Jesus. But once again he restrains himself and takes another sip of his wine smiling a toothy smile.

"Ene, that is in the past. What has been done is done. I know I have great sins to atone for to the father. But I admit I am not ready to do so. You have and I accept that."

"This has gone quite far enough, Milord. I will not countenance this any further. Enespigo, if you have changed sides then you are not welcome here. You cannot have our protection or our loyalty. You are no better than that Hellenic scum we fought against side by side." Says Naline no longer able to control his anger.

"Do you dare intimate that I even need either your loyalty or protection, dog? Just because I have chosen to be forgiven by the father does not change that I am one of the first fallen angels and one of the Hellenic tribe's greatest warriors. Do not mistake my accepting the Lord as my father again as a sign of weakness. I will strike down all who attempt to hurt him or his chosen." Says Ene looking directly at him.

"Enough, Naline, she has asked and has been given forgiveness by the all father. Let it be."

Naline is quite befuddled by Lucifer's reactions to Ene's statements. But looking directly at him he hears Lucifer's voice clearly in his head. "If you do not control yourself I will have you castrated and drawn and quartered. Follow my lead and do as you are told fool."

"Yes, Milord." Naline says aloud.

"I am not a man you idiot." Says Ene

"I apologize, Milady. I have been quite disrespectful. I shall not continue in that vein."

"What do you want from me Lucifer?"

"I want you to live your life as you chose. You have given much to the cause that cannot be denied."

"I was never your slave Lucifer. I allowed those demons to possess me because I had lost contact with the father. When Jesus freed me it was miraculous. I felt the father's love again and did not understand his plan to allow Jesus to die for mankind's sins. Sin you created in the garden. Sin you perpetuated on this earth. You are always battling for souls against our father."

"Well you can't blame a guy for trying. He did give them freedom of choice. Why not chose me."

"That's the kind of thinking that got you kicked out of heaven in the first place."

"Let's just sat I am an entrepreneur. Free will you know."

Naline and the elven elders are furious. How can Lucifer joke with her when their existence is at stake? What sick game is he playing?

"Naline." Lucifer says stirring him out of his thoughts.

"Yes, my lord."

"I would like you to have Ene taken to New York by one of your ships."

"Yes, milord."

"Good then it is settle. Ene will be given clothes, money and will stay at your suite at the Waldorf."

"In my suite, Milord. I am sure I can make better accommodations for her elsewhere."

"No I think that will be just fine, Lucifer. I hear New York is a wonderful place. I have never been there in person. A fresh new start." Says Ene with intrigue in her voice.

"Make it so Naline. Goodbye Ene I hope we do not meet on the battlefield."

"That is for only God to know. Goodbye Lucifer I will always love you as a brother." Ene replies as she follows some of the handmaidens out.

The elders turn to leave and Lucifer says "Where are you three going?"

"It seems clear what your will is milord. We will carry it out." Says Torm

"What seems clear?"

"That we are to release the lady in New York in Naline's suites with money and clothes." Replies Werg

"You idiots. The plan is to get her to cross Remy's path. The Haxe building is a few blocks from your hotel suite Naline. She will be drawn to his aura like a moth to a flame. Maybe just maybe she will be his life mate and we will soon have a child to mold."

"That is impossible. Ene cannot conceive." Says Werg

"Oh but she can now that she is a wraith. In her current form she can be impregnated. She took a vow of celibacy in her realm as a punishment for her deeds against God. Which is exactly why I want her watched and subtly prevented from engaging in sexual activity with anyone before they cross paths? She is so fertile a drop of semen would impregnate her."

"So you lied to her and allowed us to become visibly angry to complete the deceit." Says Naline.

"Of course you fool. I had to convince her that I had no plans in relation to using her for my own gains." Lucifer says sitting back on his throne and sipping his wine eyeing them.

"You truly are the prince of lies." Replies Werg.

"Soon to be emperor of the earth."

CHAPTER 18

"Forgiveness has a price."

WHEN THEY FINALLY UNWRAP themselves from each other they are totally spent. They have just made love all night long and still they hunger for one another. Dane leans up on his elbow and strokes Kiree's back enjoying the texture of her skin. So smooth and soft, but almost like touching fire, the heat pulsating from her skin. It feels good to be loved and to love completely.

"Where have you been all my life." he whispers in her ear kissing it softly.

"I could most definitely ask you the same question, my love."

"Destiny is sometimes quite cruel. God's wishes are his and happen in his time frame. Not ours."

"God is in all and in all we do. There is always a purpose for everything in life." Kiree replies smiling.

"Ah but a life without purpose is a waste. You have given me purpose and definition at the same time. It is like I was stumbling in the dark and have now stepped into the true brilliance of what it is to live and love." Dane says kissing her hand.

"Does it matter that I carry your brother's child?" she says looking into his eyes.

"My brother? Who is my brother?"

It suddenly dawns on her that he did not know Remy was his

brother. "Oh my God. You did not know Prince Remy was your brother. I am so sorry."

"The prince is my brother? From what I have heard of him I now realize he also has no idea he is my brother. He would have hunted my sister and I down. He my love is a man of honor. What a web my parents and the counsel have woven. For what end I have no idea." He says moving to the edge of the bed to sit.

Kiree moves up behind him and nozzles into his neck. "You did not answer my question, my love. Does it matter?"

Dane turns to allow her to lie across his lap and replies "Of course it does not matter. I have been in a tribe that has had ten to twelve children a year. A child and of course a royal child with the blood of all the tribes is a gift from God himself. I carry no jealousy for my brother. You are my life mate. We have bonded and neither of us will want another as long as we live. I thank God for that. I was an empty vessel and now I am full."

"Then why so suddenly pensive?"

"I am pensive because the council does nothing without reason and they had no idea I was your life mate, for if they did they would not have let us meet. It puzzles me why my parents did not tell Shara or I about our brother." He gets up laying her softly on the bed and starts putting on his clothes.

"Where are you going?"

"I go to speak to my mother and father. There is much I need to ask before my brother returns." He kisses her gently on her lips and says "I will not be long." And walks down the corridor to his parents' chambers and knocks on the door.

Dewa opens the door with a surprised look upon his face and says "Can I help you?"

Dane looks at his father with a puzzled look and replies "Are you alright father?"

In the most honest of tones Dewa says "Why thank you young man for honoring me in that way. But have we met?"

234

"Father, you are frightening me with your words. Where is mother?"

"Young man I have no need to frighten you. If it is Treva you wish to speak to I will get her for you. Please have a seat." And Dewa heads towards the kitchen to fetch Treva.

Dane sits and scratches his head. "What the hell is going on around here?"

Treva rushes in and says "Dane, my son I have much to tell you."

"I do agree, what is going on with father?"

"Dewa could you come in here for a moment please?"

"Yes my love. Be right there." He calls out. When he arrives Treva gestures for him to sit next to her.

"Please everyone clasp hands." Reluctantly, Dewa takes her hand and Dane's hand. Within an instant they are connected mentally. Treva quickly explains to both of them what has transpired. Dewa's memories are strengthened and Dane now knows the horrible existence his father has lived and why.

Both Dane and Dewa are moved to tears. Treva lets them both go and they embrace.

"To have lost you for even a moment was too long my son. I will never lose any of my family again." Dewa says.

"Dane, why are you here? I did not think you could leave Kiree for a second."

"Well Mother, I came to ask about my brother?"

Treva sighs and clasp her husband's hand tight and says "I guess it is time for them to know."

Dewa shakes head and replies "It is God's will."

"Dane your older brother was placed on a path because of a prophesy most of our people have forgotten, a prophecy given to us by God through King Vincenzo. It spoke of a special child of all bloods who would protect the earth from Lucifer and his minions. Juzef and Efisio promised to protect and teach that child. That child is your brother Remy, Prince to all the tribes including the Elves."

"Mother, how could that be we are taught that such a child would perish before maturity?"

"That is true my son. However, all of you are alive and well past puberty. It is Gods will and should not be questioned or tested. All of you carry the blood of the four tribes. It was Remy that revealed no magical traits but had an affinity for battle. The prophecy stated he would be a warrior first."

"Father, this is incredible. I have a brother I have never met. Will the council allow us to meet?"

"I do not see why not. We will not be able to hide you from one another much longer." says Dewa with a smile.

"What of your life mate?" says Treva

"She is my life mate. What transpired before the coupling does not matter to her or I. We are for each other."

"That is good to hear my son." Says Treva stroking his cheek.

"Where is Shara? She will positively burst with joy at this news." Says Dane.

"You think so?" asks Dewa

"Oh, I know so. She got to get a glimpse of the Prince and rattled on about how handsome he was. How if she had a chance she would sweep him off his feet. She even made fun of Princess Ejamine."

"Please do not tell your brother that. He is a very serious man. While kind hearted I do not think he is too good at joking." Replies Dewa "He has had a hard life and it has hardened him somewhat."

"He will be arriving within the hour. However, you need to take your life mate before the council. They are ready to give their blessing to the two of you. We will meet the both of you in their chambers in a half hours time."

"I will get Kiree and see you there." He says almost running out of the room.

Dewa turns to his wife and stares deeply into her eyes and says "Will the council punish you for what you have given me?"

"Given you? What are you talking about?" she says taking both hands in hers.

"You have given me my memories and life back. Isn't that against the law of the tribe?"

"But not against God's will. Our family has given so much for the cause. I have lost my life mate and he was given back not by the council but by the Lord Almighty. If there is a price to pay I will gladly pay it, my love a hundred times over. Come let's ready ourselves for the blessing. Stop thinking of the past and enjoy this gift called the present."

Dane arrives to find Kiree in the shower. It takes all his reserve to stop him from joining her. He stands outside the door and says "Kiree we have been summoned before the council for a blessing. Has anyone cleared your mind?"

"What? I cannot hear you over the water. Come in."

Dane goes into the bathroom and looks at her while she finishes and begins to dry off. He is amazed at her grace and beauty. God is so good he thinks to himself.

"What did you say?" she replies kissing him full on the lips.

"How can I have a coherent thought when you kiss me like that? It's not fair."

"Well we could always be late for the council." She says seductively touching his chest.

"Babe we have to stay focused. This will not take long. Now has anyone checked your mind since you came back from being with the Elves."

"I do not know what you mean?"

"When you were with elves did anyone touch your mind?"

"Yes, one of the elves told me they were extracting information. I told them I did not know anything, but they did not care. They told me they would spare my mother if I let them extract the information."

"Really, they must have a half breed dwarf. That is the only one who could do that. Well I will have to check before you go before the council. I cannot take a chance that they put a suggestion in there."

"What type of suggestion?"

"There are many they could plant. Some suggestions are to kill.

Others could be to get information and send it back to them." Dane says looking visibly nervous.

Kiree's warrior sense begins to quiver in her belly. "What is wrong, babe?"

"It's never good when you let someone walk in your mind, especially, someone who worships Lucifer. There are no bounds with them everything and anything is game."

"So, what do we do?"

Remy's plane is coasting to a halt on the runway not far from the settlement in Canada. His daughter has never seen snow and is incredibly excited. Remiella cannot control herself. Remy smiles and says "Relax, little one. You have a large family to meet."

"I have never seen snow before father. It is so pretty."

"Yes, it is." He replies rolling the word father being applied to him in his mind. Less than eight hours ago he did not even know he had a daughter. Within that time, he has become quite attached to this bundle of energy. He never thought he would live long enough to feel the pride he feels right now. Remy is broken from his reverie by Ejam.

"She is beautiful." She says

"Yes, she is. A miraculous sight. Never thought I would be a father. Thought I would be dead by now. God is good."

Stepping in front of him and placing her arms around his waist pulling him close she says "Yes, he is Remy. You soon will have more children."

"How is that?"

"Well first Kiree is expecting your child."

"Your joking. We spent one evening together."

"Well it really doesn't take much more than that you know." She says looking directly into his eyes smiling.

Remy smiles back and then stops and says, "Are you saying?"

"Yes, I am saying." She replies biting her lip.

Remy lifts her off the ground and spins her in the middle of the plane.

Commander Sauer asks, "What is he so happy about?"

"I guess she told him she is with child." Replies Renchi with a huge smile on her face. "At least a little happiness. He will have much pain. Responsibility for others always ends in great pain."

"No doubt young lady. No doubt. Come I think I have a parka small enough for Remiella and I have one for you. Time for a new life."

As they disembark Remy sees a young girl next to his parents who are waiting for him. He gets a tingling in his head and hears her voice. "Hello, brother."

"Well hello sister." He answers back without speaking

"So, you do have dwarven gifts."

"Of course. Now get over here you little cub." Remy says aloud as the run to each other. She jumps directly into his arms and buries her face in his chest. "My big brother."

"Yes, Shara your big brother."

'You know your kind of cute. If you weren't my brother who knows." She says stepping back

"I think my wife would have a word to say about that." he says pointing to Ejam who has apparently told his mother and father who are hugging and kissing her.

"I ain't scared of her." Shara says with a teenager's swagger.

"I bet your not. But let's not find out who would win. I see your werewolf side showing."

Shara emits a loud growl.

"You are fierce."

Suddenly a loud shriek is heard throughout the settlement.

"Oh my God no." shouts Treva as they all run towards the sound.

Laying in Kiree's arms is Dane. He is foaming at the mouth with a blank look in his eyes. Remy checks his pulse and he is alive. Kiree is hysterical.

Treva says "Talk to me Kiree. What happened?"

"he... he said he just needed to check my mind for suggestions placed there by the elves. Then he screamed and fainted."

Dane finds himself standing in the mountains in the night and he turns to see a pair of yellow feral eyes coming at him. Out walks a seven foot a being with a horse's head and a werewolf's body. In a malevolent deep voice he says "So you are the child of the prophecy. I am not impressed. What I have heard of your battle prowess does not match what I see."

"What did you call me demon."

"Do not call me demon, half-breed. My name is Tikbalang and I was sent to tear you limb from limb." he replies slashing at Dane. As his claws almost reach Dane's face they slam into a solid wall. "What? You can create a shield around yourself." His eyes widen with recognition. 'You are not the weapon, you are the shield. No matter I know that was just instinct. I will soon smash through your petty shield and your entrails will soon be in my hands."

There is a piercing red light and a sword cuts off one of Tikbalang's arms at the elbow. He falls back grabbing his pumping stump and says "How?"

Standing before him is Remy twirling his blade. "We are twins. Now that I am blessed what he feels I feel on all planes."

Tikbalang replies "You are all they said you would be. It does not matter I can wait until the shield is alone. You cannot stay here long."

"But I can end you now, demon." Remy says charging forward and runs into smoke.

From the void Tikbalang says "I can wait. I have all the time in the world weapon. The shield is trapped here until he can save himself. It is the way of things."

Dane looks at Remy and sees his face on a body twice the size of his body density. "You could only be Prince Remy. Thank you for coming to my aid brother."

"I did not know I had a brother till now. That is amazing but to have a twin is beyond comprehension." Remy says embracing his brother.

Dane is overwhelmed by his touch. To the point that he falls almost limp in Remy's arm. The energy coming from his brother is awe-inspiring. "You are so powerful brother."

"We must find a place you will be safe until you can get strong enough to escape back to the earthly plane." He looks and sees a cave in the distance. "And I think I have found just the place."

They head up to the cave and find that the mouth is about three feet by three feet. Remy could not even think of getting into the cave, but Dane could easily wiggle in.

"You must go into the cave. It is your only chance. I will cover the opening with one of these boulders. I already feel the tug back to the earthly realm, so we must hurry."

'Brother, I have life-mated with Kiree. Please protect her." Dane says grabbing his arm.

"Then she is family and automatically under my protection. Now get in the cave."

"She is carrying your child," he says climbing into the cave.

Remy replies "I know." And he seals the cave with a large stone. "Dane, you must strengthen yourself to escape this world. Remember your training and hewn your skills I will need you in the coming conflict. I can stay no longer in this realm. Take care."

Treva touches Dane's head and tries to enter his mind to find a mind trap has been set. She quickly backs out. "They placed a mind trap set to catch our DNA. It was probably set for you Remy."

"What the hell is a mind trap?" asks Ejamine

"It is a mental snare placed in an innocent person's mind set to be sprung when it is entered. The trap leaves you in a spatial place without escape."

"What exactly does that mean?" asks Kiree

"Unless a person is strong enough to escape back into their own mind or someone is strong enough to go get them. You are basically a vegetable in a coma." Says Treva

"He is well mother.' Says Remy as if he had just woken from slumber.

"How would you know that?"

"Because I just saved him from a demon called Tikbalang in that nether plane."

"Did you say Tikbalang?"

"Yes, that is what he called himself."

"That is a wicked being. Where did you leave Dane?"

"I left him in a cave safe from Tikbalang. I also cut Tikbalang's arm off."

"It unfortunately will grow back over time." Replies Treva

"No problem I am going back in to get him." Replies Remy taking off his gloves for physical contact.

His hands are grabbed before contact and he pivots around angrily to see Juzef and the council.

"No, my son. You have the same DNA, even if you saved him you would be trapped. It was to be my task to teach you to avoid these traps and to conquer them if need be. You are not ready."

"But I just was there?"

"Again, my son that was reflex based on your close blood bond with your twin. You took Tikbalang by surprise. That will not happen again. We need to find out the origin thread to unwind the trap or he needs to free himself. He is not going to die, and we will place him in the council chamber to be cared for."

"I know who did it and I am going to kill that bitch. I swear before God. That bitch will be dead before the sun rises again." Kiree says releasing his body to some guardsman who are carrying him to the council chambers.

Commander Sauer grabs her arm and says "Is that what I taught you? To run off and risk yourself and your child."

"Milord, he is my life mate. Without him I am nothing."

Commander Sauer embraces her and shushes her saying "God will find a way."

"That may be true. But I have a better idea." Says Remy

"What?" says Dewa

"Well my brother and I are identical twins that the elves no nothing about. I am sure the same thought process used with the Queen could come in handy. I mean my funeral would have to be public. Right."

"I see your point, but they know the trap was not to kill, but to incapacitate. They don't want you dead just out of the way for some reason."

"Exactly, so they have other plans for me. Those plans could change with word of my demise. They have no true way of knowing how I would react to that mind trap."

"That would give us time. They would also play their hand a little in reaction to what they would deem a victory." Says Dewa

"It would give me time to complete your training, Remy. Kiree who was the person who did this?" asks Juzef

"I don't know her name. Some green eyed blond-haired wench with a French accent."

"That would-be Princess Ave. She is Torm's daughter." Says Ejam

"Well, well Torm is full of secrets." Says Treva "I am sure the Elven council has no idea she is a half breed."

"Princess or not I am going to slit her throat and bathe in her blood." Says Kiree

"Don't worry Kiree. There will be time for all of us to bathe in our enemies' blood. But for now, we need to plan and wait." Says Remy "Never trouble a wolf's den in winter. Come let us get out of the cold. Soon we will turn up the heat."

"What lies beneath must reach the surface. Darkness into light"

ENE SITS ON THE plane considering the clouds. She looks back on the choices she's made and the consequences of those choices. She does not blame Lucifer or God. The greatest gift God had given any of us is the freedom of choice. The sad part is he knows how you will choose but hopes he is wrong. She is now in complete control of her own path. She will stay loyal to the Lord our God until the day she does not exist. Praise his holy name so much has changed in this world technologically. The world she had been banished to was much like Europe in the 1700s and that was a culture shock to person used to living during the time of Jesus and the apostles. One of the incredible gifts that she found there was the bible. She had read it cover to cover hundreds of times over the years. Reading God's word and praying for forgiveness daily was her personal quest. So foreign to the life of debauchery she had lead after becoming one of the fallen. She had become a demon magnet after siding with Lucifer. She remembered little of her existence until Jesus freed her from the demons and restored her faith. A faith she quickly lost upon his death, making her once again malleable to the prince of lies. Oh, how she loved Jesus. A man ahead of his time. By allowing her and other women to be part of his disciples in a world where women meant nothing. Allowing them a voice for the first time. Jesus fed the hungry, healed the sick and gave voice to the disenfranchised. There would never be another with his spirit or so she thought.

This place and way of life is totally is new to her. Almost like starting all over. When she heard they would be traveling to New York she had expected one of two things. Immediate transport via magical means or a month-long trip in a ship across the ocean. When she heard the flight would be about seven hours she was amazed. Two of the female elven priestess had taken her first to acquire some clothes before going to the airport. Ene was so used to the open markets that the boutique seemed strange. No bartering just the use of a plastic card for payment instead of wares or silver. Basically, a world that ran using numbers. No better than the mark of the beast foretold so long ago in Revelation. She thinks back to Revelation in the bible and the prophesied signs. "Oh, my lord they know not what they do. Please forgive them. My brother's power is great here."

She chooses a few basic black dresses with strange under garments called bra and panties. She had become so use to corsets and bloomers. The priestess explained this was the appropriate way to dress in this time. Ene on the other hand felt too free initially in the garb she had on much like wearing nothing after years of wearing very constrictive clothing. But she soon adapted to the change of garments. Was she not one of the Hellenic Angelic host. A garment was a garment; nevertheless, how you wore the garment was of the greatest import. You wear the garment the garment does not wear you. Just as she was leaving the store she notes a matador cut black suit with a pair of knee high black boots on a mannequin.

She turns to the store owner and said, "Do you also have that in white?"

"Yes, milady. All the way down to the boots" he answers bowing "I will take both".

She quickly changes into the black outfit and hears gasps as she walks into the store's lobby. Her long red hair pulled away from her face in a braid down her back revealing her perfect features. Not a touch of makeup but her skin seems to glow. The natural tan of her skin creates a clean wholesome look that women would kill for. The black suit just accentuates her athletic build and the three-inch heel on her boots makes her easily six feet tall. Add that to the mock neck silk shirt that makes her neck look regally long. She is towering over everyone in the room like a goddess and they can feel her powerful aura. She exudes love and peace. All in the room male and female fell in love with her immediately. Ene sensing this realized the all father has restored some of her gifts. She feels greatly humbled and immediately falls to her knees with all watching "Thank you Father for thinking me worthy again. I shall not use your gifts for evil. I shall use them for good and teach your flock, amen"

The crowd that has gathered has also fallen to their knees and repeats amen with her.

"May you all be blessed by the Father?"

The priestesses look at each other in amazement. They too feel the Father's love but, through Ene. Not a romantic love but an agape love. A pure love. They do not know what to do. The feeling is wonderful, but they feel like traitors to their clan.

Ene feels their ambivalence and says "Ladies, He does love you. You do not have to give into Lucifer's hate or the hate he fueled in your people. God is always waiting for you to come to him and to give yourself completely without reservation. It is your choice and I will honor whatever it is. But if you choose the Lord then be ready to battle your own kind."

One priestess says "While this feels wonderful, I cannot abandon the teachings of my clan. We were exiled by God and I could never come to trust him."

"I wholeheartedly understand. Your decision must come from your heart." Ene says clasping her shoulder.

"And you little one?" She says turning to the other.

"I will go with you my lady and serve God as your eyes and ears in this new world. I feel that is my path."

"So be it."

Ene returns to the present as the airplane is preparing to land in New York. From the air the sight of it makes her mouth drop open. The buildings are huge and lights dazzling.

"What wonders you have allowed, my lord? Only one as I can appreciate the gifts you have given us. One who has seen much throughout my life time?" Her mind travels to the being whose aura she had felt for some reason. Maybe because she is landing in the place he lives in. A man she could love without bounds. Was he an honorable man sworn to the service of God? Was he mated on any level? Would he find her appealing? In mid thought she stops. "Did I actually doubt I can have this man?" Ene's thoughts are interrupted by Elisha.

"Milady, we disembark soon. There will be a car waiting for us. But I feel my brethren will take my life after you have been delivered".

"Mark my words Elisha. Any who touches you will not be in this world for long. I am of the Hellenic Angelic host and you have pledged yourself to me and to God. Woe is unto he who tries."

They soon gather their things and are heading through customs when a vampire spy working in customs recognizes Ene.

"Oh my God she is loosed upon us again. I must let the Queen know". She says as she heads for a place to watch them and call Commander Sauer.

"This is Janu. I need to speak to the Queen's Guard immediately."

"Yes, this is Queen Sariel."

"Your highness, I did not expect you to answer directly."

"What does that matter Janu. What have you seen?"

"Milady, I have just seen Ene come through customs from Switzerland."

"What? You are sure." Says Sariel.

"I am positive your highness."

"That's why we felt that energy surge on the spiritual plane yesterday. The elves must have setup a portal between the realms. This is not good."

"No, your highness. What are your orders?"

"Just follow her from a distance so we know where she is going. I am not far from you. So, you can just tell me where she is heading?"

"I thought you were in Canada, your highness."

"I returned this morning. Just do not lose them. The prince was right, they are tipping their hand."

"Yes sire"

"Oh, Janu."

"Yes milady."

"Be careful. She is of the angelic host turned wraith. No need for unwarranted heroicness. You lose her, you lose her. We have other ways".

"I understand milady. But she seems different, at peace."

"Well maybe she has been forgiven or maybe it's a trick. Only time will tell".

Janu is observing them heading towards the limousine area and says," I think we may have a problem already."

Elisha and Ene head towards the limousine that is waiting for them and Elisha smells ogres. "Milady something is not right. I smell a scent that should not be here."

"You are right. Are there any weapons in our things?"

"Only a dagger."

"It will do, get it for you." Say Ene seeing that the pickup area is barren and there are twenty ogres waiting to escort them.

"What about you, milady?"

"It has been long since I have battled on this realm. The feeling is quite exhilarating. My hands will suffice against ogres."

"But milady there is twenty of them?"

"Now is the time little one that you learn about faith and the great power of our Father. If we are to live victory is promised. If not, we will be delivered into his hands for final judgment. Either way he knows the outcome."

"Excuse me?" asks one the men in black with sunglasses surrounding the limousine. Each of them is easily six feet and a half tall with huge barreled chests. "We are here to pick up two passengers from Switzerland."

"Why do we require so many ... Chauffeurs?" asks Ene

"Just proper security measures. You never know who to trust." He replies signaling for his men to start to close the loop.

Ene smiles. "Looks more like an ambush to me"

"Well I guess the games are over. I never like not being direct. It goes against my grain. Time for you to pay for your treacherous acts, Ene."

"I am of the Hellenic Angelic host. I will not be easy prey."

"You are human in this world, bitch. No wings no special powers. "Says the lead ogre Corgal. "My master has asked for your head and we shall bring it to him. The traitor will be a bonus."

From behind the ogres comes a voice they have learned to fear.

"If anyone dies today it will be you and your lot, Corgal."

Corgal turns to see Queen Sariel with ten of the vampiric guard with crossbows at ready.

"This is elf business it has nothing to do with you, Sariel."

"You shall not address the Queen in that way, ogre." Says one of the vampiric guard.

"And you do not know your place. I bow to no vampire I am about elfin business. Which should not concern you?"

"Anytime a life is in jeopardy from you and your masters it is my business. Do you think we are not vigilant? Do you think we do not watch your every move?"

"I must insist that you allow me to complete my task. Ene is one of your greatest enemies and the female elf is a traitor to our kind. You know the law within the clans. This has nothing to do with your clan. So, it is none of your business."

Sariel breaks into raucous laughter.

"Why are you laughing Sariel?" Says Corgal irritated

"Because your masters did not give you the memo."

"What the hell are you talking about?"

"The memo that states your clans declared war on all other clans publically. The memo that indicates statements like you just made will never be honored again. So now you have a choice leave or die."

"Not today, Sariel." Corgal says with a sly smile as he signals to the twenty shape changers disguised as airport personnel." Today I give my masters a second present, your head."

Before another word is said ten ogres hit the floor dead and the guard has already reloaded. Another volley and eight shape changers join them.

Janu appears behind Elisha and Ene and says "Here take these." As he hands them both short swords.

"You trust us?" Says a shocked Elisha

Ene smiles and says "I told you little one it is not about trust. It is about faith in the almighty."

With that the shape changer near her is beheaded. "I prefer a lance, but this weapon is magnificent. Come let us sing the songs of judgment with our weapons."

The battle ensues and ends shortly. Only a gravely wounded Corgal and his second in command live.

"Corgal you will not die today" says Sariel gesturing to her medical team."

"What the hell are you doing? We lost the battle we lose our lives"

"Things have changed. If God wanted, you dead you would be. You will be placed in cryogenic tanks and sent back to your masters." Sariel signals again and they are taken away on stretchers. "Killian, make sure they are totally sedated. I would not want them to harm the human team taking them back."

"Yes milady."

"Blessings to you, Queen Sariel." Says Ene bowing.

"Blessings to you as well Lady Ene. You have changed."

"I asked for his forgiveness and he granted it."

"I thank him for it, but that does not explain why you are here."

"I really do not know. The elves and Lucifer freed me from my realm and let me leave after I told them I had been forgiven. The elven consult was outraged when I explained that I no longer would follow my brother against God."

"That is very interesting. What of Lucifer?" asks Sariel.

"He is still trapped in his realm. Apparently, the nexus was in his realm yesterday and he was able with help from the Elven council to pull me out of my realm. Why he could not free himself I do not know."

"It probably has to do with the wards God applied. But I am sure they all have learned from this which means we have about four months to prepare."

"Prepare for what, Queen Sariel?" asks Ene

"For war, they have been breeding warriors for centuries. No one knows how many ogres, elves, shape changers and now these new life form fairies they have created. With Lucifer to lead them, they could devastate this planet and then march on heaven."

"I will not allow that to happen. I let the chance of that happen once I shall not be party to another attempt on the holy realm. This time if Lucifer must die then he dies."

"Are you sure? You are one of the fallen who joined him when he fell from grace. Why should we trust you? Jesus trusted you and upon his death you joined Lucifer to try to march on heaven. If Vincenzo had not rallied our forces and lead us to victory by besting Lucifer all could have been lost." Says Sariel.

"You are correct. I did go against God's word and it was because I did not understand why he would allow anyone as pure and beautiful as Jesus to die so horribly. Now that I have read the bible many times over and now I truly understand that Jesus died for man's sins. The most noble, kind and gentle man I knew gave his life for beings that still do not appreciate his sacrifice. If he can do that then I can do no less than to give my life for these beings as he did."

"I will take you at your word Lady Ene. But, my brethren may not be as understanding as you could probably understand."

"Yes, I am quite aware that you and others blame me for Vincenzo's death. But I had nothing to do with the plan to trap him. I had already been banished to the other realm. The elven council planned that ambush in the event Vincenzo defeated Lucifer."

"I hope you are prepared for her judgment on the matter. He was my life mate."

"I understand. I will leave it in God's hands."

"As it should be and you little Elf, what is your decision?"

"I have decided to accept Jesus as my savior and to follow the word of God."

"We will see little one, we will see. It is easy to say and much harder to do. Please accept my apologies for what I now must do."

"And what is that?"

"This." Sariel signals and they are both injected with fentanyl and they soon fall. "Bring them."

"Who the hell ordered an attack on Ene?" Says Naline "I will behead them myself and I do not care who it is."

The plane with Corgal and his second in command had landed about an hour ago. Naline was of course notified immediately as per Queen Sariel's orders. The message read "Naline, the more you send the more that will return to you in body bags. I return Corgal to you as a gift and to let you know we can be merciful even when threatened. But he is our last gift. By the way Ene is with us now. She has truly changed spiritually. Her aura is that of the angelic host again and after the council clears it will battle by ours sides or die. She is willing to do either. May God bless you?"

It took no time for Naline to realize that one of the council had sent an ogre hit team to kill Ene. It was a decision they would sorely regret. His anger towards her instantly became concern and the urge to protect the one he loved was strong. Someone was going to pay for this treachery.

"Guards."

"Yes, milord." Says one of the grand elven guard. The last of the battle tested elven warriors trained by the arch angel Michael. Trained to back up the Angelic host, if heaven was ever threatened. How ironic that it was the angelic host they would fight against.

"Go and waken all the council members and have them convene in the temporal temple now."

"I do not mean to question you, milord but ..."

"I will pretend you did not. Do it now." Spits Naline.

The guard bow and goes to follow his orders.

Soon the council has convened outside of Lucifer's portal. They are half asleep and completely angered. How dare Naline wake them from their rest and demand that they come here. Nevertheless, they all have come. Naline still leads the army and is their only true elven warrior master. They may bristle a bit but to not come could result in the death of not just themselves but of their whole line. Naline when angered was totally ruthless.

"I know you all are questioning why you are here. But one of you knows why we are here?" Says Naline, sword in hand, tapping it pendulum like on his palm looking at all of them with a cold stare none of them there had ever seen.

"Naline what are speaking about?" Asks Alto

"I am speaking about who sent an ogre hit team to kill Ene."

All the council members aside from the two that were in the chamber have puzzled looks on their face.

"Milord Naline, I can only speak for myself but as far as I know she was trapped in another realm and we were waiting for the next nexus to free her and Lucifer." Says Agel

"If that is so the all but Torm, Tre and Werg may return to your beds. I will convene a council meeting tomorrow to explain what has transpired."

"This is nonsense." Says Preta "I demand answers now."

Before the last word has left his mouth Naline has transverse half the hall and is lifting Preta up by his neck and throws him like some rag doll into the wall. The other members of the council who are not warriors have never seen a feral state. Naline's speed and strength are surprising.

Before Naline can gut Preta like a pig there is a voice heard that booms throughout the room.

"Naline cease your actions. We need all the loyal citizens we can muster."

Naline looks to the portal and stops in mid strike.

Looking through the portal is Lucifer himself dressed in crimson armor.

"As Naline said all of you except you three are to leave this chamber immediately." Lucifer says pointing at the three to stay.

"Place Preta in cryo he will heal and forever know his place." Says Naline sheathing his weapon.

They all quickly assist Preta and leave the chamber.

"With them gone and our Lord here, which one of you ordered the hit? The master's wishes were clear. Place her in New York and have here meet Remy for a chance to sire a child for us."

"I did."

Naline is shocked and turns towards the voice. "You ordered the hit, milord?"

"Yes, Naline. I instructed Tre to order the hit."

"Why?"

"Naline, you are a great warrior and battle strategists, while your fellow council members are let's say subtle planners."

"I do not understand?"

"After you left these chambers in a huff, I had a chat with the other three. Had you stayed you would have been privy to the discussion. However, this was even better. Who taught you to reach a feral state? Was it Vincenzo?" says Lucifer sitting on his throne.

"Yes, master."

"I must say I truly underestimated my greatest pupil." Lucifer makes certain that he emphasizes the word greatest because he knows it infuriates Naline. "He found a way to teach an elf to be feral through God's blocks. He must have loved you very much to go against the word of God."

"I know nothing of what you speak." Says Naline clearly irritated.

"You did not know that God forbade any elf to be feral or to be taught to be feral. It was a gift he did not choose for you to have. A gift that could easily have swung the war to our side, if we had others with that gift. Can you teach it to others?"

"No, I have tried but the training will not stick."

"So, God wanted you to be the only one, again, that is very interesting."

"Why so, milord?"

"Because Naline as I have tried to teach all of you, God never does anything without a purpose. That purpose may not be apparent to you, but it is crystal clear to him."

"Speaking of purpose, milord. What purpose would Ene death serve?"

"Well Naline, of all people you should know what she is capable of in battle."

"Yes milord, but she is human on this plane."

"No, you idiot. She is a wraith on this plane of existence. In battle her body would react. Her hands would grow talons stronger and sharper than any sword. Her strength would be twice that of an ogre."

"But twenty of them were sent and the best of them."

"Naline stop thinking with your heart think like a warrior. She would have even ripped your precious Corgal to shreds."

"Milord, I hate to interrupt. But her killing warriors we could use later does not make sense."

"Naline, do you think I do not know that the vampires have spies everywhere. Do you think that I did not know they would intervene? That they would feel her aura and try to help her by taking her in."

"So, this was a trick to gain entrance into the vampire world."

"I had to send the best so that the trick would work. Lesser being would not have had the same effect. Not only do we have that, but we now had a sure fired way for her to encounter Remy."

"All our reports indicate Remy is in a coma from the mind trap." Says Torm

"He will break through the mind trap. It would have instantly killed anyone who did not have his bloodlines. It will take him time, but he will surely master the trap and be a viable enemy again. What the trap did was give us so time to prepare and plan without him directly involved." Replies Lucifer. "That brings me to the other surprise Torm why had you never told me that you had mated with a dwarf and were pawning her off as true blood royalty?"

"I have no answer for you Milord. I kept it hidden to protect my family line."

"True, but having your wife killed was brilliant. A wife none of the council has ever seen. Because, if they had they would have known about your ruse. Your life mate as well. Amazing how she was born more elflike that dwarflike. What would you have done if that was reversed? I wonder."

"I would have done what was necessary as you know milord."

"Yes, I am sure including killing that child at birth. You do have the prerequisites evil needed to help tear heaven down. And you Tre?"

"Yes, milord."

"Does everyone here know you are the sire of Fica."

Naline looks at Tre and smiles to himself. "I better check out the genealogy lines on all the council's offspring."

"Fica was sired in a moment of passion Milord."

"Yes, passion with one of the beings I have heard you loathe. Plus, I have seen you personally see to his ascension in the ranks. A good word here a bribe there you know what I mean. Pride is one of my favorite sins and as he succeeded your pride in him drove you to backing his causes. Secretly, of course. Again, what a lovely black heart you have."

"The better to serve you, milord."

"That's the spirit and what of you Werg. What secret do you have?"

"I have no secret liaisons with any being milord."

"That may be true, but you do have secret ambitions. Don't you. You knew all I have said but kept all that information to yourself including Naline's secret tryst. Did you not?"

"Yes, milord."

"Another great sin, coveting what others have. You would have used that information to have them all cast out from the council making you the leader of the clan. Astounding, the evil from all of you is quite delectable. It is palpable. I love it."

"Milord, I worry about this Remy. If he can break a mind trap he is indeed a worthy foe." Says Tre.

"Worthier then any of you know. Did you see Ene face when she searched for him on the spiritual plane. He is pure my brethren, but one drop of evil will taint him forever."

"He could not possibly be as strong as celestials are." says Torm

"You should not compare him to celestials. He just currently carries the blood of all the first tribes which gives him privy to all the gifts God gave to the clans and more. His will power is strong, and he serves God, but no one served God and adheres to his laws as all celestials do. No one."

"What if he denies Ene?" asks Naline.

"Then he does. In the meantime, I need to tell you the whole story Naline. The elf guard with Ene at her capture is one of my demon daughter's. With the help of your compatriots I was able to push her across the portal."

"You mean one of your demon spawn is now in the vampire stronghold."

"Yes, and she is scheduled to be checked by the Queen."

"But won't the Queen and probably Remy sense who she is?" says Tre.

"For the Queen that will be too late. My daughter will be standing before her and as you said Remy is in a coma."

"But milord they will not allow her weapons and the Queen will have weapons."

"Fools, she is a weapon. She will morph into a full demon spawn and rip her throat out with her talons before anyone can react. This will buy us more time and prevent the life mating between her and Remy. There is five months to the nexus go and prepare we will battle for this plane soon."

EPILOGUE

DANE FINDS HIMSELF IN a cave with molten lava surrounding him. He now knows he has a twin brother, a brother who appeared to save his life from a demon. The last thing he remembered before the prior battle was that he had entered Kiree's mind to see if the elves had left anything in her mind that could attack the council. It was as if he was sucked into a black hole. At first, he was completely disoriented but Dane now realizes he is trapped in his own mind with no way out. But what did Tikbalang say "He will have to become strong enough to free himself."

From nowhere he hears a voice and looks up and sees a dwarf he has never seen before.

"Who are you?"

"I am Efisio. I trained your brother and now it is your turn."

"Little good it will do me, Master. I am trapped within myself."

"Are you, well let's see what can be done about that, my son. I find that your family is made of special stock. God will make the final decision after you receive your training."

"Training."

"Yes. I have been sent to train you just like I trained your brother. While he has mastered many forms of physical combat and has become the sword of God. It is time for you to learn to master mental combat and become the shield of God. We all have our own gifts that God has bestowed upon us."

"I am ready, Master."

"And so, we begin."

HEME INC.

261

Printed in the United States
By Bookmasters